The Gravity of Lies

The Gravity of Lies

DOROTHY DEENE

Sword and Silk Books

1353 West 48th St, 4th Flr PMB 382, New York, NY 10036

Visit our website at SwordandSilkBooks.com

To request permissions, contact the publisher at admin@ swordandsilkbooks.com.

First Edition: JUN 2023

To my flock...thank you for soaring the uncharted skies with me.

I am forever grateful for each of you.

One

I DRAW THE LINE at cockroaches.

I can tolerate a lot of things: sleeping in a cramped car, the empty hole in my stomach, pungent BO, and even breathing in second-hand smoke containing thousands of chemicals and hundreds of toxins. But staring into the devil eyes of a flesh-eating, hard-shelled, antenna-reaching roach isn't one of them.

And yet there it is, watching me, the devil roach itself, just inches from me as it teeters on the arm of the couch with its spiny legs and thread-like antennas twitching. And here I am, frozen with fear, about to be its prey.

A cold chill washes over me as I remember Uncle Richard telling me about how he and my mother once lived in a place infested with cockroaches, which he called *tiny-but-mighty beasts*. He said they could be found anywhere, like in shoes, cupboards, clinging to the walls, hiding inside the toilet rim, munching away inside cereal boxes, and even floating in a pot of soup simmering on the stove. He said one of them had found him in his bed and when he woke up, he was missing eyelashes.

That explained his right eyelid.

Eyeing my science book on the table, I slowly sit up and edge my way over to the book while keeping watch of the repulsive intruder. But that thing is one step ahead of me and leaps off the couch and darts across the floor. Crap, now my chances of being eaten have just gone way up.

Shivering, I pull the covers up to my neck and listen to the refrigerator gurgle on the other side of the wall, probably because it's empty. Like my stomach. Sighing, I close my eyes just for a second and there it is again, the haunting image of juicy meat, mashed potatoes, and bread slathered in butter. It reminds me of a story I heard once about a guy who was lost in the desert for eight days without food. He kept seeing mirages of food, and starving, he began pretending to eat the visions right up until he was rescued. He not only miraculously survived, but he was found in relatively good health.

It's gotta be worth a try. I bite into the meat and chew, and I swear it tastes like the slab of meat I was served at the homeless shelter.

I wish I was there now. That place gives out three meals a day and an evening snack.

Fiery bile shoots up my throat. Gagging, I pull my knees up to my chest and consider drinking from my mother's bottle again, even though the last two times I tried that, it made me throw up.

Taking a deep breath in, I think about how happy my father will be when we finally meet. Breathing out, I think about how when he sees me, he'll probably say something like he's been hoping for this day because he had no clue how to find me. And when he discovers what my life has been like the last few years, he'll insist I come to live with him. I bet he'll even give me my own room with my own bed, and I'll go back to public school, and every night the two of us will eat dinner together.

It's going to be perfect.

I check the walls and ceiling for any sign of said roach, but all I see are the mustard-colored water stains that have taken on a life of their own. Just last week, those shapes were clearly that of a wolf chasing a fawn across a snowy backdrop. But now, I realize it was never a wolf at all, but a lion with a bushy mane. And what was once a helpless fawn with scrawny legs and pointy ears running for its life is now a deer, one with fully grown antlers and muscular legs sprinting through the air like one of Santa's reindeer. Although I more than sympathize with the lion's ravaging hunger, I still hope the deer makes it out alive.

As for me, I've long since learned how to ration food, but the hunger inside of me lately has been hard to fill up. So I ate everything a few days ago, or rather, everything I could find... The Fruity Tooty cereal, the last of the milk, some boiled noodles, and I even scraped out that micro-thin layer of peanut butter that was stuck to the wall of the jar.

Guess I forgot all the stuff that can go wrong.

And stuff always goes wrong.

Like how my mother's in one of her funks again, which means she won't get up from the couch, which means she won't leave the apartment. She gets like this when I don't have work. She's got this notion that I'm the answer to keeping us afloat.

And I don't even know how to swim.

The mini-mart must be open by now. But I can't go without my mother. She made it clear that I must never, ever go out into the world without her. She's afraid I could disappear like her mother did the day she vanished off the face of the earth.

At least, that's what my mother told me one night in the car. It was a really cold night too; we had just gotten kicked out of the apartment where I had lived my entire life with her and Uncle Richard—that is until he died, and everything fell apart, including my mother. While the bottle of rum kept her warm, I shivered in the backseat under a pile of blankets. She started crying and saying things like she wished her mama had never disappeared.

"What do you mean, she disappeared?" I asked because my mother rarely spoke of her life growing up.

"My mama and me were staying at some motel, and one night she said she'd be right back but when she walked out that door, she never came back. She just up and disappeared into thin air."

"What did you do?"

"I went to live with my brother. He said he'd take care of me... but now he's left me too."

It was one of the longest nights of my life, huddled in the backseat of the car while she cried and smoked one cigarette after another. I was worried that all that smoke that stung my eyes and burned my lungs was going to suffocate me. I would have opened the window, but she wouldn't let me.

My mother stirs next to me. I glance over and there she is in the milky glow, just inches away from me with her mouth gaping open and a thin trail of drool making its way down her chin.

I shake her.

She moans.

"Wake up. We have to get some food. I'm starving."

She pulls the covers over her head.

"You *must* be hungry too?"

"Huh-uh."

How is it possible that she doesn't need to eat? Pulling my legs out from under the covers, I scan the room for any signs of the roach before placing my feet on the floor. Wobbling over to the other side of the bed, I plop down at the edge of the mattress and pull the blanket off her head. "We need to go to the store right now."

"What the hell, Skye." My mother wipes her mouth with the back of her hand and stretches her bony arms out in front of her. Her straw-colored hair is matted to the side of her head. I don't think she's brushed it in a week.

"I'm hungry," I insist, staring down into her pale blue eyes.

Frowning, she yanks her old brown bag from the floor and rummages through it. "Here." She tosses over a piece of hard candy. "How come you haven't been getting any work?"

I wish I had known about the life-saving candy. "I don't know." I rip off the wrapper and shove it in my mouth. "Why don't you call and find out?"

I'd be more than happy to make the call myself, but she won't tell me her passcode. Plus, she's got this fingerprint safety feature.

And even worse, I don't have a cell phone of my own because she won't let me have one. I've tried to get her to tell me why, but she won't give me a reason. I'm not sure what she's so worried about. It isn't like I have any friends to get into trouble with. I bet there's not another sixteen-year-old girl on the planet who doesn't have a cell phone *or* any friends.

But my mother doesn't answer me as she turns up the volume on the TV. "That dumb chicken picked wrong." She's almost hysterical with laughter.

My eyes water as I suck up the thick butterscotch and gaze over at the TV to see what's so funny. A woman is dressed in a chicken costume and standing next to Wayne Brady on *Let's Make a Deal.* The chicken, ironically, has just won a very large and very real cow.

I don't get why there's even a show where people dress up in costumes and make fools of themselves to win stuff. The host bites his lower lip as he shows the chicken what she didn't pick inside the box—a trip to Hawaii and two thousand dollars cash.

Chicken Lady bursts into tears.

Wayne Brady tries to comfort her.

The cow pees on stage.

My mother laughs.

"If you won't take me to the store, then I'll go myself," I shout over the noise.

She stops laughing and glares at me. "We'll go tomorrow."

"That's what you keep saying."

"Later." And she turns back to the TV.

Fine. I bolt up from the mattress and the room spins. Steadying myself, I make my way over to the only room where I can get away from her. Locking the door, I plop down on the toilet seat and squeeze my eyes shut to stop the tears. If only I were back with Uncle Richard. Why can't things be the way they were?

I chew the rest of the candy and swallow, but it doesn't change how hungry I am.

I tell myself to hold on a little longer.

My mother's 'later' has come and gone. She's been sleeping for hours. All she seems to need to stay alive is her booze and cigarettes.

Considering my present situation, I've come up with a plan, one I should have thought of days ago—first, I pour out the rest of the alcohol into the sink. Then I plan to suppress my hunger pangs by smoking every cigarette in her last pack and getting her to take me to the store.

Sitting on the toilet, I light the first cigarette and *inhale... exhale...cough.* Repeat. I continue smoking and coughing while humming some made-up tune until the cigarette is down to a butt. Only nine more to go.

Next cigarette, I picture her face when she realizes she's cigarette-less and how she'll insist we go to the store because she can never be without them. *Puff, puff.*

Starting on the third, my lungs start to seize up. Now my mouth tastes like an ashtray and I'm nauseous again.

Pulling out the cigarettes left in the pack, I break them in half and flush them down the toilet.

When she wakes up, it plays out exactly as I pictured it, but with the addition of cursing as my mother frantically searches through her bag and under the sofa cushions while muttering a string of F-bombs about how she could have sworn she had a pack left. "Skye, get ready. We're going to the mini-mart," she declares.

I'm already dressed.

Two

I SHOVE A BIG scoop of ramen noodles into my mouth and study the script. Since we got back from the mini-mart yesterday, I haven't been able to stop eating. And I'm feeling a lot better now that the creepy roach is no longer an issue. I left a trap last night; a pile of cereal on the counter and waited nearby with my weapon in hand. It was around midnight when I heard it munching away and I bravely snuck up to it. It wasn't easy, but I managed between shrieks to slam it a bunch of times with my shoe until it was dead.

My agent dropped off the movie script for an actual starring role last night. I'm going to the big audition *today*. I still can't believe I'll be reading for the producers.

Honestly, I don't get why they want to see *me*. Anyone in the business worth their salt doesn't even know my name, let alone that I exist. Maybe it's all a big mistake; maybe they picked the wrong headshot.

Considering my success so far, if I can call it that, it comes from getting hired as a human prop. I'm kind of like the human version of what they do with furniture that's placed inside an empty house to make it feel like a real home.

The fact is, I rarely book jobs from the auditions my agent sends me on, more like from background jobs. Those come straight from my stats and headshots, no audition required and no scripts to learn. Once my mother gets a call or notification that I have a job, I just show up where and when they want me and I fill an empty space. When I'm working on set, the best part is I get to eat as much as I want because craft services are like an all-you-can-eat buffet.

After reading the storyline, I think I might actually have a real chance at getting it. It's like the part was made for me. I can easily relate to the protagonist, Emily Watts, in a lot of ways. For instance, Emily is seventeen. I'm *almost* seventeen. Well, I will be in seven months. Her life suddenly changes when her mother runs off and leaves Emily, her dad, and her younger sister. Does my Uncle Richard, the only one I could rely on, dying and leaving me count? Emily's father expects her to take care of the family. My mother expects me to take care of us. Emily's dad won't talk about her mom. My mother won't talk about my father; I don't even know his first name. Emily dreams of being a singer and wants to attend an open audition that could change her life, but her father tells her no and she runs away, gets a fake ID, works at a bar, and starts getting into a lot of trouble. Okay, not exactly me. Not yet, anyway. Emily's mother is the one who finds her, and after a tear-filled reconciliation, they go home together. That's exactly how I picture it will happen when I find my father and he'll insist on taking me home with him.

All I know is if I can pull this off and book the job, I'll make all the money I need to start my new life.

Washing my hair in the shower, I realize I don't have any conditioner to tame the frizz, which means I'm going to look like I just came out of a sauna. I'd use my hair dryer, but, like a lot of our things, it got lost during one of our moves. Thing is, when my mother wants to leave a place, she's like a tornado and I don't have a lot of time to pack our stuff before she's out the door.

I've since learned to keep my important stuff in my backpack. That way, I'll always have everything I need.

Twisting my long, sandy brown hair, I tie the ends with a rubber band. I'm hoping it'll smooth it out. I dress in a tan skirt and peach waffle-knit top, the only clean clothes left in the plastic bag where I keep my clothes so they don't smell like smoke.

Gazing at myself in a mirror that's clearly incapable of lying, I pinch my cheeks and groan; not much has changed since that forever-stuck-in-my-brain day in middle school when I stupidly couldn't stop staring at Billy Miller, only the cutest and most popular boy in the entire school with all his golden blond hair and big, blue eyes, not to mention a smile that lit up the world. And yeah, he noticed me gawking at him—and after about a whole ten seconds of him staring back at me with those gorgeous eyes, I thought, *oh my god, he likes me too*!

Until he burst out laughing, and I mean that over-the-top kind where he was bent over, holding his stomach like he was in pain or something. And that wasn't the worst of it because he practically yelled out to the group of boys huddled around him that the creepy *hamster girl* (and yes, he was referring to me) was in love with him. And he wasn't talking about one of those cute furry hamsters that we all know and love, either.

All the boys laughed along with him as I stood there horrified, teetering on the edge of tears. But I managed to suck it up and give them all a stone-cold stare as I willed my legs to get me the hell out of there, but not before I gave Billy Miller and his crappy friends the finger.

I ran straight to the bathroom and cried my eyes out in one of the stalls. I didn't hear when someone else came in until they knocked on my door. Peeking through the slit in the doorframe, I didn't recognize the girl with her pixie haircut and bright pink top. She said she saw the whole thing, and that Billy was a total jerk. Then she said not to worry, that those cheeks of mine would melt away when I got older.

Thing is, I'm still waiting to melt.

Three

ON THE WAY TO the potentially life-changing audition, my mother drives and smokes with the windows up. When she blows out the toxic clouds, they swirl around and cling to everything in the car, including me. Cranking down my window, I take in a deep breath of cool, fresh air and sigh. I can't stop worrying that something is going to go wrong at the audition.

My mother, on the other hand, doesn't appear to have a care in the world as she taps her fingers on the steering wheel along to Journey's "Faithfully" like a metronome. She never has to perform for other people or stare into the eye of the camera while others judge her as worthy or not for some part that almost anyone could play.

"This is the one that's going to change our life," she sing-songs.

I stare out the window at all the restaurant signs we pass: Denny's, McDonald's, Ron's Pizza, Manna Panda. My stomach grumbles. "Can we stop and get a burger after?"

"I used the rest of the money on gas."

I doubt it was just on gas; she's got two new packs of cigarettes on the dash.

"Oh, wait, I almost forgot." She tosses back a candy bar. "I found it at the bottom of my bag this morning."

Catching it, I gaze down at the smooshed Snickers bar, and my mouth waters. I can almost taste the peanuts wrapped inside sugary nougat, all encased in a smooth chocolate layer. But I don't eat it. I'm going to save it for when I'm really hungry. I slip it inside my backpack.

The stupid song gets under my skin. The singer goes on about how he's forever hers. I stick my head out the window to drown out the words.

I bet when my father and I finally meet, he'll want to be forever mine.

I'm called into the audition room ten minutes after I arrive, which is impressive. The usual wait time for an audition is anywhere from fifteen minutes to an hour. There are only two women sitting behind the table, one staring down at a laptop and the other looking through a stack of headshots. I take in a breath, feeling the importance of this moment right down to my toes because those two women aren't the usual casting directors I see. They are the movie's actual producers and they could single-handedly change my life. My legs shake as I make my way to the middle of the room and stand on the taped X.

My stomach starts to hurt.

Both of the women look up at me. One's got a head full of prickly bleached hair and the other is wearing a multi-colored parka.

"Skye, could you sing something for us?" Parka says.

"Okay." I nod, setting my backpack on the floor next to me, confused as to why they don't want me to read first. But then, maybe they already know I'm Emily, but want to make sure I can sing. "What would you like me to sing?" I say, and I notice Prickly Hair's pink fuzzy slippers sticking out from under the table.

"Anything you feel showcases your voice," Prickly Hair says.

My mind goes blank. I can't think of even one of the millions of songs out there. I panic. *Come on, think of something,* I beg myself. Finally, a song title pops into my head: "Don't Stop Believin'." It's one of the songs on my mother's one and only cassette she owns, *Journey's Greatest Hits,* which she constantly plays in her outdated cassette player inside her even more outdated car.

I tap my foot to get the rhythm before I start to sing. After the first verse, I go into the chorus as Prickly Hair types something into her computer before stopping me. "Thank you, Skye. You have a beautiful voice, love the rasp."

"That's too bad." Parka frowns. "We haven't heard a voice like that today."

"Agreed," Prickly Hair says with a nod. "Okay, well, thank you for coming in."

"*Um,* I'd like to read for Emily." I hold up the script.

They both stare at me like I'm guilty of something. "Who gave you that script?"

"My agent."

"Who's your agent?"

"Melvin Briggs. Can I read now?"

"We feel you look a tad too young for the role. But you do have the voice," Prickly Hair says like that makes the rejection somehow okay.

"I can dress differently…wear makeup."

"We need a girl with a different look. Your face is a little too fresh," Parka says.

A little too fresh? Is it the hamster cheeks? "But—"

"We're looking for a girl who can portray the depth of Emily's struggles."

Glancing down at my black silicone bracelet, I mouth the faded words written across it: *NEVER GIVE UP*. Jackson from Mike's Instant Cash gave it to me. While he was counting out my money, I noticed the rubber bracelet on his wrist right below the small spider tattoo and I said I thought the saying was inspirational. "It changed my life," he told me and then he slipped it off his wrist and handed it to me. I told him I couldn't take something that had actually changed his life, but he said it was time to pass it on to someone who needed a reminder like he once did.

I haven't taken it off since.

Looking up at the two women, I get into character and say one of the lines in my practiced Emily voice: "But Daddy, Mommy loves us. She would never just up and leave us—"

Prickly Hair waves at me. "I'm sorry, but this audition is over.

And we'll need that script."

My vision blurs and I forget how to breathe. Grabbing my backpack off the floor, I manage to get my feet to move over to them and I drop the stack of papers on the table. "Why did you ask me to come here if you weren't even going to give me a real chance?"

Prickly Hair and Parka both stare at me, clearly confused. Guess they're not used to someone calling them out. I slam my hip into the door and it goes flying into the wall behind it with a bang.

When I step out of the room, all the girls waiting to audition are staring at me, or at least it feels like they are. Something boils in me and I want to shout, *What the hell are you all looking at? 'Cause news flash, you're probably not getting this part either!* But instead, I take off down the crowded hall, past my mother, who doesn't even notice me because she's too busy staring down at her phone, probably playing that stupid game, Candy Crush.

There's a bathroom sign up ahead and when I'm safely inside, I lock the door just in time before idiotic tears spill from my eyes. This was probably my only real chance at changing just about everything that was wrong with my life.

After splashing water on my face, I reach for a paper towel but the dispenser is empty. I check the cabinet below the sink and find toilet paper, paper towels, and a box of tampons. Ripping open the box of tampons, I pull out a handful of the yellow-wrapped tubes and shove them, along with two rolls of toilet paper, into my backpack.

I'm becoming like my mother.

"What are you saying?" my mother calls from behind me as I rush toward the exit.

"I didn't get it." I throw open the heavy black door and step outside.

She comes up to me and she pulls her frayed gray sweater around her. She's ghostlike. She hardly ever gets any sun. Next time we're at the Dollarama we should get some vitamin D.

"It's going to rain." She gazes up at the sky. "I hope there won't be any thunder. It feels like a damn earthquake."

I follow her gaze to the blanket of clouds looming above us and hope it rains before we get to the car. If I'm lucky, maybe it'll pour down hard enough to pound me right into the ground.

Sighing, I unzip my backpack, pull out the candy bar, tear open the wrapper, and sink my teeth into it. "Let's hurry." I take off down the sidewalk. *Please rain,* I beg. Halfway down the street, lightning flashes, and I count four seconds before—*boom*! I turn around to check on my mother and she's frozen on the sidewalk, her eyes as round as quarters.

"It's okay, we're almost to the car." I reach for her hand, but thunder roars and she jumps a foot off the ground.

"Hurry—hurry!" She sprints toward a building's overhang like someone's after her and takes cover behind a huge gray wall. "There's a hurricane coming!"

My mother's gotta know we don't have hurricanes here, right?

Although, she once got confused as to why the artist on the radio was singing about how it never rains in California and then, in the next breath, singing about how it pours. I didn't bother to explain that the singer/songwriter, Albert Hammond, wasn't actually referring to the weather, but that the song was a brilliant metaphor about the misconceptions of making it in L.A.

Praise to your song, Albert Hammond, which is apropos to my life. I'm here to attest, Albert, that I too have lost my self-respect; I'm under-loved, underfed, and I, too, want to go home.

Problem is, I don't know where my home is yet.

"Skye, get over here!" Her voice shrieks through the sound of the raindrops hitting the pavement, jarring my brain.

Lightning strikes… Thunder booms… The earth rattles. I throw up my arms—*come and get me, pleeease*! I squeeze my eyes shut, hoping the next lightning bolt will shoot through me.

But the only thing that shoots through me is the blunt force of my mother's fist when it slams into my back.

Four

MY MOTHER COMES OUT of the kitchen carrying a big black plastic trash bag and drops it at my feet. "Start packing, Skye. We're getting the hell out of here."

I look up from my math book. "What?"

She slams a paper on my book.

"What is this?"

"We've been evicted."

I snatch the paper up and read, *"Second notice for failure to pay."* I look up at her. "This is over two months old. Why didn't you pay the rent?"

She shrugs. "I don't remember. Maybe we didn't have enough."

"I know we had enough money to pay the rent the last couple of months, so what happened to it?"

My mother shrugs again. "I don't see you working." She grabs her bag and opens it.

It's true, I haven't been working lately. But it's given me a chance to get caught up on my schoolwork. The last thing I want is to fail homeschooling like I've failed the acting business. "Give me the money. I'll go and pay what we owe."

"No money, Skye." She stuffs the vodka bottle, cigarettes, and lighter into her bag.

"We must have *some*. Check your wallet."

"There's no goddamn money!" she snaps. "You haven't been working, remember?"

Why is it always up to me? Aren't parents supposed to work and kids are supposed to be kids? "*You* could help out and get a job, you know."

Her eyes bug out like I've offended her. "I'm busy taking care of you, little girl."

Wait. She doesn't take care of me. I'm not sure if she's ever taken care of me. That was Uncle Richard's job and since he died, I've been the one taking care of both of us.

"Pack our stuff, we're leaving."

Fine. It's not like I have a choice, anyway. I'm forced to surrender to my mother's whims. I stuff my books and papers into my backpack and take the plastic bag and start shoving in our clothes, pillows, and blankets from the floor and the couch. "Let's think about this for a second." My eye twitches. "We don't have anywhere to go."

"We're leaving."

"Where are we going?"

"Just hurry up!"

Furious, I stomp over to the bathroom and swipe everything off the counter into the bag, including the toilet paper she's stolen from various public bathrooms.

"No way I'm leaving my TV," she calls out.

I pop my head out from the doorway and watch her yank the TV cord out from the wall socket. "You can't take the TV, it's not ours."

"Come help me."

"It's not our TV. It belongs to the apartment." Although I'm still not sure why a flat-screen TV came with this furnished dump.

She ignores me and starts to lift the TV off the table like she's been zapped with some sort of superpower. "Let's go! Let's go!" She's actually got the thing in her arms and she's plodding out the door.

Dragging the garbage bag across the floor, I hoist it up along with my green denim backpack and follow her out into the hallway, where she's wavering back and forth at the top of the stairs while gripping onto that TV for dear life. When she starts inching her way down the steps, her back pressed against the handrail for support, I head over to her and, with my free hand, grab hold of the TV before she falls down the stairs.

The decrepit Toyota Corolla jerks and sputters whenever my mother puts pressure on the gas pedal. The car belongs in a junkyard, but it's the only steady roof over our heads when we don't have a place to live. But right now, I'm feeling claustrophobic with all our crap piled around me in the back seat, all because the stolen TV is jammed in the trunk.

Rolling my window down, I stick my head out and breathe. As she turns onto Highland Avenue, I realize where she's headed—it's where she always goes when she's uprooted us; the infamous heart of Hollywood.

The car moves at a snail's pace with the bumper-to-bumper traffic and when she turns onto Hollywood Boulevard, I watch all the tourists flocking the sidewalks. People from all over the world come here, intrigued by the stories they've heard about glamorous Hollywood and all the celebrity fame and fortune. They come to see it for themselves, and visit places like the Guinness Museum, Dolby Theater, Madame Tussauds, and of course, the Hollywood Walk of Fame. They eagerly hold up their phones for selfies and group photos, posing with big goofy grins while probably hoping to see movie stars.

As she drives past the Hollywood Walk of Fame, I stare out at the sidewalk of stars—stars adorned with names of people I will never know.

"One day, Skye, your name will be on one of those stars and we'll live on easy street," she says with a giggle.

My mother lives on doses of her delusions.

I pull my head back inside the car and catch her smiling in the rearview mirror. "Let's park and look at the stars."

"Not today." Her smile fades.

I don't get it. If the idea of Hollywood is so important to my mother, why won't she let me see it up close?

The traffic light turns red, and the brakes screech until the car is at a full stop. There are about a dozen people on the corner, all wearing matching yellow *I Love Hollywood* T-shirts and snapping pictures.

"See, Skye, they wish they lived here, just like us."

I don't know what she means by that, because right now we're living in a car and before that a crap hole apartment on the outskirts of L.A. I'm pretty sure if any one of those people knew how we live, they wouldn't want to trade places with us, not even for a second.

She turns off of Hollywood Boulevard and drives down a few more streets before pulling into a ten-minute free parking space on a street lined with shops and restaurants. She pushes the seat back, barely missing my legs.

"What are we doing here?" I lift up my legs and plop them on top of the trash bag.

"I'm tired." She yawns, lighting a cigarette.

Hungry, I open the garbage bag and dig through it but I can't find any food. "Where's our food?"

"What?"

"You know, the food you packed while you were in the kitchen."

"I didn't pack any food."

This can't be happening. "We gotta go back and get our food."

"We're not going back."

What the—I'm so mad, mad at her for doing this to me again. Since Uncle Richard's been gone, we never stay in one place for long, and she always has some reason for leaving. It's like she doesn't pay the rent on purpose. I know I made enough last month, so what happened to that money?

A parking enforcement car pulls up on the driver's side with flashing lights. The officer gets out and walks over to the back of our car. Does he know about the stolen TV?

My mother curses under her breath as he walks up to the driver's side with a ticket book in his hand. He taps on the glass and motions for her to roll down the window. She rolls it halfway down.

"Ma'am," he says. "Your tags have expired."

She lifts the cigarette to her mouth, breathes in, and deliberately blows the smoke out the window. He takes a step back. "Well, duh." My mother rolls her eyes. "For your information, this happens to be my brother's car, and…he died…and left me to do everything, like getting this heap of crap to the junkyard for some cash."

My uncle died two years and eleven months ago.

"I'm sorry for your loss, ma'am." He closes his ticket book. When my mother doesn't answer, he rubs his brow and scans the back seat, stuffed with me and all our crap. "Everything okay?" he asks.

No, everything is *not* okay. I look at him, deadpan.

"We need to get going." My mother turns the key and the engine groans. When she backs out of the parking space, he has to take a step back to keep from being grazed. As she drives down the road, I turn back and see him standing in the street, scratching his head.

My mother glances up at the rearview mirror and says things like how he's a stupid son of a bitch, that she doesn't have insurance and she must be really lucky. I happen to disagree; I don't think we're lucky at all.

As I stare mindlessly out the window, I observe the colors of the traffic lights at each intersection—*green, green, red, red, green.* "We should go back to the apartment." *Green.* "You know, since we haven't been formally kicked out yet." *Green.*

"I'm running on fumes." She turns into an alley and parks in a space behind a donut shop. The powerful aroma of fried dough soon fills the car and my mouth waters.

"Can I have a couple of dollars?" I unbuckle my seat belt after she cuts the engine.

"There's no money."

"Well, then we can't stay here. The sign says parking for customers only."

She stuffs her gray sweater behind her head and yawns.

Fine. I search my backpack for loose change and find a quarter, two dimes, and a few pennies. I consider using one of the twenty-dollar bills hidden beneath the flap, but I vowed to never, under any circumstances, use any of the money meant for finding my father. *"Please. Park.* Somewhere else."

"We're staying here."

Slamming my back into the seat, I gaze out the window and notice a guy standing outside the back door of the donut shop in a red apron with *Dave's Donuts* written across the front. He's staring down at his phone and holding a big pink box in his free hand. After about a minute, he makes his way over to the dumpster and tosses the box inside.

"Why's he throwing away perfectly good donuts?" I shake my head. But no sooner than the words come out of my mouth, my mother is out the door and scurrying over to the dumpster. I'd compare it to watching a horror movie come to life as she gets up on her tippy toes in her baggy sweatpants and an oversized sweatshirt. After peering inside, she pulls out the pink box.

As she trots back with the box in her hands, I slouch down in my seat and beg the universe to please make it all stop.

She gets back in the car and giggles as she throws back the crumpled lid and holds up the box, revealing a bunch of mangled donuts. Is that a piece of paper stuck to one of them? "Take one."

I shake my head until I'm dizzy. I will never, *ever* stoop so low.

"Suit yourself." She grabs a donut and takes a bite.

My stomach growls and does all these flips, and I'm spiraling into a moment of weakness from the smell of sugary fried dough. Listening to all her chewing and moaning, I swear I resist as long as I can, like a whole damn minute, before I snatch a donut from the box and shove it in my mouth. Shamelessly, I swipe up another, then another, and then two more. Five donuts later, the hole in my stomach is gone.

Bloated, I collapse back into the seat and sigh.

To say my life is humiliating is an understatement.

Five

"SHIT," MY MOTHER SAYS, peering out the driver's side window.

The guy from the donut shop is heading toward us. Cursing under her breath, she starts the car, swerves out of the alley, and zig-zags down the street. I hope we get pulled over. I hope they take me away from her and put me in a foster home or a group home or someplace I can stay while they find my next of kin: my father.

But that doesn't happen, and she slams the car to a stop in front of a car repair shop. "We're staying here for the night." She settles in with her bottle and a cigarette.

It's going to be a long night.

I should be doing schoolwork. I'm still stuck on the stupid probability distributions in the stupid workbook. I don't care about those meaningless problems—I have my own probability to work out, like how I need to get jobs that pay if I'm ever going to get out of this mess.

I wonder how things would have turned out if we hadn't come

across Bea Lester. My mother and I were staying at the shelter when Bea Lester showed up with her two kids and a black eye. She claimed her kids were going to make it big in the entertainment business. She told my mother to get me signed up with an agent named Melvin Briggs and we'd soon be on easy street. Seems to me her kids being in the business hadn't done much for them. They were, after all, staying at a homeless shelter, weren't they?

The first month I went out on auditions, I landed a national commercial and I made enough money to get our first junky apartment in L.A.

After that, my agent, Melvin, kept filling my mother's head with the idea that my immediate booking was a good omen. He promised her that if she homeschooled me (so I'd be available for auditions), we'd be rich and famous in no time.

That was almost three years ago.

I adjust myself in the seat. There's pressure in my bladder and I don't think I can hold it much longer. "I have to pee," I tell her.

"Can't you wait until morning?"

"No, I have to go bad."

"Fine." She takes out a roll of toilet paper from the glove compartment and hands it to me. "Stay by the car."

I get out and scan the area before I yank down my pants and squat near the back of the car.

Welcome to my pathetic life.

But I feel a little better now.

Locking the door, I shove the garbage bag over on the passenger seat. When I lie down, my feet hit the door. Pulling up my legs, I close my eyes and the sting of hollowness inside my heart begins to ache.

"I was wondering." My voice comes out soft. "You know how your eyes are blue and mine are brown?"

"Uh-huh." She exhales smoke from both her mouth and nose and fills the car with a cloud of certain death.

"My father must have brown eyes, right?"

Silence.

"What's his name?"

Silence.

"My father...what was he like?"

She cracks her window and tosses the cigarette out onto the sidewalk. "He isn't like anything because he doesn't exist."

"Are you saying my father...died?" The second it comes out of my mouth, I'm afraid to know the answer.

She shakes her head.

"So, he *is* alive?"

"There's no father," she snaps. "So stop asking."

How can I stop asking when it doesn't make any sense? I know something about biology and that in order to create me, there had to be a sperm somewhere in the equation. And that sperm came from a man. And that man is my father. And he has a name.

"Everyone has a father," I say.

"Dammit, Skye." She slams her hand against the steering wheel. "I told you, I told you—there's no father, he *doesn't* exist."

"Then I must have been born from an immaculate conception." I let out a dry laugh.

Silence.

"Well, I bet he'd help us if he knew we—"

"There's no one helping us since my brother left me!" My mother lights another cigarette and waves it through the air. The glowing tip flutters like a frantic firefly that can't find its way out.

Scrunching up into a ball, I suck back tears. Uncle Richard left me too, and he was the one I could count on. But everything changed the day we were watching the Dodgers versus Braves game on TV. The Dodgers couldn't seem to figure out how to overcome Newcomb's left-hander, and they were losing big.

"Uncle Richard, Dodgers aren't doing so hot," I said, but no response came. I looked over at him and at first, I thought he was sleeping, even though he never slept through a game.

The Dodgers lost that night. And so did my poor Uncle Richard. When the paramedics came, I had to hold on to my hysterical mother when all I wanted to do was make him wake up.

My mother locked herself in her room for weeks. There was never a funeral. When the social security checks stopped coming, we got kicked out of the apartment and ended up at a shelter.

"He left me too," I mumble.

"Enough of this! Now go to sleep."

Yanking my backpack up onto the seat, I dig down past all my stuff and lift up the bottom flap to feel for the bills underneath. The money's still there. But it's still not enough to hire private investigator Nick Vaas to find my father. I stumbled across his advertisement on Google when I was trying to figure out a way to locate my father even without having his name. I knew it was probably impossible to find anyone without knowing at least their name, but then private investigators popped up in my search. Of course, even they needed information about the person they would be looking for, but then I saw this advertisement: *Do you feel hopeless? Have zero leads? Not to worry, I can find anyone. Guaranteed. Nick Vaas, Private Investigator.*

One woman by the name of Margaret Dickers posted a review that said Nick Vaas was a miracle worker.

And I need a miracle.

I called his office from a payphone when my mother was in a liquor store and she thought I was in the bathroom. The woman who answered assured me that Nick Vaas could find anyone but that he requires the full $895.00 fee upfront.

Before pulling my hand out of the backpack, I grab hold of Lil' Monkey and take him out. I smooth his matted fur and stare into his perfectly round black eyes, the very eyes I've been staring into my entire life. Kissing his head, I press him into my neck and drift to familiar sounds: cars passing, a siren, a dog barking in the distance, footsteps... *What?*

I'm jolted awake. The footsteps sound close like they're outside the door. A shadow moves across the window. I squint to see if the door is locked before slipping beneath the blanket.

"There's someone out there," I whisper. But the back of my mother's head has since disappeared behind the headrest.

"Shhhh."

"Let's get out of here," I whisper, thinking she just has to put the key in, but then, the car rarely catches on the first try. When she doesn't do anything, I reach inside my backpack and fumble around for the pepper spray.

Go ahead, creep, try to mess with us.

Pepper spray ready, I strain to hear what's going on outside… Footsteps again—but they begin to fade.

When my mother sits up, she coughs and lights a cigarette.

Lifting my head up just enough to peer out the window, I scan the dark street where dangerous shadows live and breathe. We have no business being here.

And now she's humming.

At first, I'm so angry I want to scream at her, *why are you doing this to me?* But I'm too tired. As I close my eyes, I count the steady beats of my heart.

I wonder where my father is at this very minute.

One way or another, even without her help, I'm going to find him…because being with him has got to be better than this.

Six

WE'RE GIVEN CODENAMES AT Hope First shelter. My mother's 612MA (Mary adult) and I'm 612SM (Skye minor). I'm willing to be a damn number, whatever they want, as long as I get food and a cot to sleep on.

Ms. Arthur has been running Hope First for over forty years. That's one of the first things she tells us every time we come here. She shows us around the place like it's a five-star hotel, but it's just an old house full of crummy furniture and lots of rules. Everyone who comes here has to follow them, like do chores and take classes and stuff to give them the tools to live out in the world. While we follow Ms. Arthur down the long hallway, the old wood floor creaks as she recites the rules.

I already know every single one.

The woman is maybe five feet tall. Her thick, and very long, wiry gray hair is pulled back in a ponytail, and as she wobbles down the hall, it sways from side to side like the tail on a horse's behind.

Everything is timed here—eating, chores, free time, and even sleep. There are counseling groups to help the women and children and seminars to learn a trade.

My mother rarely attends any of them.

During the week, Ms. Arthur encourages the women to go out and find a job. Dozens of opportunities, including motel housekeeping, dishwashing, grocery store shelving, and some factory jobs, are posted on a bulletin board in the hallway.

No one is allowed in or out from ten at night to six in the morning. If anyone tries to leave during those hours, an alarm goes off and the offender gets kicked out.

Dinner is served at 5:30 sharp. I'm handed a plate with a slab of meatloaf, rice, green beans, and a roll. I can't recall the last time I ate something this good. The woman behind the counter keeps saying *no seconds* to everyone she hands a plate to. After I devour my food, I'm still hungry. My mother doesn't want her meatloaf or green beans and gives them to me.

After we eat, I shower and use the shampoo and conditioner that leaves my hair smelling like coconut. I stand under the hot water and only turn it off when it runs cold.

Stepping out of the stall, I wrap myself in the clean white towel I was given along with a white T-shirt, sweats, toothbrush, toothpaste, deodorant, and a hairbrush. Everyone gets the same stuff in a big Ziplock bag when they come here.

Pulling off the wrapper from the toothbrush, I look at myself in the mirror, surprised to see I look a little different. I move in closer to examine my face. Yes, older. I look a little older, I'm sure of it. Smiling, I squeeze toothpaste on my toothbrush and brush my teeth.

As I lie on my designated cot in the fresh-smelling T-shirt and sweats, a woman with a jagged pink scar running down the right side of her face goes around the room collecting dirty clothes from the women and children.

My mother's lying on the cot next to mine with her freshly washed hair. She doesn't smell like cigarettes anymore. Neither do I.

A woman three cots down hiccups incessantly. A couple of other women are snoring. When it's lights out, I pull out Lil' Monkey from my backpack and tuck him under my chin. A chorus of hiccupping and snoring fills the room.

I gotta get some earplugs.

Seven

AFTER A WEEK AT the shelter, my mother tells me Melvin has a check waiting for us. My paychecks get sent to my agent's address because we never know where we'll be living.

Melvin's outside his apartment building when we pull up and he hands us his parking pass to hang from the rearview mirror so we can park without getting a ticket.

As usual, he's wearing a polyester suit and, of course, his shiny white wingtip shoes. Whenever he moves, his gold chains jingle, especially the ones around his bony wrists. Melvin's a middle-aged man stuck in a movie out of the seventies. He believes he's the real-life Tony Manero from some movie way back when—I think it's called *Saturday Night Fever*. He told us he dreamed of being a dancer but his leg got messed up playing high school football. He says he lives for Saturday nights because he goes to a disco bar somewhere in L.A. and lives out his dream of being a disco king.

"Hey, hey, ladies." Melvin slings his arm around my shoulder. He reeks of tobacco and cheap cologne. I maneuver out of his grip.

He doesn't seem to notice and hands my mother his cigarette like he's passing a joint, and then he rambles on about how he's got a feeling good things are coming our way.

Melvin's full of shit.

We follow him as he limps to his boat-size white Buick with its shiny wheels and tinted windows. He drives down the boulevard to Mike's Instant Cash because we don't have a bank account.

I've tried reasoning with my mother about keeping our money in a bank and out of her bag and Melvin's hands, but she insists they steal people's money. I'm not sure who *they* are, but if anyone's stealing money from us, it's the guy sitting in the driver's seat.

Melvin hands me my check and waits in the car with the motor running like he's the driver in a getaway car.

I made $471.00 after taxes. I worked background for two days on a movie set, some remake of an ancient western, *The Drifter*. Clint Eastwood starred in the original movie.

On the first day on set, I was a walking prop going down a dirt road inside a fake town with horses and stagecoaches instead of cars. Then I got bumped to a speaking role which meant more pay. I was the girl going into the mercantile to buy flour and eggs costumed in one of those Laura Ingalls dresses from *Little House on the Prairie*. To add to that image, I carried a basket like Little Red Riding Hood.

When I didn't have enough money for both the flour and eggs, the store owner told me to pick between the two. My line: "But my mama needs them to make a cake for my little sister. You see, it's her birthday today." But the store owner, who clearly didn't care, told me to pick one or get out.

The drifter just happened to be in the store and overheard the whole thing. He put a gun to the store owner's head and said, "That there little girl's mama is fixin' to make a cake for her child, and I don't think you wanna break that little girl's heart, now do you, mister?"

The store owner looked like he was about to piss his pants. His hands were shaking as he placed the flour and eggs inside the basket and said to me, "We'll just call it even." He was a pretty good actor too. He even had sweat running down the sides of his face.

The drifter winked at me and wished my sister a happy birthday. My line: "Thanks, mister."

Not exactly a life-changing role or anything, but it was hands down the closest I've come to being a *real* actor.

While waiting in line at Mike's Instant Cash, I try to get my mother to look at the check before it's cashed. I want her to see what I made so she'll finally realize how much Melvin plans to take for himself. But it's no use. When I all but shove the check in her face, she slaps my hand away like some pesky fly and wanders over to the waiting area.

As I hand over my check and ID to Jackson, he waves an *I-already-know-you,-silly* hand my way.

"Hey, if you come by in the next two weeks, I won't be here," he tells me.

"How come?" I ask because Jackson is always here when I

come in.

He strokes his long, bushy caramel-colored beard with his fingers. "I'm taking my Harley and going out on the open road." He makes *vrooming* sounds while pretending to hold on to invisible handlebars.

"Where are you going?"

"Anywhere and everywhere." He raises his eyebrows and his forehead looks like it's about to crack. Jackson's clearly never used sunscreen.

"Nice." I smile, wondering if one of those anywhere places could be where my father lives. If I knew for sure, I'd ask Jackson to take me with him.

While I wait for him to process the check, I search his arms for any new tattoos. I've already seen the giant eagle, the black rose, and what looks like a snake wrapped around a skull. I notice letters on his fingers that I haven't seen before, right above the knuckles, spelling out *F-E-A-R-L-E-S-S*.

I bet Jackson *is* fearless. I bet when he's out on the open road on his Harley, he's the most fearless person alive.

"Nice to see you wearing the bracelet."

"Yeah. I really like it. Thanks again," I tell him.

"That saying helped when I needed some reminding. But now I've graduated to this." He shows me his fingers.

"That's really cool," I say. I hope to one day be more like Jackson. "I'll take twenties, please."

"I make about this much a week working at this place." Jackson chuckles as he counts the bills in front of me and puts the stack in a white envelope. "Maybe I should take up acting."

I smile. "Well, I hope you have a good trip," I say as I take the envelope.

He winks and gives me the peace sign.

I spot my mother in the waiting area, scooping lollipops out from a bowl and dropping them into her bag. I pull out four twenties from the envelope and shove them in my pocket. I'd like to take it all, but I have to be careful not to alert my mother or Melvin. If they find out, there's no telling what could happen; I'd probably never get access to my own money again.

The second I get in the car, Melvin's big hand is out. "Let's have it." He wiggles his fingers.

I clear my throat, hoping to get my mother's attention, but she's preoccupied with playing Candy Crush on her phone. I know because she chews on her bottom lip when she's playing.

I have no choice but to hand him the envelope and watch him slip bills out of the pile of cash before handing it to my mother.

Melvin turns up the radio and starts belting out a song, something about how he's walking through the shadow of death, and when he looks at his life, there's gonna be nothing left.

Melvin doesn't know it yet, but those are going to be his famous last words.

Eight

I WAS THIRTEEN WHEN I booked my one and only national commercial. It was for Stouffer's lasagna. Booking a national commercial is highly desirable because there's potentially a lot of money to be made. I didn't make a ton of money like some do, but it still airs sometimes, and that means I still get paid.

In the commercial I played the fake daughter in a fake family that sat around a table having a real dinner. There were no lines; I was hired to eat lasagna and laugh along with the rest of them.

Back when I lived with Uncle Richard, I don't remember us ever sitting at a table and eating together. My mother spent most of her time in her room, reasoning that because she smoked, she couldn't be around her brother because of his asthma. As for Uncle Richard, he ate all his meals in his chair in front of the TV and I sat on the floor beside him.

But I didn't care because we were together.

Gazing out the side window, I notice my mother's driving in the opposite direction of the shelter. "Where are we going?"

"We've got money now, and I got us a place." She turns the corner and drives toward the crap area of L.A.

"But we're staying at the shelter," I insist. And it isn't so bad there. I mean, I eat regular meals, and I have my own cot to sleep in, and I've gotten caught up on all of my schoolwork.

"That nasty ol' woman kicked us out."

"Why would Ms. Arthur kick us out?"

"Some crap about how she only has room for people who are willing to try."

"Willing to try what?"

"How the hell would I know?"

"Well, I'm not going to another junky apartment. I say we go to a motel until we can figure things out." A motel is an obvious choice. We can pay daily or weekly and leave whenever we want. There's even a cleaning service and some serve a continental breakfast every morning. But she spews out a bunch of curse words along with *over my dead body if I'm gonna stay at some bullshit motel.*

I forgot motels are a sore subject with her after what happened with her mom.

She parks in front of a rundown apartment building in a sketchy part of L.A. "This is it," she says, cutting the engine.

"How could you have gotten a place when we've been at the shelter the whole time?"

"The bulletin board's got all those ads for rentals and jobs and stuff."

A job would have been a better plan. "I hate it," I tell her. It's a never-ending cycle with her: car, shelter, apartment, repeat. "I want to go back to the shelter."

"*Skye, Skye, Skye,*" she sing-songs. "It's Hollywood, and that's where we belong."

Does she really believe that *this* is where we belong? "We're *not* living here."

"*Yes*, we are. I've got to meet the landlord and give him the rent." She gets out of the car.

"I'm not going with you!" I shout out the open window.

She stands there on the sidewalk glaring at me. "Lock the doors and I'll be right back."

She comes back a few minutes later holding up her gray sweats with one hand and dangling a key in her other. "I gotta get the TV upstairs. It could get stolen around here with the damn trunk not locking."

News flash—it's already been stolen.

When I get out of the car, she's standing in the middle of the sidewalk waving at some kid speeding toward her on a skateboard. "Hey, hey, stop!" she yells as he's about to ram her. He comes to an abrupt stop just inches from my mother.

"What's your problem, lady?" He scowls.

"I need my TV taken to my apartment."

Kicking his skateboard up into his hand, he squints at her. "How much?"

She searches her bag and pulls out a five.

He nods and follows her over to the car. The kid is big, linebacker big, and he carries that TV up the stairs like it's nothing more than a football. I ask him how old he is, thinking fourteen, or fifteen, but he tells me he's twelve and winks at me before taking off on his skateboard.

The place is way worse than I thought. It smells musty, and the room isn't much bigger than an oversized closet. It's stuffed with a saggy brown couch, a coffee table, a small metal table and two chairs near the couch, and a crusty orange chair that I plan to never sit in.

Our last place didn't have a bedroom either, but at least it was big and had a real kitchen, unlike this place which doesn't even have a wall separating the room from the makeshift kitchen. All someone did was bolt a plank of wood into the corner wall, and I'm guessing it's supposed to be a counter. There's a double burner cooktop, a wash bin posing as a kitchen sink, and next to it is a three-foot refrigerator propped up on a crate.

The bathroom is ultra-tiny. The floor is concrete and the shower head is above the toilet.

"I don't know what this place is," I mutter when I come back into the room.

"Got it for dirt cheap," she tells me while sitting on the floor and plugging in the TV cord. "I told the landlord I was looking for something with low rent." She grins, apparently satisfied with herself. *"And* you know what he said...? He said if I pick up trash around the building once a week, I don't have to pay a deposit *and* he'll give me a $150 break on the rent."

"They can't possibly want any money for this place."

"I'm paying $650 and it includes utilities."

First of all, *I'm* the one paying $650 a month for us to live in this dump. And second, there's no way she'll ever pick up trash around the building. And no way in hell I'm going to do it.

"This isn't a *real* apartment and we're not staying." I stomp my foot.

"We're staying." She stomps back.

I collapse on the chair and a cloud of dust explodes from the fabric. Coughing, I grab the garbage bag and open it, only to be met with a foul smell. "I mixed all the clean and dirty clothes together. We need to do laundry." I start pulling out all the clothes that are mixed with all our other stuff in the bag.

"The landlord said the laundry room is downstairs."

"Can we go now?" I really want to get out of here.

She shakes her head.

"Then I'll go do the laundry myself."

"No, you won't."

"But I did laundry before in our old building, remember? Besides, I'm sixteen, I'm almost an adult. I think I can go downstairs and do laundry by myself."

She looks up from the remote and pauses. "Maybe you're right. It should be safe as long as you stay in the building. But come right back."

"Oh, yeah, sure." I quickly stuff our clothes into a dirty pillowcase before she changes her mind. "I need money for the machine."

"Got some bills in my bag. You gotta come right back though."

She starts clicking and pounding the remote. "What the hell is wrong with this thing?" She shakes it so hard it flies out of her hand, hits the floor, and the batteries pop out.

Still in shock, thinking I may actually make it out the door, I swing the stuffed pillowcase over my shoulder like Santa Claus, grab my backpack and the money from her bag, and slip out the door before she comes to her senses.

There's a note taped on the laundry room door: *Closed for water leak, laundromat at the corner of Everly.* Just my luck. Heading back to the apartment, I remind myself I'm not some little kid anymore. I even reason that nothing is going to happen to me if I go to the laundromat down the block. "That is my mother's fear, and one that is unreasonable," I tell myself. Taking a deep breath, I march down the stairs and walk out of the building and stand on the sidewalk. Fear washes over me and I turn back to go inside. Wait. Clearly, I've been brainwashed, right? People don't vanish into thin air. Something happens to them like they're kidnapped or they run away or fall off a cliff or they're eaten by a wild animal or something. And none of that is going to happen to me. I pull out my pepper spray from my backpack, the one that I got from the shelter, stuff it into my jacket and start walking down the street.

I'm a little nervous, or a lot, seeing as my heart's racing, but I can't deny how good it feels to be out on my own.

There are only a few people inside the Fluff N Dry. I dump the clothes into a washer, pull out the dollar bills from my pocket and get change from the machine. The washer takes six quarters, the dryer takes three, and the detergent is five. I have twelve quarters.

I'm not about to drag all the wet clothes back, so I search the trash for soap boxes that have any soap left in them. I find three and take the boxes over to the machine and pour what's left in them into the water. Closing the lid, I sit in one of the chairs and notice a guy in a gray hooded jacket standing in the doorway and he's staring right at me.

As the machine swishes back and forth, I keep checking to see if he's still there and sure enough, he is, and he's still staring—at me. A disturbing image runs through my mind, one where he and his accomplice capture me on my way out the door and throw me in the back of a van where I'll be tied up and tortured.

I check to make sure my pepper spray is in my pocket.

I never should have come out alone.

When the washer's done, I go over and take another quick glance over by the door; he's gone. I check the room and he's nowhere in the building.

Grabbing up the handful of clean-smelling clothes, I toss them into a dryer and wait. Bored, I watch an old woman with curly gray hair and big glasses fold clothes at the table. She moves in slow motion as she smooths out each item before carefully folding it. It must take her five minutes to fold even one shirt. A hunched-over, elderly man with a potbelly and a few stray gray hairs remaining on his head wobbles in and heads over to her. They speak softly to each other until she's done folding the clothes. He takes the basket and they wobble out together.

I'm the only one left in this place. I go and check the clothes.

I have this feeling like I'm still being watched, but maybe I'm being paranoid. Stuffing the dried clothes into the clean pillowcase, I hoist it up over my shoulder along with my backpack and hurry toward the door.

Walking through the parking lot, I hear, "Hey girlie, I like you. Come here." I look around and see the hooded guy leaning against a black car.

My mother's right, I should never go out into the world alone, but maybe the real danger is other people.

Lowering my gaze, I walk quickly down the street, my free hand in my pocket, gripping the pepper spray. I turn back every few seconds to see if he's there and when I'm sure he isn't, I relax.

I pass a long row of apartment buildings in dire need of repair, with weeds instead of grass, and beaten-up old furniture left out on the side of the road. I notice a single tree near my building covered in a halo of tiny white flowers. I don't know how I didn't see it before. I wonder how it managed to survive. I go over to the tree and cup a cluster of flowers in my hand. They are soft and powdery against my skin. I press my nose into them and sniff their lilac fragrance.

"You making out with that tree?"

Startled, I look up. There's a guy sitting on the steps of an ugly green building.

"No." My cheeks grow hot. "I noticed it's the only tree alive in this crappy neighborhood."

"It's not so bad here." He sifts his fingers through his shaggy dark hair and leans back into the railing. "I see you like Lillian."

"Lillian?"

"The tree." He squints over at it.

I'm not sure what's up with this guy naming a tree, but he's cute. Super cute. "It's nice of you…watering it, I mean. The tree's pretty." I step out from under it.

"I've never seen you before," he says. "You live around here?"

"We just moved here. I'm in that building." I point to the gray apartments.

"We're neighbors then." He raises an eyebrow, places a rolled-up joint between his lips, and inhales before offering it to me.

I shake my head.

"You don't like a buzz?"

"I've never tried it."

"Here." He offers it to me.

I shake my head again. "I'm good."

"That's cool. Want to sit for a while?"

I don't budge. He's a stranger, after all. Besides, I should head back, but the thought of facing my mother scares me a little. I shrug as I make my way over and set the pillowcase and backpack down before sitting two steps below him. A whiff of a skunk-like smell fills my nose.

"You're a funny girl," he says.

"How so?"

"You smell trees, don't smoke weed, and sit two steps below me."

"Do you always talk like that?" I notice his beautiful green eyes and thick dark lashes.

He grins. "Nah. But hey, I'm Sebastian. Most people call me Bash. And you are?"

"Skye."

"Nice to meet you, Skye." He snubs out the tip of the joint and stands up. "Well, maybe we'll meet again." He makes his way up the steps and pushes open the glass door and when I blink, he's gone.

What just happened?

Hoisting the pillowcase up again, I grab my backpack and walk back to the gray building, thinking about Sebastian.

Nine

IT WAS THE SUPER Bowl, Denver Broncos vs. Carolina Panthers. Lady Gaga performed the National Anthem. Uncle Richard and I both agreed her performance and rendition were mesmerizing. Uncle Richard got teary-eyed when she fist-pumped her chest.

"I'd sure like to see you sing at one of the games, Skye. You've got a voice as good as Gaga's." My uncle wiped his eyes.

I knew I wasn't even close to being as good as Gaga. I wasn't even sure if I was good at all. But whenever my uncle caught me singing, he'd tell me I had a beautiful singing voice.

"I'll sing for you right now," I told him. Uncle Richard stood proudly with his hand on his heart while I belted out the anthem. "You are true to your name." He beamed. "Your mother was right to name you Skye Lark."

Funny, but up until that moment, I hadn't considered what my name meant. Come to find out I was named after a bird, and unlike most birds that sing from perches, the skylark sings its songs in flight.

I miss Uncle Richard.

Roaring laughter from the TV pulls me out of my thoughts. I drop my pen and sigh. All the noise is getting to me. She has that thing going all day long and I can't concentrate on my assignments and I have to finish them by next week. I'm not even sure why the table and chairs are so close to the sofa. I get up and drag the table over to the one and only window in the place.

"What are you doing?" My mother's watching me.

"There's better lighting here to do my work." I grab a chair and set it in front of the table and sit down, wondering why I didn't think of this sooner. As I stare at my stack of papers, there's a fluttering noise on the other side of the window. I gaze out the dirty glass, surprised to see a bird huddled on the windowsill.

I gently tap at the glass, and the grayish-black bird cocks its head and stares right at me. I watch it puff up and flutter its wings, and I'm even more surprised to see a nest peeking out from beneath the bird. "Guess you're stuck here too," I whisper.

"Skye, bring me a cup of that instant coffee we got," my mother calls. She's referring to the coffee she managed to steal from the shelter.

"I'll be back," I whisper to the bird.

If my father knocked on the door at this very minute and saw the way I'm living, I bet he'd say, *you're coming with me, kid.*

I'd go with him too, and never look back.

Ten

FAST ASLEEP, THE BIRD'S head is nestled inside its feathers. My mother's sprawled out on the couch, snoring.

After I finish my English and history assignments, I take a shower. Pulling out jeans and a shirt from my bag, I consider going out alone. I keep telling myself I have every right to go for a walk, even if she doesn't think so.

Maybe I'll just happen to see Sebastian again.

If I do go out, I probably have a good chance of getting back before she even wakes up. After all, it worked out when I went to the laundromat and she was asleep when I got back. Trembling with excitement, I grab the key, the three dollars on the table, and I slip out the door.

I'm not sure where I'm going, but I remember seeing a 7-Eleven not far from here. I check my pocket for the three dollars.

My stomach flutters as I step out of the building. The chances of seeing him again are probably zero. I mean, I don't know him and I doubt he'll even remember me. But then I see him right away, like last time, sitting on the steps.

My heart races as I approach him.

"Where you been?" He grins when he sees me. "I've been looking for you."

He's been looking for me? "Around," I say, trying to resist the smile that wants to creep up on my face.

"Where you headed?"

"Umm." For a split second, I can't remember where I'm going. "I'm going to…um, 7-Eleven. Yeah, that's where I'm going." I nod.

"Cool. Mind if I join you?"

"Sure, yeah, I mean, it's a free country."

He chuckles as he heads down the stairs, his strong, tan arms looking good against his blue T-shirt. He's tall, and he towers over my five-foot-five frame.

His strides are long to match his legs. I have to walk a little faster than usual to keep up.

"So where'd you live before moving here?" he asks. I glance over at him as he swipes his shaggy hair from his forehead before looking over at me.

I drop my gaze. "Not far from here." I don't dare mention we just came from a homeless shelter.

We're both quiet as we cross the street and head over to 7-Eleven.

"What are you hungry for?" he asks when we enter the store.

"I'm thinking hot dog."

He nods and we head over to the cooktop behind the glass and both pick out Big Bite hot dogs and smother them with mustard, ketchup, onions, relish, and cheese. We both get a cherry Slurpee.

I pull out the money from my pocket.

"Let me," he offers, and when he leans forward to pay the cashier, I notice a flower tattoo on his arm with the name *Lily* woven through it.

We take our food and drinks and sit over on the brick wall that divides 7-Eleven from the gas station. I wonder who Lily is.

"Dinner is served." He hands me one of the hot dogs. "You know, I made these from an old family recipe," he says.

"Oh, really." I smile and take a bite. "Delicious. I'd like to get the recipe from you."

"Sorry, but family secrets must be protected." He grins.

I laugh, curious about who Sebastian is besides being cute and funny and very tall. "Do you go to school?"

He shakes his head. "I just graduated. How about you?"

"I'm in school. Well, homeschool."

"Yeah, why's that?"

"I guess so it doesn't interfere with working."

"What kind of work keeps you from going to school?"

"I sort of do acting stuff."

"Like for movies?"

"Yeah."

"That's cool. Are you planning on becoming a big star or something?"

"Nah." I shake my head and smooth my hair behind my ears.

"I like what your bracelet says." He smiles at me.

"Thanks."

"That's what I try to do, you know, not give up even when it feels…too much." He looks down at his hot dog and takes the last bite.

"Yeah, it helps remind me of what I need to do."

"And what's that?" he asks through a mouthful of hot dog.

"I'm—um, trying to figure some things out, that's all."

"I get that." He gazes at me. I nod and sip my Slurpee. Not more than a second later Sebastian's phone buzzes. He jumps off the wall and pulls out his phone and reads the text. "I'd better head back. Nancy's watching my grandma and she needs to leave soon," he says, extending his hand to me. I'm not sure what to do. My hands are full of a hot dog and a drink. Without thinking, I shove the rest of my hot dog into my mouth and take his warm, strong hand and push off the wall.

Now we're standing there facing each other, and he doesn't let go of my hand. Should I look up at him? But what about the food in my mouth? Panicking, I remember the cutting moment when Billy Miller called me hamster face. Determined to not let Sebastian see me with bulging cheeks, I drop my hand from his and turn away long enough to gulp down the big chunk of food in my mouth. But when I turn back, he's already got his hands stuffed in his pockets. "Ready?"

I nod, and we walk quietly back.

"There's a bird on my windowsill, sitting on a nest with two little eggs inside," I say, hoping to break the silence between us.

"That's cool." He nods. "I rescued a bird once from a cat's clutches. I think it was one of those little brown sparrows."

"What happened to it?"

"I put it in a box, fed it baby food, and in a couple of days it was well enough to fly away."

"You saved him."

"Yeah, he just needed a little help." He stops when we reach the green building. "Well, thanks for the invite. It was fun."

"Thanks for making dinner."

He grins. "We'll have to do it again sometime."

"Yeah, that sounds—"

His phone buzzes again. "I really gotta get back. I gotta help my grandma. See ya around."

"Yeah, see ya." I watch him skip every other step until he's on the landing.

"Sebastian," I call.

He turns back. "Yeah?"

"Who's Lily?"

He sighs and runs a hand through his shaggy hair. "Lily's my mom."

"Oh." I nod. "Well, have a good night."

"Goodnight, Skye Girl." And then he turns to go.

I start walking back to the gray building.

I like that he called me Skye Girl.

Eleven

CAREFUL NOT TO FRIGHTEN the bird, I ease my hand outside the window and stuff a piece of bread into the corner of the ledge in case she gets hungry.

I haven't been able to get the image of me ruining the moment with Sebastian out of my head. I'm not sure what was about to happen, but I guess I'll never know now. Sighing, I gather up my papers and stuff them in my folder while reminding my mother for the third time that I won't pass my junior year if she doesn't take me to Commitment Learning. I have to turn in my books and my work and take my final test.

When she still hasn't budged off the couch, I remind her that my entertainment work permit expires mid-July, and if the school doesn't fill out the permission form so I can work over the summer, I won't be working. And I need to make money.

She gets up and scurries to the bathroom. I intersect and hand her a set of clean clothes. She's been wearing the same gray sweatpants and T-shirt for the last three days.

While she's getting ready, I clean up the cups, candy wrappers, and empty soup cans filled with cigarette butts off the coffee table.

I find myself thinking about Sebastian again. He must have been holding my hand on purpose, and maybe he was planning to kiss me. Why did I have to go and mess it up?

When we turn in my books and assignments, I take the ninety-minute Scantron test. Within minutes after I'm done, I get a nod of approval from Margaret, one of the women who run the school. She willingly fills out my renewal for a work permit, giving me a satisfactory in both grades and attendance, and she stamps it with the school's seal.

Maybe I do have some luck after all.

"Let's go to the store," I tell my mother when we get back to the car.

She drives maybe a mile before pulling into a Ralphs parking lot. "I only have sixty dollars," she tells me before getting out of the car.

It's been a while since I've been inside a store other than a mini-mart or a liquor store and I'm amazed at how much food there is. There are shelves and shelves of cereal, maybe hundreds of different kinds, and even more cookies and chips. My favorite sections are the deli and the bakery; they smell so good, but I don't pick out anything because we don't have the money for those luxuries right now, and I need to focus on quantity over quality.

I used to go to the grocery store with my mother when my uncle was alive. He'd give my mother a bank card when he got his social security deposited and we'd fill the basket twice a month. Uncle Richard worked for the DMV up until he got sick with a bad heart. After that, he pretty much stayed in his chair for as long as I remember.

I pile everything I picked out on the conveyor belt: bread, peanut butter, cereal, milk, two jugs of water, bananas, mac and cheese, and a package of chocolate chip cookies. My mother sets down a bottle of booze, a handful of candy bars, and a huge jar of applesauce. My mother happens to be obsessed with applesauce. She's got bad teeth and she says it's sweet and easy to eat. She asks the cashier for a pack of Marlboros. The bill is fifty-eight dollars and change.

When we get back, I go straight for the window and check on the bird, surprised to see her perched on the edge of the nest. And even more surprised to see one of the tiny eggs has a chip in it and the other one has a tiny beak peeking out.

I happily put the food away and make mac and cheese and peanut butter sandwiches. I spend the afternoon watching the babies hard at work as they peck their way out of the only place they have ever known, soon to be introduced to the uncertain world where they will have to learn how to survive.

Hours pass before the two tiny, pink-skinned babies are finally freed. "Guess I'll call you Mama Bird," I tell the bird as she eyes me for a split second before flying off. I sit by the window and watch over her babies, amazed at how vulnerable they are as they blindly fumble over each other, their large dark eyes still sealed shut beneath a layer of transparent skin. "I'll help keep you safe," I whisper.

Mama Bird is putting her trust in me to watch over them when she's gone.

My mother rambles on about a character on her soap named Kurt and how unhappy he is because his wife Marissa is having an affair with her trainer at the gym... *Blah, blah, blah.*

I'm sick of hearing about it but there's nowhere for me to go. It feels like the walls and my mother are closing in on me. I have to get out of here. I wait until she takes her afternoon nap before I grab my backpack, and the key, and slip out the door.

This is becoming a habit.

And one I like.

As I make my way down the stairs and out onto the street, I smile to myself. Surprisingly, everything around me doesn't seem as bleak as it once did.

I stare over at the green building and he's not there. I wonder if he's home. Curious, I make my way over and head up the steps, and peer through the glass door. A row of brown metal mailboxes lines the wall. I try the handle and the door opens. Inside, I scan the names on the boxes, hoping to see his, but there are only first initials and last names. There are at least four people with names starting with S.

But I don't know his last name.

Skipping every other step up to the landing, I count seven doors. I have no clue which one is his. As I'm about to give up and go, one of the doors opens and a girl peeks her head out.

"Who are you looking for?" She's staring at me.

"Um." I feel stupid right now. "I was looking for Sebastian's place."

The girl steps out of the apartment with a chunky baby in her arms. His tiny head is covered in tight black curls. "Who wants to know?"

"Um, well I do." Not that it's any of her business.

"And who are you, his girlfriend or something?"

"Well, no, I mean—I just—need to tell him something."

"I see. You need to tell him something, but you don't know where he lives. Sounds like you're a stalker to me."

"What? No, I'm not a stalker."

Am I?

She lets out a bellowing laugh and startles the baby, who bursts into tears. She switches him to her other hip.

"Never mind." I turn and start to walk away.

"Hey," she calls and I turn back. "You seem cool. He's number four." She points down the hall. "And he's home right now."

Who's the stalker now? "Okay, thanks."

Standing at door number four, I wonder what I'm doing here. I barely know this guy. I figure he might think I'm weird or something showing up at his door like this, but I knock anyway.

When the door opens, Sebastian is standing there squinting at me like he's unsure of what he's seeing. "Skye?" he says, like it's a question.

Maybe that girl's right—maybe I am a stalker. "I'm sorry.

I shouldn't have just shown up, but I wanted to tell you that the babies—I mean the baby birds—they've hatched and they're really cute." A sinking feeling settles in my stomach as I hear myself.

"That's cool."

"Bet it isn't every day someone you barely know knocks on your door to tell you some birds have hatched." I force a laugh.

He shakes his head. "Honestly, not until today."

I offer a shrug, feeling completely stupid. "Okay, well, see you."

His face softens. "Wanna come in?"

I nod and step inside his apartment, and my heart skips a beat when our arms brush.

"I was just making sandwiches. Are you hungry?"

I nod again and follow him through the cluttered living room past a frail-looking woman in a blue robe and pink socks sitting in a wheelchair facing a TV.

"Grandma, this is Skye." He pauses in front of her. I smile over at her, but she doesn't take her eyes off the TV. I continue following him into a kitchen decorated with yellow floral wallpaper and a shiny green linoleum floor. The room reminds me of a garden.

Sebastian yawns. "Sorry. I just got back from a ten-hour shift."

"Where do you work?" I ask, watching him spread mayo on three pieces of bread.

"Wholesale Foods. I had to do inventory before the store opened." He pulls out bologna from a package and places two slices on each piece of bread. "My grandma likes bologna sandwiches. You like bologna?"

"Yes, yes, I do."

He pulls out three more pieces of bread from the bag and sets them on the counter. "She'll only eat bologna sandwiches and cake these days." He slips a slice of cheese and thinly sliced tomatoes on top of the meat.

"I see she's in a wheelchair. Is she okay?"

He plops a slice of bread on top of the finished sandwiches. "She has bad knees," he says, cutting one sandwich into four small squares and setting them on a plate. "I'll be right back." He picks up the plate and heads to the living room.

I peer out from the doorway and watch him set the plate on top of a TV tray in front of her. She glances down at the sandwich. "Here, Grandma, your favorite, bologna."

"Should we eat with your grandma?" I ask when he comes back into the kitchen.

"She refuses to eat if anyone's in the room." Sebastian takes our plates to the table.

I sit at the little table with him. He pours water into two glasses.

"How'd you know how to find me?" He bites into his sandwich.

"I tried looking at the mailboxes but I didn't know your last name." Maybe I do sound like a stalker. "The girl down the hall with a baby, she told me your apartment number."

He wipes his mouth with a sliver of paper towel. "It's Mitchell, by the way. And the girl down the hall is Veronica. My grandma's known her mother, Nancy, for years. Nancy's been a real lifesaver. She helps look after my grandma when I'm at work."

"Where are your mom and dad?"

Sebastian runs his fingers down the glass of water. "My mom

died and my dad—he's…in jail."

"I'm so sorry," I say, wondering how his mom died and why his dad's in jail.

He nods and lowers his eyes. "I'm just glad I have my grandma. Honestly, I don't know where I'd be without her."

"I'm glad you have her too." I touch his hand.

Sebastian glances down at my hand resting on his. He smiles up at me.

"Oh, no! No!" His grandmother cries from the living room. Sebastian stumbles up from the table and rushes out of the kitchen. I follow him to find him picking up a glass of water that has spilled on the table. His grandma's chuckling.

"Lucy's funny, huh, Grandma." He glances up and sees me watching him. "I should have given her a plastic one, but I haven't washed the dishes." He sighs. "Could you get me a dish towel?"

I rush to the kitchen, grab a towel off the counter, and take it to him. "Thanks," he says, taking the towel and mopping up the water. His grandma stares at the TV giggling. I glance over and instantly recognize the iconic episode of *I Love Lucy* where Lucy and Ethel get a job at a candy factory. Lucy and Ethel are supposed to wrap each piece of candy as it comes down the conveyor belt, but when the machine speeds up, they can't keep up and the more the candy passes them by the more they panic and they end up stuffing the unwrapped candy into their mouths and inside their shirts. Uncle Richard said Lucy was a comedic genius.

"Cake." She giggles.

"Okay, Grandma, I'll get you cake, but let's go to the bathroom first." He looks over at me. "I'll be right back."

While they're gone, I walk around the living room. An air purifier hums by his grandma's chair. There's a pile of books on the floor, and bottles of medicine cover the coffee table along with framed photographs. There's one of Sebastian in his graduation cap and gown; his grandma's in a wheelchair next to him and he's holding her hand. Another picture shows his grandma blowing out a bunch of candles on a birthday cake. I pick up a photograph of a pretty young woman with long, wavy golden-brown hair and Sebastian when he was a little boy, the two of them are smiling, cheek to cheek. I know it's his mother right away; she has his same infectious smile.

Sebastian pushes his grandma back into the room.

"Your mom, she's pretty." I place the frame back on the table.

"Thanks," he says, locking the wheels on his grandma's wheelchair and placing a pink throw on her lap. When he straightens, he says, "Maybe we should exchange numbers, so you can let me know when you're around."

"Oh, sure, that sounds great but my phone—" What can I say that won't sound stupid? "I dropped it yesterday, and it's getting fixed... So, yeah, I might even get a new one, which would mean a different number, I guess."

"You can keep your number when you change phones."

"Of course." I nod. "Guess I forgot."

Sebastian takes a notepad from the table and scribbles down his number. "Here." He hands me the paper.

"Thanks." I take the paper, trying to hide my smile. "So, okay, well, when I get it back, although I'm not sure how long it'll take because they said it was pretty messed up, but yeah, I'll call you first thing."

"Great." He nods.

"And thanks for lunch." I fold the paper and stuff it in my pocket.

"It was nice." He walks me to the door. I glance over at his grandma to say goodbye, but she's asleep in the chair.

I step out onto the landing and stare up at him. His eyes dance behind the thickest and longest eyelashes I've ever seen on anyone not wearing mascara. He notices me smiling up at him and then he leans in—I think to maybe kiss me. My heart starts to race and I close my eyes.

And just when I think I'm about to be kissed by the cutest guy, an abrupt loud beeping startles me and I open my eyes.

"Sorry," Sebastian says, pulling out his phone from his pocket and shutting off the noise. He looks at me, frowning. "I gotta give my grandma her medicine."

I nod. "Yeah, of course. Well, thanks again…for the sandwich." I turn to go, but I want to stay. I want to stay and help him clean up the kitchen and look after his grandma and maybe we'll have another chance at—

"Oh, hey, Skye," he calls, and I quickly turn around. "I want you to know, I'm not some pothead or anything. I was smoking my grandma's medical marijuana." He swipes back the hair from his face. "She won't smoke it, so." He shrugs. "I did."

"Okay." I nod.

"Okay, good." He breathes out. "I'll see you."

"Yeah, I'll see you."

I turn and walk down the hall, wishing I hadn't lied about the phone.

Twelve

I CAN'T STOP THINKING about Sebastian and our *almost* kiss.

Does this mean he likes me?

Gazing out the window, I watch Mama Bird feed her ravenous finger-sized babies. I wait until she's done before lifting the window and placing half a slice of bread and a paper cup full of water in the corner of the windowsill. "Something for you, Mama Bird."

She eyes the bread.

Sighing, I stare down at the sides Melvin dropped off yesterday for a movie that I'm supposed to audition for today. I'm worried I'm not going to make it on time because my mother can't seem to break away from the TV. She says she needs to find out what's going on with Kurt and Marissa on her stupid soap.

My future lies in the balance of her fictional characters' lives.

I'm forty-five minutes late to the audition and the sign-in sheet is completely full. I manage to squeeze my name in at the very bottom. *Skye Perry. Role: Lauren.* I scan through the names and notice all the other girls here put Maya for the role. Maybe that means I have a really good chance.

The waiting room is filled with girls and their moms whispering and working on lines and sizing up the competition. Most of the girls are wearing dark clothes and their faces are caked with makeup. I'm hoping they're all dressed like that because they're auditioning for Maya, who's edgy. But then why does it look like I'm the only one auditioning for Lauren? I gaze down at my clothes: blue jeans, a white shirt, and red slip-on shoes. What the—I look like the damn poster girl for the Fourth of July.

A man pops his shiny bald head out of the audition room and studies the sign-in sheet. "Skye Perry." All the girls look up. Some of them snicker as I walk over to him. "Your appointment was at 2:10." He glances up at the clock on the wall. "It's after three."

"I know."

He pauses like he's waiting for some big excuse but when I don't offer him one, he says, "I'll have to see if they'll take you, so hang tight. We've got a lot of people here who were on time."

"Okay, thank you."

He looks past me. "Amy Lewis."

Screw this. I head over to where my mother is waiting and plop down next to her.

"Marissa thinks Steven wants her, but he'll get tired of her, and since she's dumped her husband, she's going to end up without either of them."

"You know they're not real… That it's just a show. Right?"

She squints over at me. "It's been on for over twenty years. That's pretty real."

Sighing, I lean back against the wall and close my eyes.

Every single girl has gone into the audition room and left before my name is called. I have a bad feeling as I walk in. The man and woman don't even look up from their laptops. I head over to the X. They probably hate me because I didn't come on time and they have at least a zillion other girls to choose from.

"Should I slate?"

"That's what we're waiting for." Casting Man yawns.

I look straight into the camera. "I'm Skye Perry. I'm sixteen and I'm from L.A." I turn from side to side like I'm in some criminal lineup.

"Okay, whenever you're ready." Casting Lady flicks her hand.

I start to read Lauren's part, but Casting Lady holds up her hand to stop me. "We're auditioning for Maya. I'll be reading for Lauren."

Are you kidding me, Melvin? "Oh, yeah, of course." But I didn't study for Maya. Melvin told me I was auditioning for Lauren.

Lauren: My mom and dad are always mad at me. They said I've changed. I haven't changed, they've changed. What do they want from me, anyway?

Maya: Forget about 'em, they don't know you like I do. I see you, Lauren, but they can't. They're blind to the truth. They see what they want to see, and what they want to see is their little girl, but you're not their little girl anymore. Are you, Lauren? Hell, you're almost a woman now.

Lauren: But you don't understand. I'm afraid, afraid they'll hate me if they find out. I'm afraid I'll lose them. I can't lose them. I don't want to be all alone.

Maya: Shit, I get it. I get how you feel, Lauren, but you don't have to worry, 'cause I'm here for you and I'm gonna be with you through this hell. Do you know why, Lauren? Because I'm your best friend. I'm the only one you can trust.

"That was really good." Casting Lady smiles. "It felt natural and convincingly real."

"Yes, that was quite good," Casting Man agrees. "Definitely believable."

"Really?" I'm not sure I'm hearing them right.

"Why, yes." Casting Lady tilts her head to one side, nodding. "We'd like to see you back here tomorrow. You'll be doing the same thing in front of the producers. Please make sure you dress the part of Maya, get your lines down, and don't be late."

"I will and I won't." I can't stop grinning as I head out the door before they can change their minds.

"Well?" My mother leaps up from the chair.

"They want me back tomorrow."

"You got it!" She jumps up and down.

"It's a callback, that's all." I bite my lip to keep from smiling.

"That's all? You got a callback! You got a callback!"

"Let's go." I steer her toward the elevator.

"This is the moment we've been waiting for!" She grins over at me and I can see all her yellow-stained teeth.

As she giggles incessantly, I beg the elevator doors to open and notice a penny on the floor. I pick it up. "Can we go to IHOP? I'm dying for pancakes and their strawberry syrup." I've been to IHOP twice in my life and I've never forgotten that sweet, delicious strawberry syrup.

"Melvin hasn't gotten your last check yet."

"Oh." I open my hand and stare down at the shiny penny and think of Uncle Richard and all the times we played poker with penny bets.

Sighing, I turn my hand over and watch it fall.

The elevator door opens and I step inside.

Thirteen

SOMEONE'S KNOCKING ON OUR door but my mother doesn't seem to notice.

"There's someone at the door, you need to answer it," I tell her, busy watching the babies while Mama Bird is gone. They've begun to develop feathery sprouts on their pink bodies and their eyes are wide open. I have given myself the position of bird sitter to ensure nothing happens to them when she's gathering food.

"I'm not answering it."

The knocking persists.

"Look through the peephole and see who it is," I insist, glancing down at the script. I've been trying to memorize my part because I want to be perfect for the callback.

"Fine." She pulls up her pants as she heads over to the door and looks through the peephole. "Crap, it's the landlord."

"See what he wants."

She hesitates before answering the door. I try to listen, but I can't make out what they're saying over the noisy TV. Finally, she slams the door. "This is bullshit!" She starts to cry.

"What's wrong?"

"He's blaming *me* because there was trash he had to clean up! How the hell is that my problem?"

"You said you were going to pick up around the building, remember?"

"I shouldn't have to pick up trash!"

"But you told him you would. That's why he lowered the rent."

"I got ADHD! I can't go out there and do that."

ADHD is a new one. And I'm not sure what that has to do with picking up trash. But my mother's known for making up all kinds of excuses whenever she doesn't want to do something. She can't work because she has anxiety. She can't cook because she can't be around flames or fire. She has to smoke and drink to calm her nerves.

"You said you would, so go and do it." Why did she agree to it in the first place? She has to fix this. I can't leave the birds; they're not ready to fly away yet and I need to concentrate on getting ready for my callback. Not to mention I'd probably never see Sebastian again.

"Too late, he already did the stinking trash and now he wants the hundred and fifty he took off."

"Okay, so pay it."

"I don't have it. He told me we have to pay up or get out. Can he do that?"

"No, yes, I guess… I mean, I don't know. What does the rental agreement say?" I'm so mad I can't see straight. How could I have let this happen?

She throws her hands over her face. "I never filled out anything and he wants the hundred and fifty dollars!" She shouts into the palm of her hands. "Screw him, we're leaving."

I want to shake her. Why does she have to ruin everything? "How much money do we have?"

She drops her hands from her face and sniffles. "Maybe thirty. Get the bags."

"We're not leaving," I say as she collapses on the couch and grabs up her bag. Unzipping my backpack. I pull out my jacket, Lil' Monkey, notebook paper, a baggie with toothpaste and a toothbrush inside, a brush, and finally my small wooden box. Running my fingers across the pink and purple decoupage top, I remember the day I found it at the thrift store, thinking it was the most beautiful thing I had ever seen. My mother noticed me holding it and said I could have it since it was my birthday.

I didn't tell her that my birthday had already passed.

The corners are worn now from being tossed around in my backpack for the last three years. But everything inside is exactly how I left it. I lift out my school IDs and the one and only photo of me as a baby, asleep in my mother's arms. I can't actually see her face in the picture, because it's been ripped off. My mother claims she doesn't recall how it happened.

Inside the box is some thrift-store jewelry, a blue marble that I found on the street, and a handful of Uncle Richard's shiny pennies that I won at poker. Biting my lip, I take out the envelope I started putting my money in because my backpack has a small rip at the bottom and I couldn't take any chances of losing it. Inside the envelope is Nick Vaas's phone number and a stack of neatly folded bills. My hand shakes as I count the money, I have $190.

"I'll be right back," I tell her and head for the door.

"Where do you think you're going?"

I look at her sprawled out on the couch, and all I see is a woman I *never* want to be. "I'm going to fix this." I slam the door behind me.

Standing in front of the red-painted door that has *Landlord* written in black marker above the bell, I notice a little droopy plant sitting on the dirty carpet just inches from my feet. Don't they know this plant needs water and sunlight to thrive? I consider turning back, but I can't leave now. Mama Bird still needs me. And what about Sebastian?

Biting my lip, I push the button.

In a matter of seconds, the door swings open and I'm face to face with a man holding a big fat burrito wrapped in a paper towel. The strong smell of onions and spicy meat explodes inside my nose. I'm almost drooling and have to suck back my saliva.

"I'm sorry about the trash. My mother says you want the whole rent, although I think it's overpriced. I mean, we don't even have a real kitchen."

He stares at me with narrowed eyes. "I have to pay someone to clean up. I have a bad back."

"I can do it, so can we go back to the lower rent?"

He looks up toward the ceiling for a second before he rests his eyes back on mine. "Only if it's done every Monday and on time."

"Okay. So do you still want the money, or can I do some other chore you need done?"

He licks his lips. "I still had to pay someone to clean this time."
He puts his hand out.

I seriously doubt he paid someone a hundred and fifty dollars
to pick up some trash. When I hand over the money, I have to gulp
down the lump in my throat.

"You are a good girl to your mama," he says.

I don't bother to tell him I'm not good at all. I'm handing the
money over because I have to keep the baby birds safe. At least until
they're ready to fly.

"You owe me a ten," I remind him, eyeing the burrito, thinking
it would serve as a fair exchange right now. I wipe my mouth.

He cradles the burrito in the crux of his arm and pulls a wad of
cash from his pocket. I consider grabbing the money and burrito and
making a run for it.

He hands me a ten.

"Just so you know" —I stuff the bill into my pocket and point to
the pathetic little plant on the ground— "that plant needs water *and*
sunlight or it's gonna die."

I turn away from his confused expression and wobble down the
long hall like a tricycle with a missing wheel. I swear I hear my
bones creaking.

"Hey," he calls.

A vision of him handing me a burrito flashes through my mind.
I turn back, grinning foolishly.

"Make sure you clean up *every* Monday."

I nod and watch him disappear into the apartment, where he'll
probably stuff another burrito into his mouth while counting my

money. The money that was meant for finding my father.

Fourteen

I FEEL GOOD ABOUT the two callbacks last week; maybe I do have some talent after all. So far, two of the producers said I have good acting chops. I'm still pinching myself. Last Melvin heard they'd narrowed it down to three girls. I'm one of them.

I haven't been able to sneak away for seven days now because my mother hasn't taken any naps. She says she's got insomnia.

I hope Sebastian hasn't forgotten about me.

At least I'm not hungry. We stopped at the Dollarama after my last callback and I got to pick out a crap load of junk food and about half a dozen bags of pasta and three jars of meat sauce. I've been eating pasta for days.

Her phone rings. I jump up from the chair and watch her answer it. It could be them telling me that I got the part.

"It's Melvin," she mouths.

"What's he saying?" I hover over her now. Could I have booked a major role? I can see it now—*Skye Perry*, the media will say, *once homeless girl gets her big break when she lands the part of a lifetime and enough money to find her father.* And there will be a picture of me and my father together, grinning, plastered on every social media outlet.

"Melvin said *we* have an audition today. Can you believe we *both* do?"

"What?" I'm not sure I heard right.

"He says there's another audition today."

"Wait, what about the callback?"

"He said you didn't get it."

My heart sinks. "Are you sure?"

She nods. "It's okay because he said he thinks *this* is the one."

I can't believe I didn't get the part I worked so hard for. It all feels so hopeless.

"Seriously, *you're* always falling for the crap Melvin tells you."

Her eyes narrow and she purses her lips. "He *says* the audition is for *both* of us."

"What does he mean, both of us?"

"He said it's for kids *and* parents."

I shake my head. "There's no way I'm *ever* auditioning with you."

Before I have a chance to react, she takes a swing, smacking me in the head. "You're going."

My head wobbles around like one of those bobbleheads and for a split second, I can't see straight.

My shoulders collapse as I suck back tears. She looks away from me and rubs her hand. "I'm showering." She storms over to the bathroom and slams the door.

Stumbling over to the table, I drop down on the chair and gaze out the window. Mama Bird is peacefully sleeping, her babies safely beneath her. What I'd give to be Alice right now with the *Drink Me* potion. I'd drink it too and gladly shrink small enough to crawl inside the nest where *she* would never find me.

And I'd be safe there, snuggled with the babies, warm beneath Mama Bird's beating heart.

"I think Melvin's right, this is the one," she finally says after being silent for a half hour in the car. It's taking forever to get to the audition because she only drives on streets, never the freeway; she says the car can't handle its speed limit. "I'm just not sure why they want me to audition too."

I'm pretty sure there's a miscommunication on that one.

There's no street parking anywhere near the building and the parking lot costs eight dollars. She checks her wallet and pulls out a ten. Yesterday she said we didn't have any money.

Parents and teens are pressed together like sardines in the waiting room. I make my way over to the sign-in sheet. We should just leave now. We don't have a chance.

I scribble down our names and her phone number, anyway. We stand in the corner and wait. I can't help but notice all the kids with perfect hair, make-up, and designer clothes.

I look down at my clothes and think, *gently used thrift store edition.*

At least my mother looks more normal, though. Her hair is clean and brushed, her face is scrubbed clean, and she's wearing the foundation that she found in her bag. The warm tone did a nice job of smoothing out the red blotches on her face. Her slacks and long-sleeve blouse are loose-fitting and help hide how skinny she is.

Her eyes dart around the room as she keeps watch of the people sitting on the long bench that wraps around the entire room. When two of them are called into the audition room, my mother swoops in the second they stand up and then waves for me to come over.

There's buzzing in the room, a culmination of all the whispering from the parents and resistance from the kids as their parents primp them and prompt them on how to act and what to say. It's so obvious it's the parents that mostly want this. Most of the teenagers look bored.

A woman sitting next to my mother peers over at us. "Hi, I'm Lindy."

My mother doesn't even look up from her phone. I lean forward and smile.

"This is too much, right?" The woman laughs before taking a swig of water from a gold-studded water bottle. "I don't know why I'm so nervous. I just know my Rebecca Rowe is going to get this." She glances over at a girl sitting beside her and pats her leg. The girl never looks up from her phone. "She has everything they're looking for." Lindy laughs again. Then she proceeds to drone on and on about how Rebecca Rowe has been in movies and national commercials, and is making a name for herself in the industry.

I've never heard of Rebecca Rowe.

She tells me Rebecca Rowe was snatched up by the best agency, All In, and that she got her first job from her very first audition for a national commercial. "Just look at her. She's a knockout. How could they *not* want her?" Lindy wears a goofy grin on her face.

Why does she refer to her daughter by her first *and* last name?

That's Rebecca Rowe's cue to look up from her phone just long enough to flash us a smile. I have to admit she has perfect teeth, incredible blue eyes, and clear skin.

But when I smile back at the girl, she rolls her eyes before looking back at her phone.

Thank God Lindy and her perfect daughter are called into the audition room. They are in there a good twenty minutes before they finally come out, and Lindy appears confident. She laughs with the guy who escorts them out of the room and who is clearly drooling over Rebecca Rowe.

Lindy's probably right; they'll get on the show.

When our names are finally called, my mother says under her breath, "Don't blow this."

Me?

Inside the room, a petite, curly-haired woman approaches us. "Hello, ladies, I'm Amanda Chelis." She shakes our hands. "Please have a seat." She motions to the empty chairs and she sits behind a desk cluttered with stacks of headshots.

My mother grabs my arm and squeezes it tight.

"One moment." Curly reaches over, turns the camera on, and checks to see if the red light flashes. "Okay." She settles back in the chair. "In a nutshell, what we at Greenstreet Productions are trying to do with this show is something a little different than the average audition process. We're planning to do a reality show where we get the viewers involved to vote in picking the next big thing for our new show, *Bree and Brax*. The show centers around a brother and sister moving from the Midwest to Beverly Hills and trying to fit in. Essentially, what we are looking for is interesting, dynamic, diverse, human interest, big personalities, charisma, star quality, etc."

That rules me out.

"With that said, let's get started. I'll start with you, Mom. Tell me a little about yourself."

My mother stares at Curly like a deer in headlights.

"You don't have to be nervous," Curly tells my mother. "I'd like to know a little about you, your name, where you live, and something about yourself that you'd like to share with me."

"Hmm, tell you something about me." My mother's voice raises an octave. "Well, I'm Mary…Mary, um, Perry, and I'm, oh God, how old am I? Thirty-eight, I think." She giggles. "I live in Hollywood—with her." She points to me.

Curly nods. "So, Mary, how long have you and Skye been trying to make it in this business?"

"Oh, let's see, well… Um, she started doing this a few years ago, I think."

"And what motivated you to get into the business?"

"A woman we met, yeah, her kids were in the business and she said Skye was cute and that I should get her into acting because she could make a lot of money, even make it big." She cocks her head to one side. "But she still hasn't made it big yet." She pauses. "Why do you think that is?"

"It's a tough business," Curly says. "In your opinion, Mary, do you think your daughter has what it takes to win a competition like this?"

Her head bobs up and down. "Hell, yes. She can win. She'll win for sure."

It's almost like Curly's smile might be permanently fixed on her face. "What sort of things can you do to help her get that win?"

"Anything, of course," she says, followed by a shoulder twitch.

"That's good to hear." Curly turns her attention to me now. "And you, Skye, please tell me about yourself, what your life is like, your talents, your hobbies, your goals."

"As you already know, I'm Skye Perry. I'm sixteen, I'm homeschooled, and I—" What else can I tell her? Nothing she or my mother wants to hear.

"What are some of your talents, hobbies?" She's still smiling.

I shrug. She's gotta see I've got nothing to offer.

"Just give me a day in the life of Skye."

What can I possibly tell her? That I'm currently living in a shithole, but at least I'm not living in our car? Or that I'm hungry all the time because my mother doesn't value food? Or that there's no way I'm going to be on a show with *her*?

"My life's pretty average." Lie. "You know, schoolwork, auditions. Stuff like that."

I think I see her smile fade a little. She strokes the ballpoint pen under her chin. "What would you say is the most successful booking you have done so far?"

"I did a Stouffer's commercial over two years ago. Honestly, I haven't had much luck after that though, so…I pretty much just do background work. So, yeah." I'm pretty sure Curly is agitated now because her mouth is twitching.

My mother clears her throat. Loud. I don't dare look over at her.

"Like I said earlier, it's a tough business and it can be quite frustrating at times. But that's where persistence comes in." Curly nods as if agreeing with herself. "What would you say is your ultimate goal in the business?"

I shrug. I've only got one goal, and it doesn't have anything to do with making it in Hollywood.

"Is it your dream, Skye, to try and succeed in this business?"

"I wouldn't call it my dream." I can feel my mother's eyes burning into my skin.

"She doesn't know what the hell she's talking about," my mother says.

Curly's smile is a bud of what it was.

I clear my throat. "What I mean is, I most definitely want to succeed."

"That's good because we're looking for raw talent, someone who is likable and relatable, and you have that." Curly's smile is completely gone now.

I seriously doubt I'm relatable. "Yeah, I'm sorry. My mother's right, I don't know what I'm talking about."

I need a backbone. But I need money a lot more.

"You don't have to be sorry. I appreciate your honesty and candor. If you get this opportunity, it could potentially change your life. Are you up for that?"

"She is," my mother answers for me.

"Yeah, I mean yes, I am." Maybe I should play along. There's a chance this could turn out to be something, right? "Who knows, maybe I could win this." I give her my best smile.

Yep, that came out of my mouth.

"Okay, good." Curly's smile reappears, although it's a good deal smaller. "Last question for you, Skye. If you were to be chosen for the show, would you be on board and give a hundred percent?"

"Of course, she would," my mother says.

"What do we get exactly, you know, for being on the show?" I ask.

"Good question." Curly looks down at a stack of papers on her desk. "Let's see, the winner will be given an apartment for a year right here in L.A., and like I mentioned earlier, a paying lead role on our new show."

"Holy shit!" My mother snorts.

"Sounds like a dream come true," I agree, realizing this whole thing could actually change my life.

"Good, that's what I want to hear." Curly offers a swift nod. "Well, that about wraps it up." She stands up and shakes my hand. "I really appreciate you being so candid with me, Skye." She then looks over at my mother. "We'll be sending out callbacks tomorrow."

The second we're out in the hall, my mother shoots me a look that stops my heart. "You blew it, Skye, saying all that bullshit."

I try to ignore the people who are now staring at us and say under my breath, "I was just telling the truth."

"This was our chance at a new life and you blew it!"

Why is it always up to me? "I think she really, really liked me," I insist, heading out of the building and into the parking lot.

"You're right, she did like you." She gets into the car and presses play on the cassette player. Journey's "Don't Stop Believin'" fills the car. "When we get back, I'm going to take a nap."

"Let's get something to eat first."

She reaches into her bag and pulls out the ten-dollar bill.

"Don't we have to pay for parking?"

"There was a girl stamping tickets while you were signing in." She drives toward the exit.

"Great, let's get Del Taco, it's taco Tuesday."

"I do like their iced coffee." She stops at the gate and sticks the ticket in the machine. It sucks it up, and the gate opens.

When she pulls up to the Del Taco drive-thru speaker. I ask for two orders of three crunchy tacos for a dollar thirty-nine each and a free water; she orders iced coffee and a soft taco.

While we wait for our food, I stick my head out the window. When I take in a big gulp of air, the delicious aroma of fried food fills my nose.

My mother sings off-key while tapping her fingers on the steering wheel. I sit back in my seat and when she glances over at me, she says in a pleasant voice, "Sing with me."

I find myself singing along with my mother and Journey.

And when she hands me a bag full of hot, delicious tacos, everything in my life, at least for a moment, feels good again.

Fifteen

RUNNING THE INTERVIEW OVER in my head for the zillionth time, I figure there's no way we're_getting a callback. If anyone gets a spot, it will be Lindy and Rebecca Rowe. They probably impressed the producers.

The phone rings and my mother rushes to answer it.

"Hello!" She listens and clutches her chest while doing a lot of nodding and saying, "Yes, really, yes, sure, yes. We will do that. Yes."

Once she's off the phone, she starts chanting, "We got a callback! We got a callback! Can you believe it? Oh, shit, we gotta be there in" —she glances down at her phone— "three hours!" My mother skips over to the bathroom, laughing her head off.

The building is tall and is made up of mostly windows. We are escorted to the tenth floor and through a door that reads *Greenstreet*

Productions. The waiting room is bright, decorated with a hip modern flair; long white couches, bright orange chairs, narrow black tables, tons of plants, and bold abstract art on the pale yellow walls.

There's an entire wall made of glass. I head over to the window and gaze out over the breathtaking view of L.A., the place many call *City of Angels*. And right about now, it looks heavenly from up here with all the tall buildings shimmering in the sunlight, surrounded by a backdrop of blanketed mountains and palm trees, amid a pale blue sky.

When I turn around, I find my mother by the table, grabbing handfuls of candy kisses out of a big orange bowl and shoving them into her bag.

"Please don't take those," I beg.

She grins up at me and pops one of the chocolates into her mouth.

A red-haired girl appears and has us follow her down a long hallway and into an office where a man is standing from behind the large black desk.

"Hello," says the short, stumpy man in a gray business suit and bright green tie. "Mary, Skye, I'm Eric Fields, one of the producers of Greenstreet."

After we shake hands, Eric Fields sits behind the desk. His very round face sports one of those fake-tanned orangey glows.

"We watched the two of you on video," he says, grinning, and two deep-pocketed dimples appear on both sides of his cheeks. "And we believe you both would be a good fit for the show."

My mother shoots out of her chair and, losing her balance, she tumbles to the floor.

Just let me die right here, right now.

Eric Fields rushes over and easily lifts her up and deposits her back in the chair. Oddly, he's unalarmed by her behavior.

My mother giggles.

I slump in my chair.

"I take it you accept." He chuckles and sits back down in his chair.

"You're damn straight we do," she says.

"Wonderful." He looks down at a pile of papers on the desk. "I see here you have a start date of immediately. That's important because we're filming as soon as next week."

"We've finally made it." My mother rubs her hands together, her eyes beaming.

"It's definitely the first step." Eric Fields looks over at me. "Are you excited?"

"Does it pay?"

"Good question." He nods. "Yes, it does. Twenty-two hundred plus all expenses paid, whether you win or not."

I glance down at the words on my bracelet. "Sounds really good."

"All right." He lifts up a stack of papers. "So, let me tell you a little about what's going to happen. You, Mary, and you, Skye, along with four other young actors and their parents, will live together for about a week, and we'll be following you with cameras. You'll be tested in acting skills and star quality and by the end, we're hoping to get a large number of viewers voting on who they want on our upcoming show, *Bree and Brax*. With that said, this opportunity has the potential to be life-changing." He looks directly at me now. "Skye, this is a competition and a likability factor, so you'll need to give it everything you've got."

"Of course." I smile, thinking about the money I'm going to make. It'll be more than enough to hire Nick Vaas.

"Very good." He slides a stack of papers toward us. "I'm sending the contract over to your agent for review but here's a copy in case you want your attorney to look it over. Please keep in mind, we're in a time crunch and we'll need it signed and back to us as soon as Friday, which I know doesn't give you much time, but we're moving faster than we anticipated."

"No problem." My mother snatches up the papers.

"Well then, welcome aboard." He stands up and extends his hand to me. "Are you excited, young lady?"

"*Yes*, I am. Thank you, Mr. Fields, for this opportunity." I shake his clammy hand. "When do we start?"

"Don't know how I forgot that." He chuckles. "We'll need everyone at the house as early as this coming Monday." He shrugs. "A bit short notice on this one, but that's the name of the game."

As we walk out of the building, dread washes over me. There's no way my mother can do this. I tell myself that no matter what happens, I've been handed a way out. Besides, nothing like this has ever happened to me in all the years I've been in this business.

"I'm hungry. Let's celebrate at IHOP, I saw one maybe a mile down the road." I don't mention that I'm celebrating getting the money I need to not only hire Nick Vaas but to start my new life with my father.

My mother agrees and drives to the restaurant. She pulls into the IHOP parking lot. I can't help but smile.

She tells me to order whatever I want, that she found two twenties last night stuffed in a pack of cigarettes.

"We're going to live in a big house." She grins. "That's what he said, isn't it?"

I nod and read over the menu. Everything looks so good. When the waitress shows up, I order a stack of pancakes, a cheeseburger with fries, and a chocolate shake.

My mother doesn't even flinch at my large order.

"I'll have coffee with cream and sugar, two eggs scrambled, and some white toast. And do you have applesauce?"

"No, sorry, but we do have a fruit cup."

She shakes her head. "Just the eggs and toast."

Sitting here in this restaurant, ordering food and seeing her happy, I figure this is what normal feels like. "I like our new start," I say.

"You're going to win this, Skye." My mother places her palms together and gazes down at the contract.

I pull out the strawberry syrup from the caddy and pour some on a spoon and eat it. I feel myself tingle. My mother fumbles through the contract.

"I don't get any of this." She nibbles on her bottom lip.

The waitress is back and sets down a plate with eggs and toast, a plate of pancakes, and another plate with a delicious-smelling burger and golden fries.

I grin down at all the food on the table. "We could have one of those entertainment attorneys look at it."

She shakes her head.

"Okay, well, Melvin ought to know about contracts." I shove a fry in my mouth.

My mother eats a forkful of eggs. It's good to see her eat. "Maybe we'll dump Melvin after you win," she says.

Dump Melvin? That would be the icing on the cake. It just keeps getting better and better. "When does our contract with him end?"

She pours creamer into her coffee and drinks. "*Hmm*, I don't think we have a contract with Melvin."

I should have known.

My mother drinks the rest of her coffee and holds up her empty mug high in the air. Guess she doesn't see the carafe right in front of her.

I lift it up and pour her another cup.

Sixteen

MY MOTHER HASN'T DONE anything to get ready and we're leaving tomorrow.

I wait until she's napping before I slip out the door with a pillowcase filled with our dirty clothes. I probably have about two hours before she wakes up. After I start the washer downstairs, I head straight for Sebastian's place. Maybe I'm being stupid, maybe I'm making more out of it than I should, but I have to tell him I'll be gone for a week.

Just as I'm about to knock on his door, a familiar voice calls out, "Looking for Bash?"

I turn around and see Veronica peeking out from behind her door. "He went to check out a place for Grandma Marion."

I nod. I didn't know his grandma's name was Marion. "Did she go with him?"

"She's inside. My mama's looking after her." Veronica steps out onto the landing and leans her back against the wall.

"Do you know when he'll be back?"

She stuffs her hands into the pockets of her white shorts. "Guess you two aren't a thing if he didn't even tell you he was going." She yawns. "But if you must know, he'll be back the day after tomorrow."

"Could you tell him I stopped by?"

"If you need to talk to him, you can just call him yourself. He doesn't bite, you know."

I'm about to ask why all the sarcasm, but her baby's crying from inside the apartment and someone yells for Veronica to get back inside and take care of her damn baby.

"Shit, I gotta go." She stares at me for a second and I swear it looks like she's about to cry herself. "Just call him, okay? He's a nice guy." She nods and goes back inside.

I take out my notebook and pen from my backpack and write him a note. I figure I'll take a chance and I wedge the folded paper inside the slit in the door.

After packing clean clothes and things we'll need to take with us, I stay by the window to be near Mama Bird and the babies. Endless thoughts run through my mind as I watch the bird sleep. This whole thing could end in a lot of bad ways. I'm not sure how my mother will be around all the people and cameras.

I'm worried about leaving the birds.

I'm worried I'll never see Sebastian again.

But I need to stay focused on getting the life-changing money.

As I gently push up the window, Mama Bird pops her head up.

"I'm leaving in the morning, but I'll be back," I tell her. She cocks her head to one side and studies me with her eye. "I promise no one will bother you." I spent the day picking up all the trash around the building and I made sure rent isn't due until we come back. "I'll miss you, Mama Bird."

She tilts her head even more and opens her beak, but no sound comes out.

Seventeen

WE'RE INSTRUCTED TO PARK our car in a designated parking lot in West L.A. The man at the guard's station checks our names off a list and gives us a pass to place on the dash.

I glance over at my mother; she looks nice with her hair washed and brushed and her face scrubbed clean. She's wearing makeup with a warm pink lipstick that we bought at the dollar store. Her blue blouse and tan slacks were purchased at the thrift store. They fit her perfectly.

I got lucky and found a hair dryer in an unopened box, and I picked out a pair of nearly new jeans, shorts, tops, new black leggings still in the package, a dress, and a pair of tan ankle boots.

Today, I'm wearing the cream pinafore dress with a white pullover shirt underneath. I feel almost pretty.

My mother lights another cigarette and after inhaling, she holds her breath for a long time before she lets out the smoke. "I don't want to do this show, Skye." She tosses the cigarette out the window. "You do it yourself, like the other jobs."

I shake my head. "You can't back out now. You signed a contract. *We* have to do it. Besides, it's really good money. And you know we need money. You'll be fine. It'll all be fine."

She smacks her lips for the hundredth time since she woke up this morning. "Life will be good after, right?"

"Yes, it will," I say, meaning it, and I turn my focus to a silver van pulling up next to us. A stocky man dressed in a black suit gets out. My mother and I get out of the car and I quickly grab our suitcase from the front seat. When he approaches us, he introduces himself as Oscar, our driver, and puts our suitcase in the back.

Inside the van are velvety maroon seats, little lights glowing from the ceiling, and a bar packed with drinks and snacks.

"Are you picking up anyone else?" I ask Oscar, pulling my backpack onto my lap.

"I picked up one earlier. The others will come some other way."

I nod and glance over at my mother. She's taking things out of the snack bar and stuffing them into her bag.

"Stop, *please*," I whisper.

"It's free, Skye." She grabs soda cans and stuffs them into her bag. I shake my head and look out the window at the cars zooming by on their way somewhere. I, too, have somewhere to go.

I'm just not sure what I'm in for.

When Oscar exits the freeway, he drives down busy streets before turning onto a long, winding mountain road where we pass stunning houses protected behind fancy gates. He pulls the van into a driveway, parks in front of a black iron gate, and punches in numbers on a keypad set in a brick wall. The gate opens and as the van moves up the long driveway, I peer out the window at the towering house ahead, its dozens of glistening Renaissance-style windows sparkling in the distance.

Is this for real?

"We're here, ladies." He parks the van, gets out, and opens the door for us.

"We're staying here?" My mother stumbles out of the van, clutching her bag overflowing with stuff from the snack bar.

I want to die.

"Yes, ma'am." Oscar gets our suitcase from the back and we follow him along a cobblestone path lined with neatly trimmed hedges. As we get closer to the enormous beige structure that screams gothic meets Medieval Times, its huge pillars and arches and too many windows to count makes my heart race.

We approach an elegant stone fountain in the middle of the walkway and I pause, trying to calm my racing heart—*I can do this*, I tell myself while gazing at the statue of a naked woman rising from the water. There's a little stone bird perched in the palm of her hands. I think of Mama Bird and hope she and the babies are doing well. By the time we get back, they'll soon be ready to fly.

We reach the stairs that lead up to the massive house.

"That's a big house," my mother says breathlessly.

"That there's a mansion," Oscar corrects her.

Mansion? I gaze up at it and yes, I see it now, something that incredible could never be just a house.

"We're living in a mansion!" My mother claps her hands.

Oscar laughs.

Cringing, I climb the wide steps toward the house. When we reach the massive porch, Oscar sets our bag down and says goodbye.

Not a second later, a woman appears from behind one of the huge pillars. She looks like she just stepped off the cover of *Vogue* magazine: tall, skinny, glowing yellow hair, flawless complexion. She catwalks over to us in a tight, short orange skirt, white crop top, and gold stilettos. She reminds me of a middle-aged Barbie doll.

"Glad someone else showed up. I'm Candace."

My mother looks down.

"I'm Skye, and this is my mother, Mary," I say.

My mother mutters a hello.

"Nice to meet you." Middle-aged Barbie smiles politely. "Kylie, come here." She waves to a girl who walks over to us, looking like the real Barbie doll, tall, thin, dressed in a pink skirt and pink matching heels. Her silky blonde hair flows around her beautiful face.

I prepare myself to be shunned, to be looked upon as inadequate like every other pretty girl has ever treated me. I can see it all now, the outcast girl (me) and the others.

What am I doing here, anyway?

"Like, this place is to die for," the girl says to me.

"This is looking to be better than I thought." Middle-aged Barbie does a little dance on the patio.

The girl grabs my arm and steers me away. "Don't mind my mother. She can be *really* embarrassing."

I gaze over at my mother, who looks lost.

"You're—?"

"Skye."

"I'm Kylie," she says and lets out a heavy sigh. "You know, Skye, this may seem like a good thing, but I have a feeling they're going to try and make us look like assholes, especially our parents, and that seriously sucks."

That's the exact thing I'm worried about. "I plan on staying one step ahead of them." _

Kylie runs her long elegant fingers with pink painted nails through her silky hair. "I don't know, like, these people are way cleverer than us. They, like, edit in something we say now and make it seem like we said it later, you know, cut and paste."

I'm about to agree with her when the front door opens and we're greeted by a petite woman with massive charcoal-colored hair held stiffly around her head with a whole lot of hairspray. "Welcome, I'm Rayna Mirini, one of the show's producers. Looks like we're still waiting on a few others, but please, please, come inside."

We follow the woman into the foyer and we're greeted by a long-haired guy in a plaid shirt and red baseball cap holding up a video camera.

It feels surreal standing inside this place with its shiny marble floor that flows out toward an enormous wood staircase that climbs up toward the cathedral ceiling where a bigger-than-life chandelier sparkles like diamonds above us. My mother grabs my arm. I can feel her trembling.

Rayna's rhinestone-covered phone buzzes. "I need to take care of this." She waves her phone. "Please, everyone, feel free to use this time to get acquainted."

I glance over at Kylie and her mom, and they're both texting. Looks like I'm going to be literally the only one here without a phone.

There's no way I'm going to fit in.

"Hello, everyone." A woman in a tan business-like pantsuit is standing outside the front door. "I'm Cindy Marsh." The woman steps inside the mansion with a boy that is perfectly put together, like he just stepped out of GQ magazine in his purple button-down dress shirt and tight black jeans. "And this is my son, Matt."

"Hello." He steps forward and straightens his shirt collar. "I'm Matt, and you are?"

Kylie flashes a picture-perfect smile. "I'm Kylie and this is Skye."

"Hi." I nod.

He stuffs his hands in his jeans pockets. "What do you two make of this whole reality show thing?"

"Like, we better watch our backs." Kylie snorts.

"This really isn't my cup of tea," he admits.

Kylie laughs. "Did you just say 'cup of tea?'"

Matt frowns. "You have a problem with that?"

"Like, why are you so defensive?"

He shrugs and walks away.

Kylie punches my arm. "Something's up with that guy."

I'm about to ask her what she means when a voice booms out, "Hey, hey, this is the place, right?" Behind us is a very buff, very bald man in a black tank top and baggy white pants. He's the spitting image of the cartoon character Popeye. I imagine if Popeye himself stepped out of the cartoon into human form, then he'd be standing right in front of us. "Hey everybody, I'm Dan."

A tall, lanky kid, with bleached-white hair carrying a guitar case and wearing a black Metallica T-shirt, peers up from his phone and gives us the peace sign.

"Okay, like so far, we've got an obnoxious cute guy and a bleached-out rocker. Wonder what other characters will be showing up?" Kylie whispers in my ear.

Wonder what character Kylie thinks I am?

Rayna is back and takes her place in the middle of the foyer. She instructs the camera guy in the red cap to point his camera at her. "I'm thrilled you are all here. Now, as you know, we are going to be spending the next week here. Are you all excited?"

A roar of cheers fills the room.

"Okay, everyone." Rayna claps her hands, motioning to another camera guy with a scraggly red beard to come in closer. Then she says in a very cheerful voice, "Hello, everyone. I'm Rayna Mirini, and I want to welcome you all to the mansion. This will be your home for the next few days, and I will be here for you during this whole process. Before we go up to see your rooms, I'd like to introduce our cameramen, Nick, in the red cap, and Scott, in the back. Please be aware that they will be everywhere, following you, documenting everything that's going on. Any questions?"

"Too bad cap guy is just a cameraman," Kylie says.

I glance over at her and she shrugs.

"Let's check out your rooms." Rayna moves toward the stairs.

As we all follow her, I kind of hope I'm rooming with Kylie.

But then I remember my mother. If she rooms with the other women, how will she cope?

"Hold on! Hold on!"

We all turn once again to the door and this time a woman with long dirty-blonde hair leans into the doorway, breathing hard. "Woohoo, those are a lot of stairs." She gazes up at us, laughing. "I'm Lara and this here is my triple-threat daughter, Amber." A cute girl with huge brown eyes and a head full of tight black curls smiles shyly at us.

"Welcome, Lara and Amber," Rayna calls down to them. "Looks like we're all here. Let's get you settled in."

"What about our suitcases?" Lara calls.

"You can bring your bags with you or leave them in the foyer and someone will take them up to you shortly." Rayna waits for everyone on the balcony. "After you get settled in, we'll all meet downstairs in the kitchen at 6 pm sharp for dinner."

"Where's the kitchen?" Lara puffs hard while clanking a suitcase up the stairs.

Rayna points down and to the right. "The kitchen is through that hall."

Kylie nudges me. "Like, that woman's gonna kill us all."

I like Kylie. I like her a lot.

Rayna announces that the kids and their parents will room together. Our room near the stairs is more than I could have ever hoped for. The two queen beds have floral comforters and fluffy pillows propped up against white headboards. A white desk sits by the window. The wallpaper has pretty pink and yellow flowers against a cream background.

My shoes sink into the thick carpet.

"We've made it," my mother squeals.

I shut the bedroom door, so no one hears her. "We haven't made it, not by a long shot. This is a show and it could all go down in a really bad way if we're not careful with what we say and do," I insist. I know how reality shows work, and we could be humiliated in front of all of America.

"Yeah, yeah," she moans and drops down on the bed closest to the door.

My mother's already under the covers while I unpack our suitcase and hang our clothes on empty hangers inside the closet. Someone raps on the door.

"Skye, it's me, Kylie."

I don't want her to see my mother in bed. But it's too late. Kylie's already opened the door and is peeking inside. "Like, why is your mom sleeping?"

"Umm." I shrug. "She's tired." I stand in front of her to block her view. I'm not about to explain why my mother's asleep in the afternoon.

"Come on, let's check out the rest of the house."

"Hang on a sec." I grab my backpack off the side table and slip out the door without waking my mother. As I follow Kylie down the curving staircase, I slide my hand down the smooth mahogany banister and think of Annie when she went to live with Daddy Warbucks and came down the stairs singing about her new life.

Kylie makes a left at the bottom of the stairs and opens the first door in the very long hallway. We peek into a library with wall-to-wall built-in bookshelves filled with literally hundreds of books.

Next, we find a game room with a pool table, ping-pong table, and a big-screen TV. Then a bathroom, a sewing room, an office, and a music room. The music room has pale wood floors and lavender walls. All the furniture is gray and white and faces a shiny white grand piano propped up on a velvety purple platform near a large picture window.

Kylie heads over to the piano and sits down on the bench.

"You play?"

"Yeah." She positions her hands above the black and white keys and when she plays, her fingers glide effortlessly over the keys.

"Wow, Kylie. You're good." I clap after she strikes the last note.

"I should be. I was, like, forced to take lessons for years." She steps down off the platform and grabs my hand, pulling me out of the room.

We make our way down the hallway toward the other side of the mansion and we pass a huge living room with a wall-to-wall fireplace, and then an elegant dining room with a table set for ten with beautiful porcelain plates and gold place settings, and two huge gold candelabras in the middle of the table.

Do people actually live like this?

We peek inside a room that has a lace canopy bed, an attached bathroom, and a separate entrance. And finally, we end up in an enormous kitchen that looks like it came right out of one of those dream kitchen magazines. The pale wood floors gleam and there's an entire wall made up of windows with a view of an immaculate yard. We follow the long, deep purple granite counter over to a breakfast nook with a table and chairs. There's even a fireplace in the corner.

Kylie pulls open the enormous refrigerator door and takes out a water bottle. Curious, I gaze inside, surprised to see every shelf filled with food.

"Can you believe all the food in here?"

She shrugs.

"Just look at it," I insist, pointing to the packed refrigerator.

"The devil's temptation." She sips water from the bottle.

"The what?"

"The devil's temptation. That's what food is, Skye."

"Food keeps us alive."

"Does it? Like, you must know about all the processed crap with hidden poisons. And the truth about fried stuff, like in there." She points to a box of Krispy Kreme donuts. "Like, those things cause obesity, diabetes, heart disease, maybe even cancer. People aren't doing themselves any favors by eating that crap."

Kylie shuts the refrigerator door. "I stay away from crap like that. Otherwise, I'd be fat." Kylie smooths her hand over her flat stomach.

Flipping up the lid, I gaze down at the neat (and clean) sugary donuts and pluck one out.

"Like, those things can make you fat." Kylie watches me. "And that's not what this industry is about."

"Oh, I don't know. There's all sorts of people in the industry."

"Hmm." She watches me as I bite into the doughy-soft donut that melts in my mouth.

"Didn't you hear a word I said, Skye?"

"I did." I shove the rest of the donut in my mouth and chew. "But honestly, I have one life and I want to spend a lot of it eating."

Kylie shakes her head. "You'll never make it with that attitude."

"I'm beginning to think this business is based mostly on luck." My mother and I are living proof.

Kylie laughs. "I guess I can have one if I want," she tells me as I pluck another one from the box and take a bite. But as she reaches for one for herself, her hand snaps back like she just got burned. "Nah, I can't get distracted. I have to look great. Everyone expects it." She snatches an apple from the fruit basket on the island. "This'll be enough for today." And she bites into the apple.

Eighteen

BURYING MY HEAD INTO the soft pillow, I sniff the sheets that smell like roses. Everything smells so good here. Giggling into the pillow, I can't believe how lucky I am right now.

My mother snores softly in the bed across from mine. I get up and take the hair dryer from the suitcase and my backpack from the table and tiptoe to the ultra-pretty bathroom decorated with pale pink painted walls. The sink is an enormous white porcelain bowl and water comes out of a wide gold faucet. I walk on a floor that is so shiny it looks wet.

The spacious shower stall is equipped with shampoo, conditioner, body soap, and big fluffy towels and washcloths. I can't believe my luck as I stand under the hot water that lasts more than a few minutes. I can't stop smiling as I pour the berry-scented shampoo over my head.

She's awake when I come out dressed and ready to go downstairs. I remind her to shower and brush her teeth. She groans as she opens the nightstand drawer and takes out a pack of cigarettes and a lighter.

"You *can't* smoke in here. We signed an agreement last night and one of the rules is no smoking, remember?"

"Fine." She drops the pack and lighter back into the drawer and drags her feet over to the bathroom and slams the door.

As we make our way to the kitchen, there's a buzzing of voices inside. My mother comes to an abrupt halt right outside the entrance.

"I don't want to go in there," she whispers in my ear like she's telling me a secret.

"But being on the show means we have to socialize," I whisper back.

"I don't want to socialize today."

"We're here so we can maybe change our lives. That's what you wanted."

She shakes her head. "I don't want to be around all these strangers."

"If you get to know them, they won't be strangers. You need to be friendly."

"Well, I don't want to." She folds her arms across her chest.

I glance around to make sure no one has noticed us.

"I'm going to the room. You need to come too."

I shake my head. "I can't. I have to do the show. It's my job."

"Oh." She nibbles at her bottom lip.

"I'll be fine. I'll be with the staff and producers. They're my bosses."

"I see." She thinks a minute before nodding "I'm going upstairs. Bring me coffee when you're done." And she turns and walks away.

"Hey." Kylie comes up to me. "Everything okay?"

"Yeah." I nod, but I doubt it's even close to being okay.

"*So.*" She grins. "We're trying to stay away from the parents. Come with." She slips her arm around mine and leads me out of the room. "What's up with the backpack?" she says as she steers me into the dining room.

"You girls took too long," Garrett says when we enter the room. "Matt and I have already played two games of pool. Sorry you missed out." He pours Honey Nut Cheerios into a bowl.

"Who says we wanted to play pool with you, anyway?" Kylie sits at the head of the table.

Relieved she's forgotten about the backpack question, I shove it under my chair.

Matt pushes two bowls over for me and Kylie.

"Thanks." I take them and hand one to Kylie, but she shakes her head. I pour Honey Nut Cheerios into my bowl.

Kylie peels an orange.

"How do you guys like being here?" Matt asks, gazing up from his phone.

"I like it," Garrett says. "I can use the money for some music equipment. But my dad's missing being at work. He co-owns a gym with a buddy of his and my dad's the expert on workout classes, bodybuilding, and nutrition. He's been getting a lot of texts from his clients about how they're missing him." Garrett lifts the bowl and drinks the milk from it.

"It's pretty nice here, but I hope it doesn't take too long. I've got a lot of things going on back home." Kylie eats an orange slice.

"Wish I was back home too. I'm missing some awesome auditions this week." Matt sighs, staring at his phone. "But being here means a lot to my mom."

"So where you from, Matt?" Garrett asks.

"New York."

"Where abouts?"

"Manhattan."

"That's cool. My cousin lives in Brooklyn, and he and my uncle took us to see Green Day in concert when we visited," Garrett says. "Are the auditions for a movie or something?"

"Theater."

"You a theater nerd, Matty?" Kylie raises an eyebrow.

"Quite the contrary. Not all theater actors are nerds." Matt straightens his shirt collar.

"Quite the contrary," Kylie mimics while sweeping back her silky hair. "Hmm."

Matt shakes his head and eats his cereal.

Amber appears in the doorway scowling. "I was wondering where you guys were."

Garrett hands her a bowl.

"You are such a gentleman." She giggles, taking the bowl.

Garrett grins at her. "Where do you live, Amber?"

"Georgia."

"Ugh, like, that place is infested with mosquitos and God, the humidity. I had to go there for a modeling shoot once, *never* again."

Kylie groans. "Guess you want to win, huh Amber, so you can get the hell out of that place?"

"Kylie Hanson, I happen to love my hometown, and I plan to raise my family there."

"Why the hell are you thinking about that?" Kylie pops an orange slice in her mouth.

"I don't know." Amber lowers her eyes.

"Where do you live, Kylie?" Garrett asks.

"Newport Beach."

"Oh, wow, that's totally cool, you living by the beach, surfing every day if you want." Garrett pours more milk into the bowl. "How about you, Skye?"

"Here in L.A."

"Damn, you're lucky. Sure beats my sleepy town of Ohio." Garrett shoves a spoonful of cereal into his mouth. "I've always heard this is the place to make your dreams come true." He takes a moment to chew his food. "You know that saying, the streets are paved with gold."

"The streets aren't *actually* paved in gold." I frown.

They all laugh.

"There you all are." Rayna enters the dining room. "It's good to see you getting along, but I'd like you to come back. It's time to get to work."

Gathering our bowls, we follow the clicking of Rayna's cream-colored heels to the kitchen.

"Good morning, everyone, glad to see you are all here." Rayna scans the room. Red Cap points his camera solely at her. Whiskers aims his camera at the rest of us. "Yesterday, you all had the chance to get acquainted over dinner, and we went over the house rules. Today, the kids are going to meet one of our acting coaches where they will do a little exercise."

"Is this part of the competition?" Lara interrupts.

"Everything the kids do here is considered part of the competition. Please keep in mind, you are all competing for something big."

Amber and her mother exchange a glance like they know something we don't.

"We are also going to begin interviews over the next two days," Rayna continues. "And parents, just so you know, we just want to see the kids today. Please feel free to enjoy the house, pool, jacuzzi—"

"Why can't we be with our kids?" Lara frowns.

"We want to get to know just the kids. With that said, Garrett, you're up."

When it's my turn to do an interview, Rayna takes me to an office inside the house and invites me to sit down in front of a man behind a desk. Rayna sits next to him and she introduces him as Mr. Norton, one of the producers. He's got this peculiar unwavering scowl and a pair of bushy eyebrows that furrow around his narrow eyes—that are currently staring right at me.

When he grunts a hello, it hits me that he reminds me of the Incredible Hulk. Except he's not green.

"We're here to see what we can do for you," Rayna says. "And we want to help prepare you for this opportunity."

Help me how? I doubt I have a chance at accomplishing anything more than collecting the paycheck for being here, considering I'm not beautiful and interesting like Kylie, or like Amber with her confidence. I'm not a rock star like Garret, with his cool vibe and demeanor, or sophisticated like Matt.

"I don't think there's anything you can do to help me."

Rayna's brow furrows. I bet she's thinking, *what the hell is your problem, kid? If you don't answer my question, then just go. I've got a bunch of other kids out there who actually want this.*

And I bet Hulk's thinking, *who the hell put her on the show?*

One of your dumb producers, that's who.

"Skye, why do you feel that way?" Rayna asks.

I take in a deep breath. "I don't know. I mean, I'm not like the others."

"How are you not like the others?" Rayna asks.

Folding my hands in my lap, I look from Rayna to Hulk to Rayna again and I think: *why not tell them the truth?* It isn't like they're going to kick me off the show for being honest. "I'm really not that interesting, and I'm pretty sure I don't have that *it* factor that's needed in the industry. I can't even tell you how many auditions I've been on and so far my success isn't worth mentioning unless you consider background work success."

"You are here, aren't you?" Rayna says.

"Yeah, that's true. I did get this, although I'm not sure why."

Hulk squints at me. I wouldn't be surprised if he topples over the desk, grunting some terrible monster-like sounds as he throws me through a window.

I'll keep my eye on him, just in case I need to run.

"Do you even *want* to be in this business?" Hulk speaks for the first time.

I shrug. "It doesn't really matter that much to me."

Rayna clears her throat. "What does matter to you, Skye?"

I stare back at them and it occurs to me that no one but me knows what matters to me. So, I blurt it out. "My father matters to me."

Rayna leans forward and says in a semi-eerie tone, "Can you tell me about your father?"

I shrink a little in my chair.

"Let's see." She skims through papers in a folder with my name on it. "There's no mention of your father in the paperwork or questionnaire."

"Well, yeah, because I don't know who he is, but…I'm going to find out."

"Can you tell me more about that?" Rayna asks.

The energy in the room has definitely shifted and I'm pretty sure I've become a person of interest. I look down at my hands. "I can't."

"Why can't you tell us?" Hulk says.

Because it's none of your bushy-eyebrow business, that's why.

From the corner of my eye, I see Red Cap moving in and now he's literally four feet away from me. I frown into the lens of the camera. Rayna motions with her hand for him to step back.

But it doesn't matter if he steps back because he'll just use the zoom. "Like I said." I rest my eyes on Hulk now. "I don't know anything about him."

"Maybe we can help you, Skye," Rayna says.

My leg starts shaking. "Help me how?"

"Can you first tell me a little about your situation, you know, the reason why you don't know who your father is?"

"Because my mother won't tell me anything." I press my hand deep into my leg to make it stop.

"I see." Rayna glances over at Hulk and he nods like she just spoke to him with her eyes. "Maybe we can help you find your father. If that's something you would be interested in."

Did I hear that right? "You'll help me find my father?"

Rayna nods. "We could explore the possibility."

My throat constricts and when I try to breathe in, I start choking.

"Are you okay?" Rayna's off her chair and leaning over the desk.

I nod and when I'm finished coughing, I say, "Yes, I would like that very much. You finding my father, I mean."

Rayna gets a water bottle from the shelf behind her and hands it to me before sitting back down.

I untwist the cap and take a gulp.

Rayna's got her pen in hand, ready to write. "I'll need something to give to our search team, can you think of anything that would help in the search?"

"I don't have anything to give you. My mother says... She says I've never had a father... You know, like he never existed. But *everyone* has a father, right?"

"Of course." Rayna looks at me like maybe she pities me. "What we can do is talk to your mom and see what she knows."

That's the worst idea. Rayna obviously doesn't get it. "You can't do that. I mean, it's a really sensitive subject for her. Like he probably broke her heart or something. But I still want you to look for him… As long as she doesn't have to be involved, you know, with you finding him."

Rayna shifts in her chair. "It would be a lot more helpful if she were involved."

"I get that." I nod. "But the subject of my father is, like I said, a sensitive one for my mother." My heart's thumping so hard it feels like it's about to burst out of my chest. "But maybe if she were to see him again, she'd be…well, happy, or mad, I don't know. But that could be good for the show. Right?"

"We'd need her permission," Hulk reminds Rayna.

I scoot to the edge of my chair. "What kind of permission?"

"We'd need her to sign a release allowing us to search for him, at the very least."

"Oh, yeah, of course. She'd sign a release at the very least."

"Okay. A release might work," Rayna says. "But the chances go way down without her help."

I nod.

"Okay." Rayna brightens. "If she signs the waiver, I'll see what I can do."

"She'll sign it." I swallow hard. "So, you really think you can find my father?"

"Can't promise, Skye, but we have a really good team here that does things like that." Rayna pulls out a file from her desk, sifts through the papers tucked inside, scribbles on one of the sheets, and hands it to me. "This is for your mother. It gives us legal permission to locate someone for the show. After your mom signs it, we'll get started."

"I'll give it to her right away." I reach for the paper and hope they don't notice my hand shaking.

Nineteen

MESMERIZED, I WATCH AS dust particles float and swirl inside the prism of light streaming in from the window. The second they move out of the light, it's as if they disappear. But I know they are still there, somewhere in the shadows, searching for a place to stick.

I'm like one of those specks of dust, aimlessly moving through space and time, searching for a place to stick.

I close my eyes and remember the first time I asked about my father. My third-grade teacher, Ms. Allen, said everyone had a long line of family members, and creating a family tree would help us discover all the people, past and present, who are connected to us. She had passed out a piece of paper with a drawing of a tree with blank circles hanging from the branches for us to fill in with people in our family. There was one empty circle for my father's name. Thing is, I didn't know his name. Neither my mother nor my uncle had ever spoken of him.

When I got home, I asked my mother about him and why he

wasn't around. That was the first time she said I didn't have a father.

I showed my assignment to Uncle Richard. "What name do I put for my father?" I asked.

My uncle looked at me for a long moment. "Put my name."

"But you're in the uncle circle."

"I, uh, I don't know, Skye. I don't know his name."

"But I have a father, right?"

"What did your mother say?"

"She said I don't have one."

He fidgeted in his chair and started breathing hard. "Then I suppose she's right," he said and he took two puffs from his inhaler.

"But Ms. Allen said that everyone has a mother and father, even if they don't see them."

"Ms. Allen is wrong, Skye. Put my name, Richard Kenny."

But I didn't write in Uncle Richard's name. I put Thomas Perry. I liked the name Thomas. It sounded important.

Rayna says they'll try to find my father, but I don't see how when they, like me, don't even know his name. I tell myself not to worry, that I still have Nick Vaas if this doesn't work out. And he promises he can find anyone.

Pushing myself out of bed, I pass my sleeping mother and head to the bathroom, and lock the door. Studying the paper Rayna gave me, I read a bunch of legal mumbo jumbo about giving permission and about not holding the show liable, whatever the outcome.

I glance down at my bracelet, take a deep breath, and I sign her name.

The door to Rayna's office is open. She isn't there. I go inside and there's an inbox tray with her name on it. I place the release form inside the box and make my way to the kitchen.

There's no one there when I walk in. I glance over at the mirrored clock on the wall. It's 6:30 a.m. After taking a banana from the fruit bowl on the counter, I peel it and munch away as I pull open the refrigerator door. I gather up milk, eggs, syrup, and butter and carry them over to the counter. I take a handful of cookies from the cookie jar and eat them with a full glass of milk. Then I head over to the pantry.

The pantry is like a mini-mart. There are all these different cereals, assorted canned foods, every kind of pasta, jars of pickles and jellies and sauces, tons of snacks, drinks, water bottles, and neatly stacked paper goods that fill the shelves. There's even an entire shelf dedicated to spices.

I pluck out a box of pancake mix and find a mixing bowl. I dump in the entire box of powder and add eggs and milk, then mix it all with a wooden spoon until the batter is smooth. I remove one of the shiny pans hanging from the overhead hangers and switch on the burner on the stove. Finally, I pour the thick batter onto the pan and watch it bubble into mouth-watering pancakes. When I'm just about ready to flip my ninth one, I take a moment to admire my stack.

"Smells good in here."

Startled, I drop the spatula and turn to see Garrett grinning from the doorway in a dark gray Foo Fighters T-shirt and white jeans. "You shouldn't do that." I pick up the spatula and rinse it off in the sink.

"Do what?"

"What's going on in here?" Kylie strolls in, looking as if she just came from hair and make-up and dressed in a stylish, short, mint green summer dress.

"Skye's making pancakes, and I'm starving." Garrett's staring at the stack on the plate.

"They do smell good." Kylie grabs an orange from the fruit bowl.

"How many would you like?" Garrett asks.

"Oh, no, none for me." She waves her hand. "I never touch things that come from a box."

"But you said they smell good." Garrett frowns.

"Like, all sorts of things *smell* good, but that doesn't mean they're good for you."

Garrett grabs the plate I intended for myself. "Let me make you a plate. I don't think I've ever seen you eat anything but fruit."

Kylie frowns. "Seriously, what are you, my keeper?"

"No, I just think you should eat." Garrett shrugs, piling *my* pancakes on *my* plate.

"I'm not eating the frickin' pancakes," she hisses.

"Oh-kay." Garrett takes the plate full of pancakes to the table.

"He's just trying to be nice, Kylie," I say, flipping a pancake in the pan.

"Ugh." Kylie shudders. "He's so into me, Skye, and I don't want to encourage his little infatuation."

Of course, Kylie has all the guys falling for her. Just look at her. I wonder if Sebastian feels anything like that for me.

"You're not going to eat all those, are you, Garrett?" Matt makes his way over, dressed neatly in a tucked-in button-down shirt and black slacks.

"That's the plan." Garrett chuckles, stuffing a syrupy pancake into his mouth.

Matt takes a pancake from my new stack and rolls it up and takes a bite.

"No syrup?" I ask, counting only five pancakes left.

Matt chews thoughtfully. "Frankly, I learned this method because I don't have a lot of time to get somewhere back home, and when walking or taking the subway, I often stop at a food truck and eat and walk. I find it's easier and neater to simply roll things up."

"Whatever works, man." Garrett shoves the pancake in his mouth. "Hey, I'm gonna go check out the yard." He gets up and heads for the back door. "You guys wanna come?"

"I'm down." Amber steps into the room in a cute red and white polka dot romper. I'm beginning to feel like I stick out like a sore thumb in my black leggings and oversized shirt.

"Yeah, sure." Matt nods, washing his hands in the sink.

Kylie shrugs, grabs my hand, and leads me out the door before I even have a chance to eat my pancakes.

"It's like a botanical garden here." Amber tiptoes barefoot down the path as we pass gardens with sunflower blossoms bursting out from among wildflowers of every color. We approach a narrow archway that leads us through a tunnel made of vines. We end up in what looks like a sanctuary with statues of baby-like cherubs and tall, elegant angels. Ahead of us is a bridge that crosses over a koi pond. We stop on the bridge and gaze down at the huge orange and white fish and turtles swimming and bobbing in the water.

Matt points to a bunch of turtles piled together on a rock. "Those turtles are lucky."

"Why's that?" Garrett leans over the bridge and his white hair dangles above the water like the shimmering moon.

"I don't know, maybe because they don't have to worry about anything."

Garrett dips his fingers in the water. "What's it like living in New York?" Garrett glances over at Matt.

"Manhattan is incredible." Matt shoves his hands in his pockets. "Every day I'm out there, I feel like anything's possible with all the energy, the people, the buildings, and the busy streets. It's the best feeling ever."

"Sounds amazing." Amber skips across the bridge.

"I've been there, and it smells like a rotting corpse." Kylie shudders.

"Sometimes it does smell," Matt says.

"What do you mean, it smells?" I ask, wondering how a place that sounds so incredible could smell like a rotting corpse.

Matt says, "It's a combination of humidity and with all those people in the streets who sweat, not to mention all the trash, and the city's got a lot of it, so, yeah, it can get rather raunchy before trash pickup."

"That's awful." Amber crinkles her nose.

"Oddly." Matt shrugs. "It's part of my city's charm."

Matt calls Manhattan *his* city. I've never felt like L.A. was mine. I wonder if my father lives here. I wonder if Rayna found the release form yet. Maybe, just maybe, my life is about to change sooner than I hoped.

We continue on the path surrounded by miniature palm trees and giant, leafy plants that leads us to a huge rock waterfall that flows into a glistening pool.

"This place is unreal." Garrett rolls up his jeans, heads straight for the pool, and slips his feet in the water.

Matt's next. He removes his shoes and socks and then carefully rolls up his pants before sitting beside Garrett and dipping his feet in too. "Nice."

The rest of us sit at the edge of the pool and immerse our feet in the warm, delicious water.

This place is like something from a fairy tale.

Matt stretches out his smooth, muscular legs. "What will you guys do if you win this thing?"

"Like, it wouldn't be the worst thing being on that show," Kylie says. "It could open up doors for me. But I don't want to commit to a show for years."

"Well, if I get the part, I'll be famous and make enough money so I can start my own business," Amber sings.

"And what business is that?" Garrett asks.

"I don't know yet." She shrugs. "What about you?"

Garrett paddles his feet in the water. "It'll be a good way for me to get my music out there. Those celebrity kids on TV shows often end up getting into music or, really, whatever they want. It could be my in as a musician."

"That's smart." Matt nods. "I'm not really sure about all of this. I'm happy my mom gets to see her sister who happens to live not far from here, someplace called Glendale, I think. But after being here, it doesn't feel anything like home."

"Well, one of us is going to win this thing," Amber says.

"I think they should give all five of us our own show," Kylie says.

"And it'll be about a band trying to make it." Garrett pretends he's playing the guitar.

"Or it could be more like a musical." Matt grins.

Garrett laughs. "Like Metallica meets *High School Musical*."

"And who are the love interests?" Kylie's eyebrows raise.

"Yeah, who?" Amber grins shyly over at him.

Garrett scrambles up and stands at the edge of the pool. "Wouldn't you like to know?" He winks and jumps into the water.

Twenty

RED CAP AND WHISKERS attach wireless mics to us while we sit around a huge table inside a conference room. A woman with a beehive hairdo and red pantsuit walks into the room maybe ten minutes later carrying a stack of papers and dumps them on the table.

"Hello everyone, I'm Willa Harris." She scans the room and sits down on a chair at the head of the table. "I'm an acting coach and I'm here today to get a better idea of where each of you is at as an actor. I'm also here to give you some acting pointers to hopefully prepare you for the next phase of the show. So let's get started and go around the room. Please introduce yourself, state your age, where you're from, and tell me what makes you unique." Willa Harris points to Amber. "Let's start with you."

Amber stands up and grins. "I'm the one and only Amber Vernell. I'm seventeen, from Atlanta, and what's unique about me is I dance, act, model, and sing. I've been likened to Zendaya."

"Clearly delusional," Kylie says under her breath.

Willa Harris studies her for a moment. "It would be best to be likened to only yourself." Then she motions to Garrett.

Slumped in the chair, Garrett stumbles up and pulls down his bright-yellow Rolling Stones T-shirt. "Hey, I'm Garrett, seventeen, raised in Cleveland, Ohio. Unique about me, well, I'm Korean, orphaned, and then adopted by my dad. Ever since I was a little kid, I've been obsessed with music and I'd say it comes pretty naturally to me. I compose, sing, and play guitar, drums, and keyboard." He crinkles his nose. "I brought my guitar but Rayna said I can't use it on the show, some kind of conflict of interest."

"It could be an unfair edge," Willa Harris agrees with him. "You definitely have a good look though, and it sounds like you are quite talented. Besides music, are you interested in pursuing acting?" Willa Harris asks.

"I mean, yeah, I sorta like acting, took a few classes. But I'm not gonna lie. I'm trying to make it in the music business and think doing something like this could get my name out there. Open some doors. You get me?"

"I got you." She grins for the first time. "It appears your goal is musical fame."

Garrett nods. "Yeah, that about sums it up. I mean, I've seen musicians get on TV shows, and the next thing you know, they've got the platform for their music."

Willa Harris nods, smiling. "Thank you for being so honest, Garrett. It'll be interesting to see your acting chops." She nods and points to Matt.

Matt stands up, wearing khakis and a light blue dress shirt, the clothes he changed into after Garrett splashed him when he jumped into the pool.

"I'm Matt Marsh, I'm seventeen, and I live in New York. I'm not sure if it's considered unique, but I live for performing. My passion is theater. I think about being on stage every minute of the day. I love everything about it and I've got my eye on making it big."

"Theater can be unforgiving," Willa Harris says. "But it sounds like you've got the right mindset, Matt."

"Absolutely. I've been working in the theater since I was eleven and I know how demanding it can be. But I'm willing to work as hard as I need to."

"I like your perseverance, Matt." Willa Harris produces a broad smile. "I'm sure you have a lot to bring to the table." And then she points to me.

I stand up and look around the room. They all clearly have goals and dreams. "I'm Skye Perry. I'm sixteen and I live in L.A. I'm not sure there's anything unique about me, though."

Willa Harris asks, "What is your passion, Skye?"

I'm not sure I'm passionate about anything. I shrug.

"Is there something you feel you're good at?"

"Um, maybe singing."

"All right, we have a musician and a singer." She nods. "But I think, Skye, you might want to ask yourself what you want."

My vision blurs. I don't need to ask myself what I want because I already *know* what I want, and it has nothing to do with making it in this business. I nod and look past Willa Harris at the words written on the wall-to-wall dry-erase board. *Your regrets aren't what you did, but what you didn't do. So I take every opportunity.*

Cameron Diaz.

I sit back down.

Willa Harris points at Kylie. "You're up."

"I'm Kylie Hanson, I'm seventeen, I'm from Newport Beach and I don't know if you can call it unique, but I've been modeling all over the world since I was nine. My most recent runway was for New York Fashion Week. It was incredible, especially since I got to keep one of the dresses."

What I'd give to be even a little like Kylie Hanson.

"Quite impressive, Kylie. Sounds like you are doing well. Thank you." Willa Harris looks out over the room. "Lots of talent in this room, from what I've heard. So okay, let's get started. First, I'm going to pair you up and give you a prompt. From the prompt, I want you to step into a character and create a scene and be as natural and believable as you can when interacting together. With that said, Amber, Garrett, you're up. Come stand in the middle of the room so we can all see you."

The camera crew is armed and ready.

Amber giggles as she heads over with Garrett to the open space.

"Garrett, you start with *I'm sorry to tell you this but—*"

We wait for Garrett. Amber stands there twisting her tight curls.

"I'm sorry to tell you this, but—" Garrett laughs. "Sorry. Let me try again." He shakes himself like a wet dog. "I got this." He stands still now and looks at Amber and says, "I'm sorry to tell you this, but you didn't get the lead role or any other part for that matter."

Amber stares at him wide-eyed. "You've got no one better than me for the part... And when your movie flops?" She slams her hands on her hips. "And it *will*...because *I'm* not in it."

"Look, it's not personal. I need a big-name actor, not a no-name...like you."

Amber's dark eyes glaze over. "Why're you being a jerk, Garrett?"

"Face it, dude, you're not gonna make it in this business."

"Screw you!" Amber heaves back tears.

"Okay, you can stop there." Willa Harris holds her hand up. "I think there were some interesting moments. Garrett, you had too much hair covering your face, and we need to see your face to connect with you. Although I like parts of what you both did, Amber, you came on a bit too strong without any backstory. It felt like you were being yourself, and not in character."

"Hey, Amber." Garrett rubs her arm. "I was just acting."

Amber storms back to her chair, frowning.

"Next up, Matt, Kylie, and Skye. Let's see what you three can do with the same line. Kylie, you'll start with, 'I'm sorry to tell you this, but...' and make us believe you."

Kylie looks up at the ceiling and closes her eyes. "I'm ready," she finally says, standing beside Matt. Kylie looks straight at me and says, "I'm sorry to tell you this, but" —Kylie bites her lower lip— "your father and I are getting a divorce."

It's my turn to say something. "I—I know I've been a pain lately, but I promise you both, I won't be any more trouble."

Matt approaches me and rests his hand on my shoulder. I look into his eyes and could swear I see the pain in them. "It has nothing to do with you, sweetie." He glances back at Kylie. "This is about your mom and me. Isn't that right?"

Kylie nods.

Matt turns his attention back to me. "Your mom and I are going to make this as easy as possible for you. And don't ever forget how much we love you."

Kylie comes over and meets my gaze. "Yes, we *both* love you very much." And then she hugs me.

Matt's eyes are brimming with tears as he watches us hold one another. Is he really crying or is it stage crying? Before I can even blink, he throws his arms around us both. "You can always count on us," he breathes out. I can feel his body trembling.

"You can stop there." Willa Harris waves over at us. "I liked the way you all worked together. It was tight, heartfelt, and believable. I have to say, Matt, there was something compelling in how you delivered your lines. Must be all that stage experience. Great job."

"Thank you." Matt nods, shoving his hands in his pockets.

Amber raises her hand.

"Yes, Amber?"

"I was wondering what you thought of *my* performance. You know, how good *I* was?"

"Like I said earlier, you had the intensity." Willa Harris straightens the papers on the desk. "I just think you could work on getting out of Amber and into your character. *Become* the character you are portraying, and respond like the character would respond. You all did a good job. My suggestion to all of you is that you continue to stay in the moment, and make sure you put yourself into your character and *be* that character. You only get one shot at getting noticed. Does that make sense?"

We all nod.

"I'd say we got a real competition here. You feel me?" Kylie slaps Matt's arm.

Matt scrunches up his nose. "Yeah, I feel you."

Twenty-One

WHEN WE GET BACK, Matt and Amber head up the stairs and Garrett, Kylie, and I make our way to the kitchen. Popeye's at the counter slicing up apples and popping leafy greens into a blender. When he sees us, he greets us with an *ahoy matey.*

Kylie grabs water from the refrigerator and tells us she'll be right back. Garrett goes straight for Popeye. I'm surprised to see my mother at the back table and I make my way over to her. "I didn't know where you were," she says with her eyebrows raised. "I thought you disappeared but that man over there" —she points to Popeye— "said you'd be back any minute."

"I had to do an acting thing for the show because this is a job, remember?" I lean in and whisper. "And we're getting paid a lot of money."

"A cameraman wanted me to do an interview."

I lose my breath. I can't let her do an interview at all. She could mess up my chance at finding my father. "Did you do it?"

She shakes her head. "I told him I'd only do one with you there.

He took someone else, the lady that talks real loud." My mother's referring to Lara, of course.

"Don't interview without me, no matter what, okay?" I now have to worry about Rayna saying something to my mother about the release form, so I've got to make sure she doesn't do any interviews until then.

"I'm going to the room. It's almost time for my soaps. You need to come."

"I can't. I'm still working," I tell her.

"Then don't leave again." She lets out a long wheeze.

"I won't. I'll be right here the whole time, just think of this house as the set."

She nods and turns to go and as I watch her walk away, she seems so tiny and frail.

Minutes later, Lara's voice vibrates the walls when she walks into the kitchen with Amber at her side. She's already complaining about what a joke it is that she's being kept from her daughter when they're supposed to be doing this show together.

Popeye looks up from the blender and rolls his eyes.

"You don't agree, Dan?" she grunts out and plucks a can of Coke from the refrigerator.

"This is about the kids, not us, Lara." He pours the green gunk into a glass.

"Guess it wouldn't bother you, Dan, seeing how your kid is just a musician."

"Just a musician." His eyes bulge. "You don't know what the hell you're talking about. My kid's a musical genius."

Red Cap slinks around the kitchen, holding his weapon. Popeye notices and stares blankly into the camera before walking out of the room, holding his green drink up in the air like he's about to give a toast.

Lara lets out a wicked snicker.

Kylie and her mom are in the kitchen now. Candace does her beauty walk in silver stilettos and a shimmering white dress like she's just won the Miss America Pageant. The only thing missing is her crown. "Coffee, where's the coffee?"

Lara groans. "Now, I know you know how to get yourself a cup of coffee, Candace."

Candace shoots her a look. "What the—" But Red Cap swoops in and hands her a cup of coffee. I don't even know how he did it that fast while holding a camera.

"Why, thank you! You are such a gentleman." Candace flashes one of her perfect model smiles at him.

Red Cap blushes.

Garrett comes over to me and says quietly, "It's like a war zone with that lady. Let's check out the music room."

I nod and willingly follow him out of the kitchen.

Matt's already in the music room, sitting on a cajón. Garrett goes straight for his black tattered guitar case with a huge holographic Metallica sticker on the front.

"That's cool you brought your guitar." Matt raps his hands on the box.

"I never leave home without her." He opens the case and pulls out a shiny white guitar. "We should play some tunes." Garrett slips the guitar strap over his shoulder.

Amber and Kylie come into the room and they thank Matt for texting them where we are.

I wish I had a phone.

Amber veers off to one of the overstuffed chairs and giggles while gazing down at her phone.

Kylie and I plop down on the couch. "What could that girl possibly think is so funny?" Kylie nudges me.

I offer a shrug.

Kylie scrolls through a ton of photos on her phone, showing me one of her and another girl hugging. "This is Alissa. She's my BFF, and she's going to the Paramore concert without me. I can't believe I'm missing that concert."

The girl in the photo looks a lot like Kylie: skinny, pretty, but with pink hair.

"Is she a model, too?"

"Nah." Kylie continues swiping through photos of herself, her friends, and a very buff guy with curly blond hair leaning against a red sports car. She tells me that's her boyfriend, Jake. Then she shows me endless pictures of her mother dressed in skimpy lingerie. "You gotta admit my forty-something-year-old mom looks hot." She smiles.

"She does," I agree. "That's cool that she's still modeling."

"Modeling is her life. Even my grandma is still modeling. I'm the third generation to take on the Hanson brand they've worked so hard to create." Kylie sighs. "I want to, like, make my mom and grandma proud, but I can't see myself doing it my entire life. I mean, I've got my own dreams."

"What does your mom say about that?"

"My mom won't hear of it; says I already have a clear path for carrying on the Hanson tradition." Kylie nudges me. "Let me see your phone."

I freeze.

"Hey, you girls wanna sing lead?" Garrett calls. "I know you said you like singing, right Skye?"

I nod.

"What song do you plan on playing?" Kylie asks, forgetting about the phone.

"I'm thinking 'Sweet Home Alabama,'" Garrett says, strumming his guitar.

"I got keys." Kylie jumps up and heads over to the piano.

"Rad." Garrett gives her a thumbs up. "Hey, Skye and Amber, you can sing the verses."

"You bet." Amber grins.

"You both know the lyrics, I assume."

"Sure do." Amber springs up from the chair and heads over to me.

I don't actually know the verses by heart. My mother hardly ever listens to any other music besides Journey.

Garrett comes over and hands us each a wireless microphone. "Hey Amber, sorry about earlier today, I was just fooling around.

It's just acting, right?"

"It's okay." She looks down, hiding a small smile. Does she have a thing for him?

"Awesome." He grins at her. "So let's do this. You two take a verse. We'll all sing together on the chorus." He heads back over to Matt and picks up the guitar and begins to play. Garrett's suddenly transformed into a rocker with his cool stance and expert playing, not to mention great hair. He gives a nod to Matt and Kylie to begin playing.

"I noticed you don't have a phone." Amber leans in to me. "Don't worry, I've got the lyrics on mine." She holds up her phone.

I nod, embarrassed but grateful.

Garrett gives a thumbs up and Amber nudges me. "You got this." She nods. I swallow hard and sing into the microphone.

Garrett grins over at me. Matt carries us with the beat and when we get to the chorus and everyone joins in, what happens is the sweetest harmony, one that has us all smiling.

I find myself singing out with unexpected confidence as I remember Uncle Richard telling me that I had a talent for singing.

I spot Whiskers standing in the doorway. The camera's red light is blinking.

Amber nudges my arm and when I look over, she's smiling at me.

I smile back.

And I keep singing.

Twenty-Two

MY MOTHER'S SLEEPING WHEN I leave the room to find Rayna. I have to ask her how the search for my father is going. I check the office, but she isn't there.

A burnt smell hits me when I enter the kitchen. Lara is bent over the sink, mumbling to herself as she scrapes blackened eggs from the pan. Garrett and Popeye are at the blender chopping fruits and vegetables. Amber's sitting at the table, texting.

"Good morning, everyone." Rayna scrunches up her nose as she scans the room. "I instructed everyone to be down here at nine sharp."

After a few quick texts, the others show up within minutes. That is, everyone but my mother. Luckily, Rayna doesn't seem to notice as she lectures us on kitchen safety rules.

"All right, everyone." Rayna runs her tongue along her glossy lips and motions to Red Cap to point his camera at her. "Today is going to be exciting. You all have an audition today."

"Oh, my Lord!" Lara howls.

Rayna checks her phone. "You'll be leaving in about forty-five minutes, so do any last-minutes quickly. And good luck."

"Are we going?" Popeye asks.

"No parents—"

"Again?" Lara huffs. "Seems like our kids are doing this without us."

Rayna nods. "That's right. We want to see if they can do it on their own. We know the parents are dedicated, but whoever wins, we need to know that *they* really want this."

Red Cap moves in on Lara.

"I get it." Lara fake laughs for the camera. "What are we supposed to do while they're gone?"

"You're free to hang out here or, if you wish, to leave the premises. Just coordinate with Madison, and she can arrange transportation. Her number is on the house rules list." Rayna points to the type-written list of rules and contact numbers hanging on the wall. "But I'd like everyone back no later than four when we'll be conducting some interviews. I'll see you then." And with a quick wave, she walks out of the room.

Kylie approaches me. "No parents, thank God."

Candace makes her way over to us and strikes a pose. "I want you to win this, Kylie. You, being a television star, will be good for business."

"I'll do my best." Kylie nods.

"I know you will." Candace blows her a kiss. Her phone rings and she smiles at me before she answers and walks away.

Kylie sighs and looks over at me. "I'm going to freshen up my makeup. You coming?"

I want to go with her, but I've got to talk to Rayna before we leave. "Actually, I forgot to do something. I'll meet you outside."

Luckily, I find Rayna standing outside her office. "Excuse me, Rayna."

She looks up from her phone. "How can I help you, Skye?"

"I was wondering… Did you get the release my mother signed? I left it on your desk?"

She squints thoughtfully. "Yes, I did. I gave the go-ahead to begin the search. I'll keep you posted."

"Okay." I suck in air. "Thanks."

"Now go break a leg today." She smiles and looks back down at her phone.

Feeling like I'm going to burst, I run upstairs to check on my mother. I don't even care that she's in bed watching TV. If this works, I won't need the money. All I need is my father. "Rayna said we're going on an audition today."

"I'll get dressed."

"Parents are supposed to stay here."

"While you go where?" Her eyes widen.

"To the audition with one of the producers and the camera crew. I'll be fine, it's just another job. I'll be back in a few hours."

She shakes her head.

"I'll be fine. It's just like when I'm on set with other jobs and besides, I have to do it."

"Don't leave their sight."

"I won't."

"I don't like it here," she says.

How is that possible? This place is amazing. *More* than amazing. I don't have to keep one eye open here like I do in the car, or listen to all the creepy noises coming from people at the shelter, or feel afraid someone is going to break into our sketchy apartment and kill us. And you know what, I'm not some loser anymore, 'cause I'm fitting in and I have no intention of them ever knowing what my life is really like. And now I have to make sure she doesn't get us booted off before they might actually find my father.

"I'll be back later." I grab my backpack off the chair. "Remember, don't give an interview."

"I'll stay here until you get back. And don't leave the house."

I'd explain it to her all over again, but then I figure it's not going to make a difference.

We enter a building on Wilshire Boulevard and follow the camera crew into a huge room on the eighth floor. We're instructed to find a seat around a conference table where a woman with big-rimmed glasses and ginger colored hair pulled up into a messy bun has been sitting since we got here. She hasn't acknowledged us even once as she busily sifts through stacks of papers. Red Cap and Whiskers stand around waiting too.

We keep glancing over at each other, shrugging and clearing our throats as she continues to ignore us. Maybe it's a test of some kind. I watch the clock on the wall to see how much time passes before she looks at us.

Four minutes and counting.

She finally makes a sound, a sniffle while she reads something.

Five minutes, thirty seconds. There's a lot of eye contact around the room, followed by eye rolls, shrugs, and snickers.

The woman sneezes and there it is. She peers up at us through the big-rimmed glasses. "Anyone wearing perfume?"

Silence.

"I specifically told Rayna to make sure no one wears perfume." The woman sniffles. *"Or* cologne." She pulls out a tissue from her bag and blows her nose.

She removes her glasses and her eyes are swimming in liquid. She blows her nose into another tissue. I feel bad for her and wonder if this will be aired on TV.

Sneezing again, she pulls her bulky beige bag up onto the table and after searching through it, she pulls out a box of tissues and an inhaler. "Excuse me," she says before sealing her mouth around the inhaler. Taking a swift deep breath in, she holds it before breathing out.

"All right. I'm Hannah Lewis, and I'm casting for *Bree and Brax.* We're looking for someone to light up the screen and get kids watching. We've noticed a consistency in low ratings of our network shows and we're hopeful that this fresh concept of doing a reality show will change that." She sniffles. "We're hoping to build excitement and interest and create a more personal connection with each of you as the viewers watch you go through the process of living and competing together." She clears her throat.

I'm not sure how I fit into this group. I don't see kids looking up to me. I'm usually hidden in the background, like Waldo in those *Where's Waldo?* books.

Hannah blows her nose into another tissue and drops it on a growing mound of used tissues on the desk. "I'll be giving each of you sides from a script, and I want you to show me why you're the one for the role."

"What about me? Are you casting for a half-black, half-white girl?" Amber calls out.

"Who are you?'

"Amber Willis."

"Amber, we are simply looking for talent and star quality to fit these roles."

Amber beams. "Then you've found your girl."

Hannah smiles politely. "Remember, everyone, to always give everything you've got because that moment could be the one that catapults your career. So always, always put your best foot forward." Hannah blows her nose again. "Here is the synopsis: Bree and Brax have moved from a small town to a big city and are attending a new school. Popular at their old school, they find themselves lost in their new one. Having made a few unpopular friends, they are determined to find a way to create their own kind of popularity and have all the opportunities popular kids get. Bree and Brax juggle home life, a quirky friend group, and growing up, and they do it with mishaps, misunderstandings, and those bonding and teachable moments."

Amber claps. "Sounds like a great show."

Hannah chuckles at her enthusiasm. "Okay, let's get started." She passes out the sides. *"Hmm,* let's see, Amber, you read for Bree; Kylie, you read for Rachel, and Garrett, you read for Brax."

Red Cap and Whiskers move in.

EXT. SCHOOL—HALLWAY—MORNING

Bree is standing by her locker with her brother Brax when the most popular girl in the school, Rachel Fleming, walks toward them. Bree tries to get her attention by waving. But when she waves, her hand hits the locker door, which hits Brax's books he was carrying, and one falls off the stack and hits Rachel.

Rachel: What the hell is your problem, loser? (She checks her leg for damage).

Bree: (quickly picks up the book and looks up at Rachel) It's my fault. So sorry, Rachel.

Rachel: So the new girl knows my name. (She smirks)

Brax: (fumbling with his books, he laughs nervously) My sister and I were thinking we could have lunch with you sometime, you know, get to know each other.

Rachel: Get to know each other. (Laughs). And that would be a no.

Brax: (Moves in close to Rachel) Bree was actually kind of popular in our school back in Ohio. You two have a lot in common.

Rachel: (rolls her eyes). We have nothing, nada, zero in common. Look at me... (she stands back) and then look at her.

Bree: (Her face turns beet red).

Rachel: Okay, that was fun, (she fake yawns) you can stay away now. (She walks away, her entourage of girls following).

Brax: (frowns) Bree, you don't need someone like her, anyway.

Bree: Yes, Brax, I really do.

"And scene." Amber bows.

"Impressive." Hannah sniffles.

After everyone has taken turns reading multiple parts, Hannah jots down her final notes. "Good job, everyone." Hannah's nose glows like Rudolph's. "Your ride should be waiting for you downstairs."

And then she blows her nose long and hard.

Twenty-Three

WHILE WE'RE WAITING IN the living room for Rayna to show up with the results from today's meeting with Hannah, Red Cap has all the kids sit lined up on the couch and instructs the parents to stand behind their kids. I can feel my mother's finger twitching behind me. I can hear her shuffling from one foot to the other. Kylie is on one side of me and Amber on the other. Next to her is Garrett, then Matt.

Rayna enters the room and stands in front of us. "First of all, great job, everyone. Hannah was quite pleased with all of you. With that said, she felt there was someone who especially stood out today. But before I get to the results, I need to express my disappointment. I was informed that someone wore perfume, even though you were instructed not to, and because of that, she had to end the session early. Please don't let something like that happen again."

We all nod.

"Okay, let's get to it. Kylie, you particularly stood out to Hannah." Rayna smiles over at Kylie. "She said you were very real and convincing."

Candace squeals.

"How does this work, I mean, what about the guys getting a chance at a role?" Popeye says from behind us. "Are they looking to cast more than one of these kids seeing how there's roles for both girls and guys?"

Rayna's phone buzzes in her hand and she glances down at her phone. "I can't quite answer that." She smiles briefly before gazing over at Popeye now. "But yes, there are multiple parts that will need to be cast. I suppose the outcome will lie heavily on the viewers' votes, which could possibly result in more than one winner."

Lara clears her throat. "Does Kylie being the winner mean our kids have less of a chance now?"

"Not at all. This is only one challenge, and trust me, there's more to come. And please remember, the viewers will be casting their vote after we've gone through all the challenges."

"So does that mean even if they do great on all the challenges, they could still not get chosen?" Lara adds.

Rayna puts on her best smile. "Please, try not to stress. We'll have to see how this all turns out."

"That's not very reassuring," Lara says.

Rayna's phone pings and she glances down at the screen. "I'd better get going, but thank you all. I will be available later to answer any more questions you may have." And with that, she steps out of the room.

Everyone's chatting as they head out of the room. I get up and turn to see my mother, who looks at me, confused. "What's going on?" my mother asks.

"It was just some judging. Everything's fine."

"Is it done? Can I go back to the room?"

"If you want, I guess."

"Then let's go." She turns to leave.

"I can't. I have to work."

She turns back and considers what I said. "Don't you leave then."

"I won't."

She nods and turns to go.

A loud bang comes from the kitchen followed by some wicked laughter.

The first thing I see when I walk in is Lara hovering over the sink, clutching a big watermelon like it's a football. Popeye's just feet away in a yellow muscle shirt; his huge biceps twitch.

Red Cap and Whiskers are armed with their blinking cameras.

Lara drops the watermelon in the sink and slowly pulls herself up. With blue eyes blazing in Popeye's direction, she says in a shrill voice, "My daughter's outshining all the other kids, Dan. Hell, y'all should take a lesson from my Amber."

Kylie appears from out of nowhere and pokes me in the arm. "That woman's delusional."

Amber shoots Kylie a look as she flies past us.

"Amber's been acting and modeling since she was six," Lara continues. "She's got the look, the talent, and that casting woman, whoever she is, doesn't know what she's talking about. Amber's the only real threat around here."

"Well, that's not true, Mama," Amber says.

Lara turns to her daughter with her mouth gaping open. "What the hell is wrong with you? That's the completely wrong attitude, young lady."

"What the hell is wrong with *you* is the question." Popeye shakes his head. "I don't know what planet you're from, Lara, but maybe you could learn a thing or two from my kid."

Lara flippantly waves a hand at Popeye. "I seriously doubt it."

"Really? Can your daughter play five instruments and compose music?"

"She doesn't need to do those things. She's beautiful, she can act and dance, and that's the business we're in, Dan. *Not* the rock 'n roll business."

Popeye lets out a low chuckle. "There's more to this business than just looks. It's called talent, and my kid's on the verge of making it big."

"If that's true, Dan, then *why* is he here?" Lara shoots him the evil eye. "This is for acting, not fiddling with a guitar."

"He's here because he's talented and has a good chance at winning, plain and simple."

Puffing out her chest, Lara shakes her head. "You're sadly mistaken, Dan. Your kid's the least likely to win this. He's just a musician, and that's not what they're looking for. Admit it, Dan, you're jealous because you don't have a chance."

Popeye takes a step toward Lara. Garret walks in and immediately steps in front of his dad, blocking him from Lara. He whispers something in his dad's ear. Popeye nods, and without looking at Lara, follows Garrett out of the kitchen.

"I called it!" Lara chuckles.

Popeye spins around and knocks into Red Cap, making him lose his balance and almost drop the camera.

"Sorry, man." He helps Red Cap regain his footing, then turns his attention back to Lara. "What the hell's wrong with you?"

Lara starts yelling a line of obscenities, all directed at Popeye.

Luckily, Rayna appears, waving for a timeout. "Calm down, *please!* Let's remember, there are kids here."

"I didn't start this shit!" A bright pink hue washes over Lara's face.

"Yeah, ya did," Popeye growls.

"Doesn't matter who started it." Rayna motions for Whiskers to move the camera in closer. "Let's remember why we're here."

"We're here to win this competition," Amber mutters.

"Yes, Amber, you are all here to try and win." Rayna scans the room with a stern look. "But *your* job, parents, is to support your kids during this process. Agreed?"

"Agreed," Matt's mom, Cindy, calls from the doorway. "Our kids are counting on us."

Lara's shoulders droop. "Sorry, Dan," she mutters.

"Yeah, me too." Popeye nods.

"Let's all regroup tonight," Rayna suggests. "I won't be here, but I'm going to call in for Chinese."

I bow out of the kitchen to check on my mother and maybe get her to come down for dinner. The second I open the door, I detect the smell of smoke and find her standing by the window with a cigarette between her fingers.

"What are you doing?" I quickly shut the door.

"What does it look like I'm doing?" She turns back to the open window and exhales the smoke. "See, I'm blowing it out the window."

"You *can't* smoke in here. Do you want to get us kicked out?" I scan the room for any fire hazards and notice a bottle of vodka on the nightstand. "Where did you get that?"

"There's a cabinet in the kitchen with a crap load of them in there." She laughs, seemingly satisfied with herself. "Everything's free here. Remember?"

"You shouldn't be drinking."

"I distinctly remember that woman saying adults could drink."

"Just don't smoke in here. It smells and I don't want to get kicked out."

"Don't worry, I've got this." She holds up a can of deodorizing spray.

"We're having dinner soon, so get ready to come down and eat with everyone. We're getting paid for being here and it's a lot of money."

She tosses the cigarette out the window. "I am kinda hungry."

There's an elaborate spread of delicious-smelling food in the kitchen. Each carton has a little card in front of it with the name of the dish: garlic shrimp, scallops, lemon chicken, sweet and sour chicken, Mongolian beef, sautéed vegetables, fried rice, white rice, noodles, egg rolls.

My mother piles food on her plate and even says hello to Popeye. He invites her over to the table where he and Cindy are sitting.

"Come with me," she insists.

"Okay, but let me get some food first."

"Skye, there you are!" Kylie heads over to me, waving chopsticks in the air. "I'm going to try everything here."

I grab a plate from the counter. "I'd like to see that." I half-smile, glancing over at my mother. Cindy's talking to her. Maybe this is what my mother needs to start feeling better about this.

Both Kylie and I load our plates with food from every box. I start to head over to my mother but Kylie steers me out of the kitchen and leads me out the front door. "This is more like it." She sits on the steps where we have a clear view of the fountain. "I need a break from Lara's mouth," Kylie groans.

It is nice out here on the porch with just the two of us. I can't help but worry about my mother though.

"I should probably go check on my mother."

"She's fine. She's with the grown-ups." Kylie hands me chopsticks.

Kylie's right. Besides, Rayna's not even here to ask my mother questions. "I've never used chopsticks before."

Kylie laughs. "Here, like this." She shows me how to pinch

the sticks with my thumb and index finger and tells me to rest the bottom stick on my ring finger and the top stick on the middle finger. "It's that easy," she says, clicking her sticks.

Even though I follow her instructions, no matter how hard I try, I can't get any of the food to stay between the sticks long enough to get anything into my mouth. We can't stop laughing.

While I practice picking up sticky rice, Kylie tells me about Jake, her boyfriend, back home.

"He texted me today. Let me read you what he said: *Kylie, you shouldn't have left, I want you to come home. I think I'm falling for you. I've never missed anyone this much.*" She smacks a kiss on her phone, where an image of the blond guy leaning against the red sports car fills up the entire screen. "He is lucky to have me."

"Does he go to the same school as you?"

"No way, he's like twenty-five. He works at an investment company."

"Isn't he kind of old?" I say as I attempt to master the fine art of picking up food with chopsticks and actually getting it in my mouth.

"Older guys have things, Skye, like jobs and houses and cool cars. Jake has a Porsche, and he takes me to really expensive restaurants and shows, and, like, some really upscale parties. Hell, he sends me twelve long-stemmed roses after our dates."

"He must be in love with you."

She leans in and whispers, "More like I'm good in bed."

I don't know what to say to that. The only experience I had with a guy was when I met Jeffrey Redman while we were working as extras on a movie set, and he kept looking over at me and smiling.

At lunch, he took me by the hand and led me behind a trailer. He said I was pretty, and he shoved his tongue inside my mouth. He tasted like tuna. But then he reached inside my shirt and started squeezing; I thought he was going to break a rib and I pushed him away.

After staring at me in disbelief, he laughed. "You don't have anything to feel, anyway." And he left me there with my shirt pushed up to my neck.

I haven't eaten tuna since then.

"Your parents let you go out with a man?"

"My mom thinks it's cool and my dad goes along with whatever she tells him because he's her house-husband." Kylie stuffs garlic shrimp in her mouth.

"House-husband?"

"Yeah." She chews her food. "Like, he takes care of the house and my mom makes the money. Good thing, because she doesn't even know how to make toast." Kylie snorts. "What about your dad? What's he like?"

"I've never met him."

"Like ever?"

"Uh-huh."

"I forgot. Did you say you have a boyfriend?"

I wonder if Sebastian got my note. "Not exactly."

"Have you ever had one?"

Swallowing a piece of spicy chicken, I'm starting to get nervous with all these questions. I wish I had some water. I feel like a loser being sixteen and never having a real boyfriend. She's waiting for an answer. Thing is, I like hanging out with Kylie and I don't want her to think I'm weird. She's the closest I've ever had to a real friend. And I like it. "There is this guy I met, Sebastian, but we were just getting to know each other right before I came here."

"Like, what did he say when you told him you were leaving? You can tell a lot by what they say."

"I didn't see him before I left."

"O-kay…but you've talked or texted?"

I shake my head and swallow hard. "I don't have a phone."

"How on earth do you not have a phone? Everyone in the whole entire world has a phone."

"It's impossible, Kylie, for everyone in the world to have a phone."

Kylie laughs. "Here, you can use mine. Call him." She hands me her pink diamond-studded phone.

I shoo it away. I'm not about to admit I lost the paper where a cute and very interesting guy that I think wanted to kiss me wrote his number. "I use my mother's phone when I need to," I lie. She'd probably kill me if I touched her phone.

Kylie shrugs. "Here." She hands me a fortune cookie. I crack it open and pull out the slip of paper. But before I can read it, Kylie's on her feet. "I gotta go to the bathroom."

I stuff the little paper in my pocket and follow her inside to check on my mother, but she's not in the kitchen. Popeye and Garrett are the only ones there.

"Do you know where my mother went?" I ask Popeye.

"She said she was going to look for you."

"Did she say anything else?"

"I don't think so."

"Okay, thanks." I leave the kitchen and check the downstairs bathroom, but Kylie isn't there. I head up the stairs and stop at Kylie's room before checking on my mother.

"Kylie, are you in there?" I press my ear against the door.

"I'll be right out," she calls from inside her room.

I wait until she comes out. "Are you okay?" I ask.

"Yeah. I think the shrimp made me sick. But I'm good now." She gathers up her hair and puts it in a scrunchie that she's pulled off her wrist. "It's getting boring around here, don't you think?"

I shake my head. "I like it here."

Kylie turns to me and shrugs. "Someone with no life would."

"What's that supposed to mean?"

"It means you can't possibly have any kind of life. I mean, like, you don't have a phone, you don't wear makeup, and those clothes."

My heart plummets. I'm shocked and I don't know what to say. Stupid me for thinking she was my friend. I turn away from her.

"Hey, don't be mad." She grabs hold of my arm.

I yank my arm out of her grip and face her. "So what if I don't have a phone, or don't look exactly like you? What's it to you anyway?"

"Hey, look, I'm not trying to be mean—"

"But you are being mean and I actually thought you were my friend."

"I am, I am your friend and…and I'm sorry." Kylie's face is all scrunched up as she throws her arms around me and hugs me tight.

When I struggle to get out of her arms, she hugs me tighter.

"I'm not good at this friend thing," she whimpers. "But I want to be."

All my defenses deflate.

And I hug her back.

Twenty-Four

RAYNA STOPS ME ON my way to the kitchen and I just know that *this is it*—the moment I've been waiting for. "Skye, I'd like to speak to you for a moment."

I nod, trembling with excitement as I follow her down the hall where she stops in front of her office, the anticipation killing me.

I'm holding my breath when she turns to me and says, "I have some concerns about your mother, Skye. Some of us have noticed she isn't present the majority of the time and she hasn't responded to my texts."

The air seeps from my lungs like a balloon with a slow leak. It's not my fault, Rayna, that none of you bothered to figure out something isn't right with my mother before you invited us here.

I clear my throat. "Oh, she isn't feeling good, maybe a cold or something and she doesn't want to get anyone sick."

Rayna purses her lips. "Yes, I don't want anyone else to get sick, either. How are you feeling, Skye?"

"Great. I'm great," I squeak out, and just when I'm about to ask her about my father, her phone rings. Before she answers it, I blurt out, "I was wondering if you had any updates about my father?"

"Nothing yet. But don't give up hope." She nods and answers her phone and walks into her office.

I don't have to tell her that I plan to never give up.

There's commotion coming from the kitchen, which has become the norm. Lara's voice is the loudest, and she's complaining again. She's going on about how unfair it is around here, and that she's being kept from her daughter.

As soon as Lara sees me, she assigns me to toast duty. We're encouraged to make meals together. Rayna believes it's a way for us to bond.

As I put bread into the six-slot toaster, I'm worried my mother's going to blow this for me. I can't let anything get in the way of my father being found. I glance around the room, looking for Kylie, and see Red Cap sitting at the table eating cereal. His camera is propped up next to him, pointing at Lara. The red light is on.

Amber's sitting on the counter engrossed in her phone while her mother whisks eggs in a big bowl. Lara says she's going to have *a talk* with Rayna. Amber mumbles something to her mom, jumps off the counter, and strolls out of the room.

Kylie enters the kitchen and smiles over at me as she heads over to the fruit bowl and plucks out a grapefruit.

Lara looks over at Kylie. "You know, Amber's only real

competition is you, Kylie, and maybe…possibly Matt," she says. "As for Garrett, he doesn't have a chance. Still don't know why he's here." Lara pours the eggs into a pan sizzling on the stove.

Red Cap gets up and hoists the camera on his shoulder and positions the camera so it is pointing right at them.

"Like, why are you so insecure, Lara?" Kylie says as she peels off the skin of the grapefruit.

I laugh.

"You." Lara points a finger at me. "Not sure why you're here, either."

"What's the matter with you?" Kylie says, biting into a sliver of grapefruit.

"What's the matter—it's Barbie bitches like you thinking you have something over my Amber."

"Don't you call my friend that," I say.

Lara glares over at me and licks her lips like she's about to eat me. "You, little girl, don't even come close to holding a candle to my quadruple threat." She leans into the counter and her long stringy hair sticks to the side of the bowl.

I make a mental note to never eat Lara's eggs.

"Shut up, Lara," Kylie says.

Lara swings around and straightens her spine. "Looks like your Barbie mama didn't teach you any respect." She grabs a spatula and pushes it through the bubbling eggs.

"Like, you only wish you looked a quarter as good as her," Kylie says.

Lara freezes, the spatula dangling in mid-air above the pan.

Kylie slowly licks her lips. "The truth hurts, huh?"

Lara drops the spatula on the counter and jerks around, swinging her arm, almost hitting Kylie in the face.

"Get away from her!" I shout.

Lara spits out an angry laugh. "Looks like you got a little spunk in you after all, unlike your mama. By the way, is she retarded or something?"

Without thinking, I blindly grab the first thing I see, which happens to be the pan on the stove. I'm not sure what I planned on doing with it, but the handle burns like fire in my hand and I let out a scream as it goes crashing to the floor, landing just inches from Lara's feet.

Stepping back, Lara stares in horror at the mess on the floor. "You idiot!"

I stand there, shocked, the palm of my hand throbbing and burning.

Kylie wiggles in between us, careful not to step in the gooey eggs sizzling on the floor. "Ever since we've been here, you've been bashing everyone in this house. The truth is, you and your kid aren't that special—so shut the hell up."

"Why, you little bitch!" Lara spits out.

Popeye appears and I can almost hear the rescue music as he bounds past Red Cap. "What's going on here?" He stops in the middle of the kitchen, surveying the scene.

Lara chokes out, "None of your damn business, Dan." She raises her hand to quiet him before he speaks another word.

"She's bullying us—called us bitches," Kylie tells him as she leads me over to the other side of the kitchen, grabs ice from the freezer, and places it into my burning hand.

Popeye thrusts his hands on his hips, shaking his head. "You can't speak to the kids like that."

"*You can't speak to the kids like that,*" Lara mocks. "Just shut the hell up, Dan. Don't make me kick your sissy ass."

"Go ahead and try." Popeye takes a step toward her. But only a step.

"Come on, a little closer now." Lara's face turns beet red.

Garrett's in the room now and darts over to Popeye and grabs hold of his shoulder. "She's not worth it, Dad."

And then, shockingly, Lara starts crying. Cindy's in the room now and she rushes over to Lara. "It's okay." She rubs her arm. "This is all a little overwhelming, isn't it?"

Lara nods, rubbing her eyes. "Look at this mess."

"Easily fixed." Cindy grabs paper towels, bends down, and wipes up the eggs from the floor. "Guess we won't be eating these eggs." She smiles up at Lara.

Lara sniffles. "If my dog was here, he'd have it cleaned up in no time." She lifts the pan off the floor.

"Really? What kind of dog is he?" Cindy asks.

Matt touches my arm and I look over at him. "You okay?" he asks.

I nod, even though my heart sinks to my feet because now I've gone and blown everything.

Twenty-Five

MY MOTHER AND I are called into Rayna's office.

I'm shaking so hard, clearly aware that I have gone and messed everything up. I managed to break house rule number 5: *Destructive or violent behavior will lead to immediate removal from the house.*

My mother wants to know if we're going to do an interview. I have no choice but to tell her about what happened in the kitchen, or at least parts of it. But I assure her I'll explain to Rayna that although I did grab the pan in the heat of the moment, I had no intention of doing anything with it and I dropped it solely because it was burning my hand.

Both Red Cap and Whiskers are standing in their respective corners, cameras ready. Rayna comes in and sits behind the desk. This time, she isn't smiling.

"Okay, first let me say I know there's been a lot of tension in the house. Lara can be a bit overbearing—"

"I just want to say I'm sorry for what I did. It was stupid of me grabbing the pan, but I only dropped it because the handle was burning my hand."

"I understand it was an accident, but someone could have been hurt. Let's not have that or anything like that happen again. Got it?"

I nod, but I'm still shaking because it's probably not over yet.

"Now that that's out of the way, the reason I called you in is because I have some interesting news." She leans back in her chair and smiles. "We believe we made contact with your father, Skye."

There's this split second where it feels like everything stops. I'm literally frozen as I stare at her smiling face. But then my mother starts screaming.

I stumble up from my chair to get away from my mother. "When can I meet him, Rayna?"

"What the hell is going on here?" My mother grabs the back of my shirt and pulls me back.

"Mary, *please*." Rayna's eyes raise in concern. "Remember, you signed a release form allowing us to look for him and—"

"Don't know what the hell you're talking about—I *never* signed anything and you have no right to put your nose where it doesn't belong."

"It doesn't matter now. He's been found!" I cry.

My mother shoots me a look, one that's sharp and dangerous. When I blink, she's swatting at me like I'm a swarm of bees.

"Mary, please calm down." Rayna gets up from her chair but stays behind her desk.

"Don't you *dare* tell me to calm down!" The blood has drained from her face. She drops her arms and collapses in the chair.

Rayna swallows hard and picks up her phone. Maybe she's

planning to call the police. "It seems we have a misunderstanding here." She looks directly at me. "Isn't that right, Skye?"

Before I can answer, my mother shouts, "Oh, you better believe there's a misunderstanding!"

Both cameras are on us. I look down at the floor, about to burst with happiness.

"I can see this is a delicate subject for you, Mary."

"I don't need *you* to tell me how I feel."

"Our intention was to help you reconnect, have him come to the show, and talk to you and Skye, but—"

"You—" My mother points a stiff finger at me.

"Mary, please," Rayna says.

My mother turns her attention back to Rayna and points that same finger at her. "She doesn't have a father! Now put a stop to this or I will sue your ass." She whirls around. "And get that goddamn camera out of my face!" She swipes at Whiskers' camera.

Rayna's eyes are wide and she motions for Whiskers to back off.

"Let's go, Skye." My mother yanks the wireless mic from her shirt and throws it on the floor.

"Please," I beg. "What if he's really my fa—"

"Shut up!" she spits out while grabbing my arm and dragging me toward the door with unusual strength, a lot like when she stole the TV. I don't protest or try to get away. I let her pull me along, even when Whiskers is right in front of us, recording the most humiliating moment of my life.

She paces back and forth across the room, waving her arms around, shouting things like "Rayna is crazy," and "What the hell have you done?"

"But he *could* be my father?" I mutter, huddled on my bed.

"He isn't your father!" she bellows, and I have to cover my ears. With no way to escape, I press my back into the headboard and pull my legs close to my chest. She stops pacing and stares up at the ceiling like she's either thinking or looking for something before turning to me with fire in her eyes. "What the hell is wrong with you?"

"What's wrong with you?" I blurt out, which shocks me as much as it shocks her. When I see her coming at me like a charging bull, I have no time to get away before she leaps on my bed. I jerk back and my head slams into the headboard. She glares at me with a blind fury. There's no telling what will happen next, but I'm pretty sure it isn't going to be good.

There's a loud bang on the window, startling us both. I look over and there's a crow perched on the flower box, squawking at the top of its lungs.

My mother jumps off my bed and she mumbles something about how there's no way he knows who she is. She grabs her cigarettes from the drawer and tears at the pack.

Did she just admit I have a father?

"Not a goddamn chance," she says to herself and lights one of the cigarettes that are now strewn all over the nightstand. After a few puffs, she opens the drawer and pulls out a bottle of liquor, twists open the cap and guzzles it down.

I glance back at the window, but the bird is gone. When she collapses on the bed, I'm grateful her back is to me. Quietly, I crawl inside the covers head first, needing to get away from everything that hurts. Lying still underneath the weight of the comforter, I feel safe inside the darkness.

When I close my eyes, a vague image of a man is there in the distance. Even though I can't make out his face, I know who he is. *"Dad, Dad,"* I call, but he doesn't seem to hear me, so I run toward him, trying to get close enough for him to see me.

But no matter how hard I try, I can't get close enough.

Twenty-Six

I'M SUFFOCATING.

I thrash and kick until I untangle myself from the covers. Once my head is out and I can breathe in the room's cool air, everything that happened comes rushing back and all I can think about is that my father's been found.

I've got to fix this.

Her phone pings on the nightstand. She isn't in her bed. Or anywhere in the room. It pings again and I stumble out of bed and gaze down at the screen. It's a text from Rayna: *Mary. I need you and Skye to come downstairs to the office in twenty minutes. Please reply.*

I check the time, surprised that it's only five-thirty. It's been an hour and a half since Rayna said she found my father.

The bathroom door flings open and my mother makes her way back to the bed without looking at me.

"Rayna just texted us to meet her downstairs. Text her back and tell her we'll be there."

She shakes her head.

"You made a lot of threats. You need to tell her you're sorry—"

She spits out a laugh. "We're getting the hell out of here."

"Please, we have to fix this. You can't deny—please, just text her back, tell her we'll meet her and then I'll forget about this and never mention him again." I don't mean it. But I have to get her to fix this so I can find out who he is. "Let's finish the show and if I win, our life's gonna change and we'll live somewhere nice, and you'll have a new car and life will be easy. That's what you want, right?"

The look on her face chills me to the bone.

We're alone in Rayna's office. There are no camera guys or cameras, no audio devices attached to our clothes. I whisper over to my mother in the chair next to me, "Tell her you didn't mean to threaten her. We have to stay a little longer so we can get all that money, and then I'll try and win. Then we'll forget it ever happened. Okay?"

She doesn't so much as twitch a muscle or blink as she stares at the wall in front of us.

A tall, stick-thin man in a steel-gray suit walks in and introduces himself as Jonathan Martin, an executive something or other. He walks right past us and doesn't even shake our hands. He signals to a guy in a blue uniform standing by the door. Jonathan Martin sits in the brown leather chair meant for Rayna.

Where *is* Rayna?

"Look, I'm going to be straight with you, Ms. Perry. We take threats very seriously." He rests his hands flat down on the desk. "And although I sympathize that you don't feel comfortable with the idea of seeing Skye's father, I believe it could have been dealt with differently. My concern is, Ms. Perry, that we can't have people threatening us." The sunlight streaming in through the window creates a halo above his head.

If Jonathan Martin is an angel, he's the angel of death.

"Bullshit," she says under her breath.

"It appears you are still very upset." He frowns. "I'm afraid I'm going to have to ask that you and your daughter leave the premises. You'll be escorted to your room by the gentleman outside the office. Please pack up your things and Oscar will be waiting outside to take you back to your car."

I turn to my mother. *"Please,* fix this."

"We have a contract," she says.

"Yes." Jonathan Martin frowns. "And if you've read it, you'll recall that on page fourteen, under article 14f, it states we have the right to revoke the contract under conflict of interest—this being one of them. With that said, Ms. Perry, we will need you to pack your things and exit the house immediately."

"Please, Mr. Martin, *we* are very sorry and you should know—" I drop to the floor on my knees, begging...like a dog. "You should know that—"

Jonathan Martin raises a hand to stop me.

My mother pulls me up by the shirt. "Let's go, Skye."

Following her out of the room, I hear voices coming from the kitchen as we head up the stairs. I've got to find Kylie and tell her I'm leaving. But when I turn around, I bump into the guard following us.

This must be what it feels like to be a criminal.

Twenty-Seven

OSCAR DROPS US OFF near our car, sets our suitcase outside the van, and drives away. I keep telling myself it will be okay, that it's not even close to being over. If my father has really been found, nothing's going to change that. I just need to figure out a way to find out who he is.

"Mama Bird will be glad I'm coming home." I dump my backpack on the seat.

"Who?" My mother drags the suitcase over to the trunk.

"No one. I mean, I'm glad we're going back to the apartment." I go over to help with the suitcase and I see a stuffed black trash bag in the trunk. "What's this?"

"Our stuff. I told the landlord we weren't coming back."

"Why would you do that? We were paid up and I cleaned around the building, for God's sake."

"I didn't think we'd need that place anymore, but it looks like you screwed that all up, didn't you?" She slams the trunk, leans against the car, and pulls out a cigarette from the pocket of her gray sweater.

This can't be happening. She must be confused. "We've only been gone like five days. What about the rest of our stuff?"

"I figured we didn't need it, thought we were going to start a whole new life." She lights the cigarette with a shiny gold lighter that I've never seen before. She must have stolen it from the mansion. "I'm pissed about my TV, though."

I almost can't believe what I'm hearing. "When could you have possibly taken our stuff to the car?"

"Remember when you were picking up trash? And you didn't even notice." She smiles at that.

I don't understand what's happening. My chest tightens. What about Mama Bird? I promised I would help watch over her babies. And if we don't go back, I'll never see Sebastian again.

"You've got to go and talk to the landlord… Tell him we don't want to leave after all."

She takes a long drag from the cigarette. "You never liked that place, anyway." She tosses the cigarette on the ground and gets into the car.

I rush over and get in the passenger side. "We *have* to go back to the apartment."

"No." She turns the key and the engine grinds and sputters.

"*Please,* please go back."

"Shut up!" she shouts, turning the key again. The engine catches.

The guy inside the ticket booth waves at us as the gate rises.

I don't wave back.

I can't stand sitting next to her so I scramble over the seat. But when I pull myself over, my shoe accidentally hits her in the head. "You ungrateful shit!" she screams, and the car starts to swerve and almost sideswipes a red Prius. She slams on the brakes, and she freezes right there in the middle of the road. Horns blare.

Closing my eyes, I don't care if they hit us.

But when a black truck comes too close, its brutal horn snaps her out of it. Pounding the gas pedal, she starts driving again while screaming just about every obscenity ever created until she pulls into a nearby gas station and slams the car into park. I don't waste any time and get out of the back seat and run straight for the bathroom, grateful the door is unlocked and no one's in there.

"I'm never going back!" I scream inside the four walls. When I take in a breath, I'm hit with the pungent smell of urine.

Is this all there is?

When I come out of the bathroom, the sun is low in the sky. It'll be dark soon and I have no home to go to, no bed to sleep in. I get back in the car and find her slumped in the driver's seat, smoking a cigarette. "I want to go back to the apartment," I tell her.

My mother doesn't say a word as she tosses the cigarette out the window and puts the car into drive. She swerves out of the lot and goes over the curb with a thud, causing the cassette player to start playing "Don't Stop Believin'". She bangs on the player and the door flips open. Who the hell has cassette players in their car, anyway?

Something wells up in me and I can't keep quiet any longer. "I want to know about my father."

She ignores me as she pushes in the door to the player, but it keeps popping open. Cursing, she bangs on the release button, and then forces the cassette out of the machine and bashes it against the dash until it cracks open. A long strand of magnetic tape explodes like confetti.

"Tell me!"

"Shut up!" she screams. I glance at her reflection in the rearview mirror. Her face is all crumpled up.

"Please—"

"Shut up, shut up, shut up." She drives down the street waving the broken cassette, screaming and crying about how I screwed up her life.

I sink into the seat.

She throws the mangled tape on the dash, slows down, and starts to sob.

I drop my head on the seat, relieved she took it out on Journey instead of me.

Twenty-Eight

RAYNA SAID SHE FOUND my father and wanted to set up a meeting. That means he must want to meet me. So what am I doing here? I can't let him slip away.

My mother's slumped in the driver's seat, snoring softly. I reach for the bag on the passenger seat and take out the bottle, twist open the cap, and drink. It burns going down my throat. I remember the time we were living in the car in the dead of winter and I was shivering cold. My mother insisted I drink with her; she said it would keep me warm. We drank from a bottle of rum. It didn't taste good, but it did take away the cold inside my bones.

I was fourteen.

Pushing open the door, I turn the bottle on its side and watch the liquid pour out into the gutter. When it's empty, I twist the cap back on and shove it inside the bag.

Once I'm out of the car, I gingerly shut the door so she won't wake up. I move at a fast pace down the street and don't slow down until I turn the corner. It's still dark and everything is so quiet. It almost feels like I'm the only one left in the world. I keep walking, unsure of where I'm going.

I wonder if Rayna told the others about what happened to us. It would be good for the show; all that drama with the crazy woman and the pathetic kid might be more interesting than the Lara drama. Doesn't matter now. It's not like I'll ever see any of them again.

As I'm waiting for the streetlight to turn green, the sun begins to rise above the mountain, casting a warm glow in shades of orange and yellow. When the light turns green, I cross the street and go straight for the 24-hour donut shop. The place smells like freshly brewed coffee and warm baked dough. My mouth waters. I gaze at all the donuts in the display case, ones that remind me of the time I ate from the trash. I pick out a chocolate chip muffin and a coffee, dump in creamer and sugar, pay with the five-dollar bill I've had since we went to the mansion, and head back.

"Where the hell have you been?" she yells the second I get into the car.

"I took a walk." I shove my backpack on the floor.

"Don't you *ever* do that again! You could vanish, disappear without a trace, do you understand?"

No, I don't understand. I don't want to live in her world anymore. But right now, I'm too tired to argue, so I lay down on the seat and close my eyes.

When I wake up, we're parked in front of a liquor store. "Come on," she says as she gets out of the car. I stumble out of the back seat and groggily follow her into the store. This is my opportunity to pick out some food. I grab two pre-made turkey and cheese sandwiches, Cheetos, candy bars, a can of Orange Crush, and a big bottle of water, and dump them on the counter alongside her bottle of booze, a crap load of candy, and two packs of Marlboros.

We sit in silence in the car as I eat my sandwich with the windows rolled down in hopes of getting a slight breeze now and then. "Why didn't you take the TV if you knew we weren't coming back?"

"I figured we'd be rich from you winning."

I wonder what world she's living in.

Thing is, I've got to find a way to check on Mama Bird and the babies and talk to the landlord about leaving them alone until they fly away. I want to see Sebastian and tell him I lost his number, tell him something…something about how I don't want to lose touch because I don't know where I'll end up after I meet my father. "Let's get your TV."

"Good idea," she says and starts the car.

That was easy.

As I follow my mother over to the gray building, I glance over at the green apartments and wonder if Sebastian is home. "We'll have to ask the landlord to let us in," I say.

"Oh, I've got the key, never gave it back." She laughs. What's so funny? Has she forgotten all that has happened?

I wait while she opens the door. My heart is thumping hard. I can't wait to see what the babies look like.

"It's still here." My mother races over to the TV. I dart past her, anxious to see the babies; they must be covered in feathers by now. Peering out the window, my body instantly runs cold... I have to blink a few times, sure I must be seeing it wrong, but what I see is *nothing*... No Mama Bird... No nest... No babies.

I scream at the top of my lungs.

"What the hell is wrong with you?" My mother comes up behind me, grabbing my arm. I yank out of her grip and shove the table away from the window and the chair slams to the floor.

"Mama Bird!" I cry, pushing open the window. But I can't bring myself to look down.

"Who the hell is Mama Bird?" Her voice cuts through me.

Jerking around, I almost knock her down. "Get away from me! You are so oblivious to everything!" I burst into tears and run past her out the door. *Maybe they are okay, maybe I can save them,* I tell myself as I stumble down the stairs and race around the building, searching everywhere for them, screaming for them when I can't find them.

When my voice gives out and my wobbly legs can no longer hold me up, I collapse on the hot cement and weep.

I hear him calling out my name. I force open my eyes, and there, in the bright sunlight, is Sebastian kneeling beside me. "It's okay, Skye Girl, I'm here."

"I promised Mama Bird," I mutter.

"Let me take you home."

I want to tell him that's all I ever wanted. "I don't have a home," I murmur. He scoops me up like a helpless child and he carries me away. I gaze up at his face, which feels familiar and safe. He heads up the steps to the green building, through the glass door, up a flight of stairs, and into his apartment, where he lays me down in a bed that is warm and soft. "You're going to be okay," he says, pulling the covers over me and kissing my forehead. "Now just rest."

I don't resist.

I willingly close my eyes and sleep.

Twenty-Nine

THE SECOND I OPEN my eyes, everything from the last few days comes flooding back. I turn over and he's in the room with me, hunched over a desk. I whisper, "How long have I been sleeping?"

"All night." Sebastian twists around in the chair. "Are you feeling better?"

"Yes." I nod, sitting up in his bed. "How did you find me?"

"Luckily, I was outside watering Lillian, and I heard screaming. I was surprised to find you there."

"The baby birds died. I should have been there—"

"It's not your fault." He comes over and sits down beside me.

Maybe that's true. But I should never have trusted my mother. I look around me. "Where's my backpack?"

"Hanging on the door." He points over to it.

I nod, relieved, and gaze around the room. There are all these elegant drawings of skyscrapers etched on large sheets of paper hanging on the walls. "Did you draw those?"

He nods.

"They're amazing."

"Thanks. I'm hoping to become an architect."

"You planning to go to college?"

He shrugs. "I was. I mean, I thought I was going to Arizona State like my buddy, Adam. We both got in on scholarships and they have a really good architectural program. But I didn't accept it because, well, my grandma was sick and…I couldn't leave her." He gazes over at his drawings. "But she's been getting worse the last few months and Adam's mom's friend works at a nursing facility in Scottsdale that specializes in dementia. She said there was an opening if I wanted to place my grandma." Sebastian bites his lower lip. "I'm taking her tomorrow. I'm having trouble wrapping my head around all of it, but I know she'll get the care she needs." Sebastian looks over at me and the sadness in his eyes makes my heart ache for him. "It's hard because I wanted to always be there for her like she was for me. It feels like everything's changing so fast."

I take his hand and squeeze. "I know what you mean."

Sebastian sets out a clean towel and one of his shirts on his bed and says he's going to make breakfast. I shower and come out to the kitchen wearing his long gray T-shirt that stops just above my knees.

"That looks better on you," he says.

I grin and watch him pour orange juice into two glasses.

"Hope you like pancakes."

"I've actually had dreams about pancakes if that's any

indication."

He chuckles and places two plates stacked with pancakes on the table and sits down.

"I didn't see your grandma?" I sit across from him.

"She doesn't sleep good at night and usually wakes around nine or ten."

I stare down at the delicious-smelling food. "Thank you for breakfast."

"My pleasure." He gulps orange juice from his glass. "I was thinking, Skye, your mom's probably wondering where you are. Maybe you should give her a call?"

Staring down at the pancakes, I feel queasy. "I don't have a phone."

"You still haven't gotten your phone back?"

"I never actually had one. I should have told you, but I was... embarrassed."

"I don't want you to ever feel embarrassed." He takes my hand. "You can use mine to call your mom."

I shake my head. "I don't want to call her. I'm not going back."

"What's going on, Skye?"

I look into his eyes and all my defenses deflate, and I'm suddenly telling him things. Telling him about how I needed to find my father. It comes out easy too, even the part about how my mother won't tell me who he is, and about how Rayna said she found him, and finally, how my mother sabotaged my chance at meeting him.

"I'm sorry you've gone through all that," he says, squeezing my hand. "Not sure why your mom's keeping your father from you, but maybe he's a bad guy or something."

"I don't think so." I shake my head. "It's something else, it's like… There's someone she's protecting. But I don't think it's me. Whatever the reason, I'm going to find him."

"First things first," Sebastian says. "We gotta get you a phone."

Nancy comes over to stay with his grandma while we go to buy a phone. When the salesman places the small black phone in my hand, it feels like I've been given the key to my cell.

"Thank you so much!" I throw my arms around Sebastian and hug him. His number is the very first I put as a contact into my phone.

"I wish I didn't have to go," Sebastian says as he drives me back to our street. "But I'll be back the day after tomorrow if it goes well with my grandma."

"It will," I reassure him. As he gets closer to the gray building, I want to tell him to take me with him. But then I see, from the corner of my eye, her beat-up car parked on the opposite side of the block.

My heart sinks.

Thirty

MAMA BIRD STARES DOWN at her babies' lifeless little bodies splattered on the ground. When she looks up at me, she cocks her head to one side…knowing I'm to blame. She flies over to me, lands on my chest and begins pecking my eyes out. I throw my hands up to my face and feel for my eyes. When I open them, I look around me and realize where I am. I'm in a gas station parking lot and I'm squished in the back seat of the car.

Her phone pings. She sits up and yawns as she reads the text. "Melvin got our check from that show."

Good. Once I get my hands on the money, I'll be calling Nick Vaas to tell him everything I know. I bet he'll easily find my father in no time.

I push open the door. "I really need to pee," I tell her and without waiting for her to answer, I get out and shut the door.

When I come out of the bathroom, she's watching me from the open window. "What is that you're wearing?" she asks when I get back to the car. I look down at the shirt and smile. I haven't taken it off since Sebastian gave it to me to wear.

I don't answer and slam the door shut. I may never take this shirt off. I feel close to him with it on.

We're back in Melvin's car; he's taking us to get my money. He babbles on about having a plan. I don't listen; I don't care about his plan. I keep checking to make sure my phone is still in the front pocket of my jeans.

I wait in Jackson's line. He grins at me when I step up to his counter. I slip my check into the opening between the glass and he studies it. "Looks like you've been busy workin'."

"I'm done with this business," I tell him.

"Really? How come?"

"Because I'll be living with my father…just as soon as I find out where he is," I tell him. "So, how was your trip?"

"Dude, it was incredible. I met the woman of my dreams. Crazy, right? I mean, my lady's got a Harley." He laughs. "We've been talkin' about gettin' hitched in Sturgis."

"Where's Sturgis?"

"South Dakota. We'll be goin' in August for the motorcycle rally." Jackson counts my money and puts it in an envelope. "I haven't told anyone yet." He leans in close to the opening in the protective glass and says in a quiet voice, "But I'm quittin' and getting Bella, and we're gonna go where the wind takes us until we end up in South Dakota."

I smile and take the envelope from him. "I wish you and Bella all the best." I don't mention that I won't be coming back here.

"Thanks. Oh, and good luck finding your pop." Jackson gives me the peace sign. "Be fearless." He winks.

That's exactly what I plan to do.

Outside, Melvin is talking on the phone while sucking on a red lollipop. As soon as he sees me, he hangs up.

"Where's my mother?" I glance up and down the street.

"She went to find a bathroom." He's got his hand out.

I pull out four fifty-dollar bills from the envelope and hand them to him.

Fearless.

He peers down at the money as if he's confused. "Gimme the rest." He yanks the lollipop out of his mouth and chuckles.

"You're lucky to get this." I frown. "Think of it as your going-away present."

"What the hell, hand it over." He wiggles his fingers at me.

"I'd take it if I was you because you see, Melvin, I'm being generous by giving you any of it. If you have a problem with that, we can head on over to the police station so they can look into how you've been handling my money. You have your financial records and contract, right?"

Melvin's eyes bulge and then he breaks out into one of his stupid grins. *"Ah,* I get it. You're playin' with me."

I shake my head. "I'm not playing and as of right now, you are no longer my agent. Not that you ever were—legally."

His grin fades. "Don't think Mary's gonna like this."

"Let's see what the IRS has to say. You know, about all the cash you've been taking off the books. They would probably want to know about that."

"Screw you, Skye." Melvin stares me down, and I stare back. I'm not going to let him win. Not anymore.

Melvin blinks.

You lose, Melvin.

"This is bullshit." He throws the lollipop up in the air and we both watch it fly up as far as it can go before gravity pulls it back down and it smashes into a million pieces when it hits the pavement. "This isn't over." He straightens his stupid yellow bowtie before whirling around on the heel of one of his wingtip shoes, pausing briefly before limping down the sidewalk toward his car.

I pull out all the money I need to hire Nick Vaas, shove it in my pocket, and breathe.

Thirty-One

THE NEEDLE ON THE thermostat shoots red, and within minutes, steam seeps out from the hood. It's gotta be over a hundred in the car because my mother's got the heater on full blast, insisting it cools the engine. My clothes stick to my skin.

She pulls up to a liquor store and parks. "How much money do we have?" She tosses the envelope over at me.

I don't have to count it. "One thousand, one hundred and twenty-six dollars," I tell her. That's what's left after I took the rest of the money I needed.

"I thought there was a lot more than that." She shoves her stringy hair away from her sweaty forehead.

Now she pays attention.

"Gimme it."

I toss over the envelope with my money.

"Let's go." She gets out of the car.

"I'm not going. I'll lock the door."

"Fine." She gets out of the car and slams the door.

The second she walks away, I pull out my phone from my pocket and text Sebastian.

Me: *How are you?*

Seconds later, Sebastian replies: *Good. She's been stressed with all the cars going by on the road. I bought dark sunglasses for her at the gas station, which seems to help. We're almost there.*

Me: *Maybe while you're there you could stop at the college and ask if you can still get in for the fall semester. I mean, couldn't hurt, right?*

Sebastian: *I thought about it, but I'm pretty sure they have strict rules and I missed the deadline.*

Me: *My mother's coming, gotta go.*

Sebastian: *Okay, talk later.*

My mother carries a water jug to the front of the car, and after lifting up the hood she curses as she pours water into the radiator.

"I'm not sleeping in the car anymore," I tell her when she gets in.

She wraps her hands around the steering wheel; there's a swollen pink burn on her index finger.

"Melvin won't answer or call me back." My mother blows on her finger.

"We don't need him anymore."

Her eyebrows furrow. "I'll keep calling." She starts the car and pulls out into the street.

"It's way too hot to stay in the car anymore. We need to stay at a nice hotel until we figure things out."

I'm not sure why the mangled cassette still sits on the dash; a reminder of the life I'm living, I guess. "Like that one." I point to a small hotel with a nice courtyard. "It'll have a TV and we can shower," I tell her. I'm shocked when she pulls into the hotel's entrance and parks.

"This is a hotel, right?" she asks when she gets out of the car.

"Yes, it is," I say, although I think it's more like a glorified motel.

Check-in is easy. The woman takes our money and hands over a key. Before I even have a chance to lock the deadbolt on the door, my mother is sprawled out on the only bed in the room. "This was a good idea." She reaches for the remote and switches on the TV. One of her soaps is on and within an hour, she's asleep.

I head out to the pool in the middle of the courtyard. No one is around. I grab one of the foam rings leaning against the wall and get in the cold water in my shorts and bra, and spend the afternoon floating and smoking cigarettes I snuck from my mother's pack.

When my skin starts to shrivel, I lie on a lounge chair and bake in the sun. I'm hoping to look more like Kylie, with her healthy glow.

Back in the room, my mother stirs from the bed. My stomach growls when I see a picture of a juicy hamburger on the cover of the *Welcome to Aires* menu on the table. "I'm ordering food and having it delivered to our room."

"What?" she mumbles sleepily from the bed.

"I'm going to order room service. What do you want?"

She peers out over the maroon-colored bedspread. "Grilled cheese and applesauce."

After ordering, I switch on the air, grab my backpack, head over to the bathroom and shut the door. Taking out Lil' Monkey, I smooth his fur and set him on the counter. After emptying all the stuff from my backpack, I pull out the envelope.

A huge sense of relief washes over me as I count the money. I have enough to hire Nick Vaas. Pulling out my phone, I punch in his number even though it's a Sunday. It rings a bunch of times. No answer. No voicemail. I plan to call first thing in the morning and tell Nick Vaas about what happened on the reality show; that should give him a good lead. A message pops up on my phone.

Sebastian: Everything went well. Driving back soon.

Me: How did she seem when you left?

Sebastian: Better than expected. She liked her room, ate dinner with the other residents.

How are you?

Me: I'm good.

Sebastian: Can you get away tomorrow?

Me: Yes.

Sebastian: Where are you? I'll come get you.

Me: Aires Hotel. Do you know where it is?

Sebastian: I'll find it. Does eleven work?

Me: Yes. Perfect.

Sebastian: Can't wait to see you.

Me: Can't wait to see you too.

I smile down at my phone. This must be what freedom feels like.

The food from room service arrives on a tray. My mother whimpers when she sees there's no applesauce. I ignore her and munch on a French fry.

"Would've liked applesauce," she says.

The second I bite into the hamburger I think I might throw up. But I chew and swallow because I haven't eaten anything all day.

When I'm done, I take a shower, careful not to rub my sunburned skin. I wash my clothes with the complimentary soap and I hang them on the towel rack to dry.

When she's asleep, I turn down the volume on the TV and carefully slip a pillow between us before I get into bed. After checking to make sure my phone's on silent, I tuck it under my pillow.

Holding Lil' Monkey to my chest, I reassure him that everything's going to be alright if we can just get to tomorrow.

Thirty-Two

I LEARNED HOW TO play poker when I was seven. Uncle Richard and I made bets with the hundreds of pennies he kept in a huge glass bowl. He taught me all the possible ways to win: Two Pair, Three-of-a-Kind, Flush, Four-of-a-Kind, Straight, Straight Flush. And, of course, the ultimate Royal Flush—Ace, King, Queen, Jack, and 10 all in the same suit. Uncle Richard said he had never gotten a Royal Flush in all the years he'd played and he was still holding out for one.

It was my eleventh birthday. There were three chocolate cupcakes with white icing on a plate; mine had a pink candle in the middle. I was so excited about eating it that I forgot to make a wish before I blew out the flame. Looking back, I should have wished for Uncle Richard to never leave me.

We played poker all afternoon. After maybe forty hands, I set my cards down on the table: 10, Jack, King, Queen, and Ace in all hearts. Yes… I got the infamous Royal Flush. Uncle Richard stared down at the cards for a long time before he looked up at me with tear-filled eyes. "*You done good, kid.*" And then he gazed back down at my cards for a long time with his wrists resting on the table and the palm of his hands pressed together.

I think he was praying.

I dress in the jean shorts and maroon V-neck top I washed in the sink last night. Except for being a little wrinkled, they don't smell of cigarettes. My red sunburned skin has lightened to a pale pink, but it still stings a little. While I blow dry my hair, I keep telling myself that no matter what happens, I won't let my mother stop me from seeing Sebastian.

Opening the bathroom door, I peek out and she's sound asleep. The bottle of vodka is half empty. Every tense muscle in my body relaxes.

I head down to the end of the balcony so I won't have to whisper when I call Nick Vaas. I make a mental note of this pivotal moment, the one where Nick Vaas, private investigator extraordinaire, is going to tell me he'll find my father. My hand trembles as I hold the phone to my ear... One ring... Two rings... A prerecorded message: *The number you have reached is no longer in service.*

What?

This can't be right. I must have called the wrong number. I punch in the numbers again, but it plays the same message. I listen to the whole thing: *The number you have reached is no longer in service. Goodbye.*

I suck back tears and kick the wall. I kick it again, wondering what the hell I'm supposed to do now. I make my way back to the room. I go over and stare down at my mother as she sleeps. I'm so angry. I want to shake her, make her tell me who my father is.

Snatching her phone from the table, I punch in her code that I saw her use when we were in the car the other night. I'm in. I scroll through the texts and—Kylie?

Hey Skye, it's Kylie, got your mom's number from the list of contacts. You okay? Rayna won't tell us anything. Call me, please.

Why didn't my mother tell me Kylie tried to contact me? I pull out my phone from my pocket and add Kylie's number to my contacts.

Next, I look for Rayna's texts, but they aren't there. Did my mother delete them? I check her voice messages; they're all from Melvin.

Scribbling a note on the hotel notepad, I tell her I've gone out.

Sebastian's there waiting outside the hotel. "Skye," he calls when he sees me. His arms are wide open and I run to them. "I missed you so much," he says breathlessly, holding me close. His strong arms and kind words are like a lifeboat.

"I missed you too, Sebastian."

We walk hand in hand through the parking lot and he stops in front of a big, brown station wagon. "Your chariot awaits." He opens the passenger-side door.

The inside of the car is immaculate and smells like brown sugar. The steering wheel is wrapped in a pink fluffy cover. I smile over at him. "I take it you like pink?"

"Although I do like pink," he says with a grin, "it's my grandma's car. But I guess it's mine now." There's a flicker of sadness in his eyes. He starts the engine and it purrs like a kitten.

We drive down the road and he's quiet. "You okay, Sebastian?"

"Honestly." He glances over at me. "I don't like being away from my grandma." He looks back at the road. "I've been feeling out of sorts since I took her there, and it's like I'm not sure where I even belong anymore. I think I've got to find a way to be closer to her."

"You were going to go to college in Arizona, right?"

He nods. "Yeah, but my chance has passed."

"Did you stop in and ask when you were in Arizona?"

"Yeah, but I doubt it'll work out." He shrugs. "So, anyway, where would you like to eat?"

"We've passed two Starbucks already and I've always wanted to go inside one."

"Great choice." He nods, and after a short drive, he turns into the popular coffee shop's next location.

The place is buzzing with people either waiting in line or sitting at tables with their specialty drinks while working on their laptops or staring at their phones. We order two iced mochas and breakfast sandwiches and find a vacant table outside. As I nibble on the deliciously warm sandwich, I notice Sebastian watching me.

"Have you thought much about what your next move is

concerning your dad?"

"I'm not sure, but now that I know he's out there, I plan on finding a way to meet him and soon." I take a sip of the frothy drink topped with whip cream and chocolate drizzle. I don't think I've ever tasted anything this delicious. "But I still don't have his information."

"The show has to know it, right?" He bites into his breakfast sandwich.

"Yeah." I nod, feeling hopeful again. "The show must have his information."

"Maybe you can call and ask for it."

"I don't have the number, but I think I know who might." I pull out my phone and call the only other number besides Sebastian's in my contacts list.

"Skye!" Kylie squeals when she hears my voice. "Damn, girl, I thought I lost you forever."

"I'm sorry I didn't call you back. My mother never gave me the message. But I have my own phone now."

"Moving up in the world," she says. "Like, I've been worried about you. Rayna wouldn't tell us why you left."

"It's a long story," I say. "So, who won?"

"No one yet. It's been so weird since you left. They, like, had us leave the mansion. We're all staying at a hotel while the viewers vote and they'll have us back at the end of the week to announce the winner." Kylie chuckles. "Lara's been going berserk about how she and Amber will be moving to L.A. soon."

"I don't miss that," I admit. "So, I was hoping you could give me Rayna's number."

"Yeah, of course. I'll text it to you."

"Great, thanks."

"You gonna fill me in on what happened?"

"I will. I'll call you later, though."

"Okay, texting now. Call me."

"Thanks so much, Kylie. I will."

Sebastian and I both stare at my phone, waiting for her text. When it comes through, I click the number and it rings.

Rayna answers with "Hello, this is Rayna."

"Hi, Rayna, it's me, Skye... Skye Perry."

"Oh, my goodness. How are you, Skye?"

"I'm okay. I know you have my father's name and number and I'm hoping to get them from you."

Silence.

"Rayna, are you still there?"

"Yes, I'm here. Look, Skye, the thing is, I can't give out that information."

"Why not? You found him and you planned to have us meet."

"Yes. But as you recall, you misled us."

I gaze down at the whipped cream melting in my cup. "I know, but I had to. And I don't regret it. My mother wouldn't have allowed you to look for him. Please, Rayna, *please* help me."

"It's against policy to disclose any information obtained by the show. I'm sorry, but I have to get going. But I do wish you the best. Take care, Skye."

The phone goes dead.

I look up at Sebastian, shaking my head. "She told me she can't give me his information." There's no denying that Rayna holds my future in her hands. "I have to go and talk to her in person." I check Kylie's text. "She's at 5728 Wilshire Blvd."

"Let's go," Sebastian says and reaches for my hand.

Thirty-Three

THE GIRL BEHIND THE information desk has an eyebrow piercing. I try not to be rude, but I can't stop staring at the little cross dangling over her eye. I wonder if it interferes with her vision. "Rayna will see you now." She absently swipes the silver cross from her eye, but it ends up dangling in front of her pupil again.

Rayna is waiting outside her office with a taut look on her face. Our eyes meet and I feel like I've done something wrong. "Skye, I shouldn't be doing this, but…let's go into my office."

I follow her into the small room. There's a brown desk, a bookshelf, a filing cabinet, and three chairs. The only thing hanging on the wall is her credentials and a clock. I assumed anything Rayna had, including her office, would be as glamorous as her. She sits behind the desk stacked with folders and papers and she motions for me to sit down.

"Is he my father, or was it all a publicity stunt?"

She leans back in her chair and sighs. "Originally, we did think it would be good for the show, but no, we believe he may actually be your father. He was, as I remember, very interested in knowing more about your mom and agreed to meet you both. Although he wasn't sure he wanted it aired."

Hearing her say that sends butterflies swirling inside my stomach. "What did he say when you told him it wasn't going to happen?"

Rayna's mouth tightens. "He said he wanted your mother's number. He was pretty insistent, but the odd thing was he called her Kary, not Mary. I tried correcting him, but he insisted her name was Kary."

I don't understand what she's trying to say, probably another misunderstanding. "Did you give it to him?"

Rayna shakes her head. "No, we can't give out personal information."

"Without his name, there's no way I can find him. Doesn't that seem wrong to you, that I'm not allowed to even know my own father's name?" She doesn't answer me. "You can just give me his name. I mean, surely you can't get in trouble for *that*."

Rayna sighs. "I wish I could, but there are policies I—"

"Screw your policies, Rayna. *You* found him, you said so yourself, and I don't have a chance of finding him myself if I don't even know his name."

"I'm sorry, Skye, I can't help you."

I eye the folders on her desk. My father's information must be inside one of them. "You're the only one that can help me."

Rayna rests her elbows on top of the folders and runs her tongue over her lips. "I wanted to help you, but you lied to me and forged your mom's signature."

"You're right, I did, and I'm sorry. But I was desperate after you said you could maybe find him. All these years and my mother won't tell me anything, not even his name. I have a right to at least know my father's name, don't you agree?"

Her gaze moves to the window. "I sympathize with you, Skye, I do." She looks back at me now. "But I can't jeopardize my job. It's simply out of my hands."

Jumping up, I bang my fist on the desk, startling us both. "Actually, it *is* in your hands." When she shakes her head, I realize I'm done here and make my way to the door. I find myself standing on the threshold between how my life is now and what it could be.

When I reach the lobby, the automatic doors open to the outside, but I stop dead in my tracks. If I leave, I will have lost all hope of finding him.

"Skye, wait!"

I turn back and see Rayna coming toward me.

"Phew." She stops in front of me, laughing nervously. A large group of people head toward us and she steers me away from the door. "I thought I had missed you. Here, I forgot to give you this." She hands me a book.

I gaze down at the title: *Ten Acting Techniques Every Actor Should Know.* I look up at her, confused.

"Seems there was a name on the back of your birth certificate. That's how we found him."

I've never seen my birth certificate. I asked to see it once, but my mother said she didn't know where it was.

I asked if she'd send for another one.

She agreed to but never did.

"Look, Skye, I want to help." Rayna searches my eyes. "Inside—this book has that information you're wondering about. I'd suggest you open the book immediately." She sucks in a breath and says, "No matter what happens, I hope you find yourself in all this." She touches my arm. "Read the book today, okay." I nod and she walks back into the building.

A small boy darts past me, chanting, "*Make a wish, make a wish and it'll come true.*" He runs straight for the fountain and tosses a coin into the water. A woman in a frilly yellow hat calls to him, asking if he made a wish, but he doesn't seem to hear her, pretending now to be an airplane, his curly black hair bouncing around his head. He zooms past me, not paying attention, and bumps into me. The book slips from my hand.

A piece of paper falls out and flutters in the breeze. The boy races after it. "Here, lady." He runs up to me and hands me the paper, and when he grins, I notice his two front teeth are missing.

"Thank you." I smooth out the paper and gaze down at what's written on it: *Jason Mackey,* followed by a phone number. Jason Mackey? My finger brushes over the name and it occurs to me what this means. Clutching the paper to my chest, I burst out laughing.

"What's so funny?" the little boy asks.

"I'm just so happy."

"Me too!" He laughs and skips off. "Come on!" He motions for me to follow. And without thinking, I follow him, and soon I'm skipping around the fountain too, clutching the paper with my father's name... My father's name is Jason Mackey!

The little boy stops skipping and turns to me, holding out his hand. "Here, you can make a wish." I look down and there's one shiny penny in the palm of his hand.

"Oh, thank you." I smile down at him. "But it looks like my wish already came true."

The boy runs off chanting, "Wishes do come true, wishes do come true."

And he throws the coin into the fountain.

Thirty-Four

MAILBOX FULL SAYS THE generated voice on the other end of the phone.

The station wagon idles. I look over at Sebastian and shake my head. I try texting the number again but it keeps coming back as undeliverable. "If I can't get a hold of him, I'll just find out where he lives and go to him."

My heart leaps when my phone rings. I hold my breath as I check the screen. It's Kylie.

"Hey, Skye. Well, we just finished meeting with Rayna and her people. They said we'll be filming the results show early next week to announce the winner. So, like, we're just waiting. How about you? Did you talk to Rayna? Because I asked her and she wouldn't tell me."

"Yes, I did, thanks."

"Okay, great, but like what's going on with you? You gotta fill me in. Where are you, anyway?"

I read the sign above the restaurant in front of us. "We're parked in front of a place called Nick's Cafe. It's down the street from where Rayna works."

"What the— We're up the street from you and, oh God, we're bored to death waiting for our parents. They're having their own meeting with Rayna and who knows how long that's going to take. Hey, we'll come down and see you."

Before I tell her not to come, she hangs up.

We wait by the car for maybe fifteen minutes, and with every minute that passes, I want to tell Sebastian that we should go. I need to get back to locating my father. But it's too late; I spot them bounding down the street.

"Skye, you've got some explaining to do." Kylie throws her arms around me. "And who's this?" She glances over at Sebastian.

"Hi." He smiles over at them. "I'm Sebastian."

"So this is the guy." Kylie grins over at me as everyone introduces themselves.

"Hey, I don't know about you guys, but I'm starving," Garrett says and heads over to a vacant table outside the restaurant and waves the server over. Soon there's a frenzy as they order omelets, waffles, fruit salad, and an ice cream sundae.

"I don't get what the holdup is for this show but I'm ready to get back home." Garrett taps his fingers on the table. "I've decided to start a band and get serious about my music career."

"Hope it's not me that wins. I really want to get back home." Matt sighs.

"My mom overheard Rayna on the phone talking about how the show needed to be canned," Amber says.

"Can they do that?" Garrett asks.

"They can do whatever the hell they want," Kylie says.

Everyone's now talking over each other and my leg shakes under the table. I glance over at Sebastian and he shrugs. I don't have time for this.

The server arrives with a tray of food.

"I don't know about any of you, but I'm going to miss you guys," Garrett says, stuffing a huge piece of his spinach and cheese omelet into his mouth.

Matt gazes over at Garrett. "Same."

"Me too," Amber says.

"What is this, a funeral?" Kylie pops a tangerine slice into her mouth.

The server is back and sets down a huge sundae overflowing with whipped cream, fudge, nuts, and a bright red cherry on top in front of Sebastian and me. Sebastian smiles at me and hands me a spoon.

"The lovebirds." Kylie winks at me.

"Skye, tell us what happened. Why did you leave?" Amber squeezes a huge glob of ketchup on her omelet.

All eyes are on me now. My eye twitches in response. "Um, it's kind of a long story."

Garrett glances at his phone. "We've got time."

"Come on, what gives, Skye?" Kylie elbows me.

My face grows a prickly kind of warm. I look down at the ice cream that's already melting.

"Skye's looking for her father," Sebastian offers, scooping a spoonful of fudge off the side of the glass.

I shoot him a look. His eyebrows raise and he mouths *sorry*.

"Why haven't you told *me* about this?" Kylie frowns.

I'm not sure what's going on here. I haven't known any of them for very long and yet they insist on knowing things about me that are certainly none of their business. It isn't like they're my friends or anything.

But in the split second when I look up at them, all I see are genuinely concerned faces and my defensiveness deflates. "Sebastian's right. I'm trying to find my father."

"How's the search going so far?" Matt asks and they all lean forward, gazing intently at me.

My eye twitches. "It's been hard, I mean, until Rayna—I don't know if I should be saying this, but Rayna said she'd try to find him and she did, but my mother got pretty upset and we got kicked off the show."

"That's terrible." Amber shakes her head.

"Yeah, it was." I nod. "But the thing is, I have his number now, but it just goes straight to a full mailbox and texts come back as undeliverable. I need to find out where he is because I'm going to go to him."

"Wow! That's courageous." Garrett drums his fingers on the table.

"How come you didn't tell me?" Kylie asks.

"Honestly, I've never told anyone, not until recently." I glance over at Sebastian. He takes my hand and squeezes it.

"Okay, so you plan on going to him. How can we find out where he is?"

I'm not sure why Kylie is saying "we". This is my search, my father, my problem. *"We* don't. I've got this."

"I can't speak for anyone else here, but I plan to help you find your dad," Kylie says.

"Yeah, me too." Garrett gives a thumbs up.

"Me three," Matt chimes in.

"Don't forget me." Amber raises her hand.

"Guys, that's nice of you, really, but it's okay. I've got this."

"You need our support, Skye. This should be a group effort," Kylie insists.

"I think it's beautiful that you want to find your dad," Amber says.

"Oh, God," Kylie groans.

"You should keep calling," Garrett says.

"What's your dad's name and number, Skye?" Matt pulls out his phone.

"Jason Mackey." I tremble when I say his name and read off his number.

Matt types in the information and within seconds shows me his phone. "Jason Mackey, forty-three, lives in San Jose and also lived in Los Angeles. There's even an address."

I gaze at the screen and I have to catch my breath. "Do you think it could really be him?"

"Yeah, I do. He has the same phone number."

My heart races when I see that the numbers match. My father lives at 1404 Mellonroe Street in San Jose. I know what I have to do.

"I'm going to San Jose."

"How're you planning to get there?" Kylie asks.

"I'll figure it out. Maybe take a bus or train or something."

"If that's what you want to do," Sebastian says. "Then I'd like to take you."

My eyes well up with tears. "Sebastian, are you sure?"

"I want to take you, Skye."

"I'm going," Kylie says.

"Count me in." Garrett flips his hair back. "I'm ready to get out on the road."

"I'll go too," Matt says.

"You guys can't all go without me," Amber insists.

I'm getting nervous about this talk of all of them going. "Guys, really, it's nice that you want to come along, but really—"

"We're gonna need a car to fit the six of us," Garrett says as if he didn't hear me.

"I've got a station wagon. It'll fit everyone." Sebastian looks over at me and by the look on my face, he probably wishes he kept quiet.

Kylie's eyes widen. "It's like a new car, right?

"1976 Chrysler Town and Country," he says with pride.

"Like, I don't think I can be caught dead in that." Kylie shakes her head.

"Really, guys, you don't need to come with me."

"Not sure if my dad will let me," Garrett says. "Unless I can think of something he'll say yes to."

"Tell him you're staying with me, over at my aunt's house in

Glendale," Matt offers.

"Yeah, that could work."

"Hey, what about me?" Amber frowns. "Who do I say I'm staying with?"

"Are you sure you can get away from your mama?" Kylie snorts.

"If I have a sleepover, I can."

"Girl, you're killing me. Tell her we ran into Skye and she invited us to have a sleepover at her very fancy house."

"How long will we be at her house?"

Kylie shakes her head. "You do know we're not actually staying at her house, right?"

"Yes, I get it, geez." Amber rolls her eyes. "We're going to find Skye's daddy."

"Right. So if Skye, let's say, meets her *daddy* tomorrow, we can be back by tomorrow night."

"But that'll mean I'm lying to my mama." Amber frowns.

"Not exactly." Kylie pats Amber's hand. "You'll actually be *with* Skye and me, just not at her house."

"Yeah, but my mama doesn't like Skye," Amber says and turns to me. "Sorry, Skye."

"It's okay." I shrug.

"Perfect." Kylie nods. "So to clarify what we're doing: Garrett, you'll tell your dad you're staying at Matt's aunt's house, and Matt, you say you're staying at the hotel with Garrett, and Amber and I will tell our mothers we're staying at Skye's."

My chest tightens. I can't let this happen. "Look, guys, it's really sweet that you want to do all this for me, but I think I'll just fill you in on what happens when I get back. I mean, what if something were to happen?"

"We can only hope something happens," Kylie says.

I shake my head. "I mean something bad, like an accident, or—"

"Stop worrying, we'll be fine," Kylie says. "Besides, we need to get away after all the crap our parents put us through."

"Speak for yourself." Garrett frowns. "My dad's awesome and supports me a hundred percent."

"Then why are you going?" Kylie squints at him.

"I like the idea of being out on the road."

Kylie flicks her hair back over her shoulder. "Okay, it's settled. Let's call our parents." Kylie waves over to the server. "Check, please."

As we make our way to Sebastian's car, everyone's on their phones making calls to their parents.

"I'm going to call my mother," I tell Sebastian and stay back. I punch in her number and hold my breath. "It's me, Skye," I breathe out when she answers the phone.

"Where the hell are you?" she yells into my ear.

"I'm with the kids from the show."

"What are you talking about? You know you must *never* leave me—ever! Come back here, Skye, right now!"

"I'm not coming back—not until I find my father."

"What the hell are you talking about?" she screams so loud I have to yank the phone away from my ear. "You come back here now!"

"No. I'm going to meet him."

"This is bullshit, Skye. You stop this now, do you hear me?"

"It would help if you'd tell me what you know about him."

"Enough! Get back here in the next few minutes or—"

"I'm not coming back—not until I meet my father."

She screams out a string of obscenities through the phone.

"I gotta go, bye," I shout, doubting she even heard me and I end the call.

As I walk back to the car, I'm a little shaky and more than a little scared. I'm not sure if what I'm doing even makes any sense, but it's all I have right now. Maybe I should go back.

But when I look up, they are there, waving and calling for me to hurry up, and it occurs to me I'm in control for the first time in my life.

I walk a little faster, waving back.

"Wait, I don't have any of my things, no clothes, makeup, anything," Amber says from the back seat.

"Wish I had my guitar. I never go anywhere without her," Garrett says.

"It's going to be a long car ride," Kylie groans, sandwiched in between Amber and the door. "Move over."

"Sorry." Amber scoots over toward Matt. "I can't believe I'm really doing this, or that my mom actually said okay. I feel so—so *free*." She giggles.

"Why can't someone sit back there with you, Garrett?" Kylie

hisses.

Garrett pops his head up from the third row. "'Cause I called it. And man, it's so spacious back here. Bash, I like your ride and I'm loving that I can wave to all the people behind us."

"Thanks, man." Sebastian smiles in the rearview mirror.

"Seriously, you should let one of us sit back there with you, Garrett." Matt squishes into the door to get away from Amber's fidgeting.

"Nah, I'm good, dude. Besides, you get to be with the girls." Garrett laughs.

"Are you sure you're okay with this?" I whisper to Sebastian as he starts the car.

"No. But here we go." He grins over at me and puts the car in drive.

Thirty-Five

SOMEONE FARTS.

Kylie gags and rolls down the window. "Don't do that again, asshole."

"That's where it came from." Garrett laughs.

"My seat belt keeps coming undone." Amber clicks it a million times. "It won't stay in."

"Sorry, that one's tricky, just keep shoving it in until it locks again," Sebastian says.

"Why on earth would you want a car like this, anyway?" Kylie asks.

"It was my grandma's, and it's full of memories."

"That's so sweet," Amber says.

My phone won't stop buzzing. I have eight missed calls from my mother and one voice message. I tell myself not to listen, but I need to know she's okay. *Skye, Skye, I don't know whose phone I'm calling but if you know Skye, tell her to come back. Tell her I need her to come back—*

A sick feeling washes over me, hearing her desperation dripping in my ears. But I can't let her stop me. Not this time.

I turn my phone on silent.

"That's Queen; can you turn it up, Bash?" Garrett calls from the way back. Sebastian raises the volume on the radio and Garrett starts singing about how he's a poor boy and Matt joins in with how he doesn't need sympathy. Amber and Kylie join in.

Sebastian grins over at me. "It's a great song," he says and breaks out singing along with the rest of them. Soon the car is filled with all their voices, some on key, some not, but it all sounds kind of perfect.

I gaze out the window, the road melts under us, bringing me closer to my father.

"Are we getting close?" Amber sighs.

Sebastian peers into the rearview mirror. "We still have a few hours to go."

"I'm getting carsick," Amber moans.

"I'm starving," Garrett groans, rubbing his stomach.

"I have to pee," Kylie says.

"Food helps car sickness," Amber insists. "Food, I need food."

"Food, food, food," they all chant from the back.

Sebastian glances over at me and we laugh.

"Pizza." Garrett points to a sign up ahead that's shaped and painted like a slice of pizza. "Bash, follow that sign!"

"Yes! I want pizza!" Amber squeals.

"You okay with stopping?" I ask Sebastian.

"I can eat." He nods and takes the next exit, which gives way to cheering and clapping as he follows the signs that lead to the town of Bayside, and the red and white house-shaped restaurant with ivy strewn around the door.

Entering the pizza place, the man behind the counter calls out to us, "Welcome to Mama's Pizzeria."

"Smell that pizza." Garrett rubs his hands together and heads over to the man waving us over.

"Choose any slice or you can order a whole pizza made any way you like—and you must know, all of our pizzas have Mama's special sauce, and you will *love it*!" The stout man grins.

We check out all the huge slices of pizza behind the glass—there's cheese, pepperoni, meat lover's, vegetarian, Hawaiian, and pesto. We agree on a jumbo pepperoni pizza. Kylie rolls her eyes and orders a salad without dressing.

The restaurant is buzzing with people. Matt spots a table that seats six. The tables are decorated with red and white checkered tablecloths, red paper napkins, and glass vases filled with red and white carnations.

When the piping hot pizza arrives, Kylie nibbles on lettuce while she watches us eat. Matt notices and says, "Live a little, Kylie. You look incredible. You can afford to eat a slice."

"Thanks, Matty, for the compliment. But *not* eating that glob of dough drenched in fat and grease is exactly why I look the way I do." She pops a cucumber in her mouth.

"Don't know how you can pass up pizza." Garrett starts on a second slice. "Just one bite and you're hooked." He shoves the pizza in front of her face.

"Get that away from me!" Kylie swats it away.

"Okay, relax, geez."

"What's up with all those Polaroids?" Matt points over at the back wall with maybe hundreds of photos stuck to it. "I'm going to check it out." He gets up and strolls over to study the photos. "Hey, guys," he calls from across the room. "There's actually famous people in these pictures—Drake...Selena Gomez, Steve Carell...Jennifer Lawrence...Michael Jordan...and Arnold Schwarzenegger."

Curious, we all head over to see for ourselves. Every photo has someone famous posing with a pizza and a little old lady with a head full of frizzy gray hair.

Amber follows the line of photos with her finger all the way down to the other end of the long wall. *"Ooh,* it's Harry Styles!" she shrieks.

"Wait. That's Brandon Arch." I point to a photo of the actor posing with the same little frizzy-haired lady.

"Who's Brandon March?" Kylie asks, gazing at the photo. "Oh wow, he's gorgeous."

"Brandon Arch, you know, the actor who starred on *Station 44.*" I know because I worked with him on set as one of the human props being rescued from a building on fire. Brandon Arch played Kip Larson, the courageous and undeniably gorgeous paramedic.

"Oh, right, I recognize him now." Kylie touches the photo. "I liked that show—well, I liked Brandon. The show was lame."

"Did I hear someone mention Mr. Arch?" the owner calls as he approaches us.

"I worked with him on *Station 44,*" I tell him.

"*Really.*" His droopy eyes widen. "Mama fell in love with Mr. Arch when he came here for our pizza, he said to her she's the most beautiful woman he has ever laid eyes on." He chuckles and calls out, "Come, Mama, come, we have a star right here who works with Mr. Arch himself!"

"Who is it, Antonio?" The tiny frizzy-haired lady who's in every photo comes rushing toward us. "Tell me, Antonio, where is he, where is he?" She's breathless with excitement, squinting as she scans the room.

"No, Mama, Mr. Arch isn't here. This actress right here" —he points to me— "starred with none other than Mr. Arch himself."

"*Ah Mia*, lucky girl." Mama's eyes light up. "I'll get the Polaroid!" She turns and waddles over to the counter and comes back with a black Polaroid camera.

"I'll take it, Mama, you get in the picture with the actress—I'm sorry, your name?" He's looking at me.

"Her name is Skye Perry," Kylie obliges. "Remember that name." She winks over at me.

"Skye Perry who worked with Mr. Arch." Antonio grins. "Get in close to Mama."

I look to the group for help, but they're too busy giggling.

"What about them?" I point over at them. "They're all actors too."

Antonio freezes. "What? So many young stars, good for business, like Selena and Justin, but oh, so sad they broke up." Antonio lets out an exaggerated sigh, motioning for them to come over. "Mama, more young stars, good for business. Go get the pizza."

Mama disappears behind the counter again, only to return carrying a huge pepperoni pizza. She positions herself and the pizza smack in the middle of us.

"You, tall one, come." Antonio points at Sebastian, who is observing from a few feet away.

Sebastian shakes his head. "But I'm not—"

"Come, come." Antonio waves him over.

"Yeah, come, come, Sebastian," we all say in unison.

Sebastian heads over to us shaking his head.

"Okay, okay, *squeeze* closer, more, a little more," Antonio says as he looks through the camera's tiny viewfinder.

"Wait, wait." Mama hands the pizza to Amber, licks her fingers, and uses them to smooth back her hair. "Okay, I'm ready." She slips one hand under the tray and she and Amber hold up the pizza.

Antonio lifts the camera again. The other people in the place are watching us, maybe trying to recognize us from a TV show or a movie. "Okay, good... Say *cheese.*" Snap. Antonio grins from ear to ear as he pulls out the film and holds it carefully between his fingertips. "Now *mangia*, and we wait for the magic."

Mama bats her eyelashes at Sebastian. "Ah, such a handsome and very tall young man." She giggles.

"That was kinda weird." Sebastian laughs after Mama is back behind the counter. "Even though I'm not an actor, I kinda want to be one now."

Garrett steps up to him and shakes his hand. "Well, consider yourself having made it 'cause we're about to be inducted into the wall of stars."

"I'm finally getting the recognition I deserve." Matt chuckles, and we head back to our table.

"I gotta say, this pizza is rad." Garrett helps himself to another slice.

"The tangy sauce and doughy crust reminds me of the pizza back home." Matt nods, folding his pizza in half and taking a bite. "Delicious."

"It's because of Mama's secret sauce," I say, eyeing Sebastian.

"And a family recipe must always be protected." He winks at me.

"Inside joke?" Kylie's eyebrows raise.

We laugh.

"I don't know what all the fuss is about, it's *just* pizza." Kylie yanks a slice from the tray and bites into it. *"Mmm,* this pizza is AMAZING."

"Look at this!" Antonio waves a photo in front of him. "You must leave me all your names." He beams as he heads straight for the wall of stars and places the photo next to the one of Brandon Arch. "Perfect."

We all get up and follow Antonio to the wall and examine our photo.

Matt grins and snaps a picture of our picture with his phone.

"This was fun." Sebastian also snaps a photo. "But I think we better get going."

"I have to use the ladies' room." Kylie heads to the back of the restaurant.

I follow Kylie to the bathroom, thinking I should go before we leave. When I open the door, I hear her throwing up in one of the stalls.

"You okay, Kylie?"

The toilet flushes and Kylie swings the door open and comes out of the stall. "Couldn't be better." She washes her mouth out and applies lip gloss. "You coming?" She pulls open the door.

"I'll be there in a minute."

Kylie nods and walks out the door.

After using the toilet, I wash my hands and call the number again. It goes straight to voicemail. I try texting but it comes back as undeliverable. I have a bad feeling about this.

"Did you get through to your dad yet?" Amber asks when I get back in the car.

"No one answers. I guess I didn't think it all the way through."

"You have his address, you could go and knock on his door," Garrett suggests.

My stomach starts to hurt. "I guess so."

"He'll probably be in shock when he sees you standing there," Amber says.

"What do you plan on saying to him?" Matt pulls dental floss from his teeth.

"I'm not sure."

"Seriously, dude." Garrett leans over the seat. "You keep dental floss in your pocket?"

"Don't underestimate the daily practice of dental floss. I've never had a cavity."

"It just occurred to me, what if he doesn't live there anymore?" Amber says.

"Guess I'm taking a chance."

"I think you're courageous." Kylie rubs my shoulder.

"But what if he shuts the door in your face? Then what?" Amber frowns.

"Why are you guys throwing all these what ifs at her?" Kylie says.

I hold on to the door handle and squeeze, and when I look out the window, everything's a blur.

Thirty-Six

THEY'RE ALL ASLEEP IN the back.

Sebastian drives down a long stretch of road while some song about how *everything works out if you let it* comes out of the speaker. I roll down my window; my chest feels tight and I'm having trouble breathing.

I take deep breaths. Sebastian lowers the volume. "We're getting close. Do you want to go straight to the address?"

I nod and lean my head against the window.

I imagine my father is a businessman living in a big city apartment or a big, beautiful house. He dresses in suits and goes to dinner parties where they discuss important projects while eating steak and lobster. He dates, but nothing serious. He lives alone and has an extra room meant for me because he hopes to find me one day.

Sebastian turns on Mellonroe and drives through a nice suburban neighborhood. Most of the houses have flower gardens and trees, and every house has meticulously cut grass. He parks in front of a yellow house.

My father doesn't live in a big city in a high rise like he does in my daydreams. My father lives in a small yellow house.

"Want me to go with you?" he asks.

"I'm okay."

"I'll be watching. Just give me a wave if you need me."

I nod and open the door. What if he slams the door in my face? What if he's a bad guy, after all?

Walking up the path leading to the porch, the grass is well-manicured and there's a bunch of rose bushes off to the left, and a big oak tree on the right. My father must have walked this path at least a million times before.

Heading up the steps, I glance over at the swing and a small table on the porch. I peer into the white coffee mug sitting on the table. No cigarette butts inside. My heart flutters as I stare at the pale wooden door.

Showing up like this without warning could throw him off. I'm not sure he'll even want to talk to me. I turn around and Sebastian is watching, just like he said he would. I nod, turn back and force myself to knock on the door. A dog barks from inside the house.

When no one answers, I head back to the car. "I'm going to leave a note."

"Good idea." Sebastian searches for a pen in the glove compartment.

I pull out my pad of paper from my backpack. Sebastian hands me a pen. I write: *For Jason Mackey: Hi, my name is Skye and I believe I am your daughter.* I write down my number and ask him to call me. I leave the note tucked inside the crack in the door, right above the doorknob. When I get back to the car, everyone's awake and they're all looking right at me.

"What happened?" Kylie leans forward in her seat.

"Nobody answered, so I left a note."

"I'm sure he'll get the note soon," Sebastian says.

Braiding her hair, Amber looks up and sighs. "Not if he doesn't live there anymore."

My heart sinks.

"Leave my girl alone, Amber," Kylie hisses.

"Sorry, Skye." Amber reaches over and rubs my shoulder.

"It's okay," I say.

"Look, since we have to stay for the night, I've got an idea," Kylie says. "While we wait for him to call, let's go down to the beach. It's not far from here and we can stay at one of the hotels. My treat."

"I definitely need to get out of the car," Matt groans.

"Oh, yes." Amber drops her head on the back seat. "I'm getting car sick."

Sebastian looks over at me. "What do you think, should we stop?"

I nod. "It looks like we'll need a place to stay the night."

We end up at a seaside village that's buzzing with people enjoying summer break and the warmer weather. Beachy merchandise stands and quaint little shops decorate the sidewalks. There's an assortment of restaurants with outside tables and colorful umbrellas.

Kyle stretches her long limbs. "You're going to have to share that seat, Garrett."

Garrett laughs and sings out something about *I win, you lose*.

"First things first, we need to go shopping. I have to get Skye something to wear for her big moment." Kylie ignores Garrett. "There's a boutique across the street." She points it out. "It should have what we need."

I shake my head. "I don't really want to go shopping."

"Girl, you *must* have something pretty to wear for this momentous occasion."

I glance down at my clothes. Whatever I wear isn't going to change anything, especially if I don't even get the chance to meet him.

"I'm gonna head over to the surf shop." Garrett looks over at Sebastian and Matt. "You guys coming?"

Matt nods and heads down the sidewalk.

"You want me to come with you?" Sebastian takes my hand.

"I don't think you'll exactly enjoy dress shopping." I smile up at him. "You go ahead."

"Alright, see you in a while." He gives me a hug and I watch him as he heads over to the guys.

"Come on." Kylie motions to Amber and takes my hand. "You'll be okay without him for an hour, Skye."

We both laugh.

"Girls' day out," Amber sings as we walk across the street.

Sarah Beth's Boutique smells like a field of wildflowers. Amber and I follow Kylie through the cheerful place with racks of colorful clothes, jewelry, and a variety of hats, purses, and trinkets displayed on shelves and hangers along the walls.

After I try on four dresses, Kylie and Amber insist I get the white dress because Kylie says it complements my tanned skin and flounces when I walk, making me look feminine.

Her words exactly.

"You look like a princess." Amber hugs herself.

Kylie insists I pick out white sandals to complement the dress, and she tells me they're a gift. She picks out bright pink sandals for herself and makeup from assorted baskets on the counter. Amber buys a frilly yellow hat and sunglasses.

"Don't worry; he'll call," Amber says as we lean against the side of the car, waiting for the guys to get back.

"I hope so," I say.

Amber peeks out from the top of her sunglasses. "He will. I can feel it."

Kylie tilts her head. "I didn't know you were a psychic, Amber."

"Maybe I am." Amber glances down the street for the hundredth time. "Does anyone happen to like Garrett, you know, like-like him?" She pulls her new hat down over her braids.

Kylie laughs. "Why? Do you?"

"I don't know, maybe. I mean, he *is* really cute and so incredibly talented."

Kylie rolls her eyes and pulls a pack of sugarless gum from her purse. "I was thinking you two would make a cute couple." She offers

Amber and me a stick of gum. Amber giggles as she takes a piece. "But I'm still not sure about Matt. I think he's hiding something."

"Like what?" I take a stick of gum, glad we're talking about someone besides me.

"Not sure yet, but don't worry, I'm good at figuring people out." She rolls up the gum and pops it in her mouth.

"Have you figured me out?" Amber asks.

"Oh, hell yeah."

"Okay, Kylie, what do you know about me?"

"All right, Amber, if you insist. First of all, I think you don't actually care as much as you claim you do about any of this acting stuff, you just think you do because your mommy wants it. And I think you're hiding something, which is something that would surprise a lot of people. But you're too afraid to say anything because you're afraid of losing your mommy's approval, not to mention you're a coward."

Amber's bottom lip quivers. I put my arm around her and she drops her head on my shoulder and cries.

"I've certainly got a knack for this," Kylie says, taking her new lipstick out of her purse.

Amber lifts her head off my shoulder and sniffles. "Sometimes I think you're just plain mean, Kylie Hanson."

"So I've been told." Kylie shrugs and applies her new pink lipstick.

Thirty-Seven

A ROOM AT VILLA by the Beach with no view of the ocean is two hundred dollars a night.

"How about a room *with* a view?" Kylie asks the man behind the counter while holding out her credit card.

"We should get two rooms," Amber insists.

"You got money?" Kylie snaps.

Amber shakes her head and her hat tips over her face.

The man looks up from the computer screen and shoves his metal-framed glasses up his long nose. "We don't have any other rooms available right now."

"Let's sleep in the car," Garrett suggests.

"No way in hell I'm doing that," Kylie says. "We'll take the room with no view."

"If you insist." Garrett gets in close to her and flutters his long lashes.

"Dweeb." She pushes him away, and he pretends to stumble.

"Geez, no love for the rocker." He throws his hand to his heart.

"I'm sure you're loved." Amber grins over at him.

"Really?" Kylie grunts.

"I've never slept in a room with guys before." Amber ignores Kylie. "And I don't think I should."

Kylie squints at her. "You're kidding, right?"

I check my phone for the umpteenth time.

"No, I'm not kidding, Kylie." Amber grabs a brochure from the counter and walks away.

"Are you sure there aren't any other rooms?" Sebastian asks the guy behind the counter.

"It's summer, man, that's all I got."

"Fine. We'll take it." Kylie drops her credit card on the counter.

When the door opens to our room and we step inside, Amber frowns. "There's only two beds and there's what, six of us?"

"There's a couch, maybe it folds out into a bed." Garrett goes over and pulls off the cushions. "Yep, sleeps two."

"I call this bed." Amber sits on the bed by the window.

"Reality check, Amber, today you're not all that." Kylie tosses her purse on the bed. "We'll do two girls in one bed. The lovebirds can have their own bed, and Matt and Garrett take the fold out."

"How about it, Amber? You sleep with me?" Garrett winks.

Amber stomps her foot. "Garrett Ritchie, I sleep alone."

"Not tonight," Kylie reminds her. "And you better not snore or drool or breathe in my direction."

Sebastian and I share a smile.

"I don't know about you guys, but I'm going to check out the beach," Garrett says. "You guys coming?"

Amber gathers up a few of the bathroom towels and we all head out to the sand. Garrett takes off running toward the ocean.

We pass groups of people under colorful umbrellas, teenagers playing frisbee, and little kids building sand castles.

"Well, I know what I'm going to do." Amber dumps the towels in my arms and does cartwheels in the sand.

"I don't know about that girl." Kylie shakes her head as she struts through the sand in her pink sandals.

Garrett's already swimming in the water by the time we reach the shore.

"I'm going to check audition notices." Matt takes a towel from me.

"Looks good out there." Sebastian pulls off his shirt and jeans, revealing navy blue boxer briefs and a lean, muscular body. He glances over at me, smiling. "You going in, Skye?"

"I think I'll hang here. You go ahead." I give him a thumbs up. He nods and takes off toward the water.

"You got a good one," Kylie says as we both watch Sebastian until he disappears into the water. "But who's Lily?"

I'm about to answer her when Amber cries out, "Hey, I don't have a bathing suit! I should have gone back to the hotel before we left and packed. I hate not having my stuff and now I can't go in the water, not that I like the ocean all that much but—"

Kylie rolls her eyes. "What does your bra look like?" She starts to pull up Amber's top.

"There are people out here." Amber swats her hand away.

"Trust me, no one cares." Kylie pulls at her top again and peeks down the front. "Yellow bra, cute. Matches your hat. How about your underwear?"

"Don't touch me." Amber takes a step back. "But if you must know, my underwear is purple, why?"

"*Hmm,* guess it'll do as a bathing suit."

"I'm not going out there in my underwear," Amber says.

Kylie shrugs and pulls off her top, revealing a pink lacy bra. "Think about it. What is a bikini but a bra made of what, polyester and nylon, some Lycra for durability?" She moves her hands over her smooth stomach. "Bras, underpants, bathing suits… It's just another way to make money off us women."

"Fine." Amber pulls off her top and drops it in the sand. "I'm going for a swim, but I'm keeping my shorts on."

"How about you, Skye?" Kylie twists her long hair and ties it in a loose knot.

"Nah, I think I'll hang here just in case I get a call."

Kylie nods and steers Amber toward the water.

I check my phone. No messages.

Shading my eyes against the bright sunlight, I watch Kylie and Amber run toward the water in their bras and smile when I see Sebastian rising from the water, all sleek and beautiful. He waves when he sees me. I wave back.

I gaze out at the massive ocean; the world around me is so much bigger than the world I've known. I want more than anything to share it with my father.

"You'd love it out there," Sebastian calls out as he jogs up to me. "Come with me for a swim."

"I've never actually been in the ocean before and I—I don't know how to swim."

"That's okay." He holds out his hand. "Let me take you out there a little ways. I promise I won't let anything happen to you."

I don't tell him I don't believe in promises. People break them all the time, like how I broke my promise to Mama Bird and the babies.

Amber approaches us, dripping wet with her hand outstretched. "I'll hold your phone and backpack. Want me to answer if it rings?"

"Yes, thank you." I reluctantly hand over my phone and backpack.

"It's okay, I'll watch for the call. Go have fun."

I nod and take Sebastian's hand and we make our way into the massive ocean. The weight of the water wraps around me and I'm afraid…afraid I'm going to be swallowed up and all I can do is squeeze his hand. "I won't let you go," he says. But I still feel afraid.

A seagull swoops past us. Startled, we both laugh. In the distance, I notice a wave coming toward us. "I'm scared!" I cry. I'm scared of drowning. I'm scared my father doesn't live in that yellow house anymore. I'm scared he read the note and he doesn't want to talk to me.

"Hold on to me until it passes." Sebastian wraps his arms around me and I cling to him as the wave slams against us. I waver a little, but I don't fall.

"You did it." Sebastian grins down at me.

"I did!" I laugh.

We make our way out of the ocean. I feel a lot better when we're back on land. Sebastian suddenly stops and turns to me, searching my eyes. "There's no place I'd rather be than here with you. I really like you, Skye."

I gaze into his smiling eyes and my heart is bursting with happiness. "I really like you too, Sebastian."

He grins down at me and takes me in his arms and kisses me with his salty, sweet lips. When our lips finally drift apart, we smile into each other's eyes and hold each other as the cool breeze brushes over our sun-kissed skin. And in those moments, there in his arms, as he smiles down at me, it feels as if the hollow parts of my heart are no longer empty.

"Do you hear that?" Garrett gets up and scans the beach. "The music's coming from over there." He points to the pier in the distance. "I gotta find out who's playing." He shakes out his hair like a wet dog. "You guys down?"

We trudge through the sand, following Garret until we reach the pier. There are food vendors and people selling homemade jewelry and various trinkets. We make our way to the end of the pier where there's a crowd of people and music booming.

We stay close behind Garrett as we inch through the crowd. Someone steps on my foot and a girl screams in my ear. Sebastian takes my hand and we stay on course, pushing our way through to keep up with Garrett. A group of girls stare at Garrett, maybe mistaking him for one of the band members as he pretends to play an air guitar. They clear a path and let him through. We stick close behind.

When we reach the front, I can see the band. Five musicians are performing on stage, all with boldly colored hair, and their faces are made up with eyeliner and mascara, and even black lipstick. The purple-haired drummer leaps off his seat and twirls his sticks before slamming them down on the drums. The lead singer struts around the stage in tight, shiny black pants and spiky yellow hair, and he has big black teardrops painted on his cheek. He screams into the microphone, the words impossible to make out.

"They're playing 'Right out of the Jungle!'" Garrett shouts. The crowd moves in and shoves us forward. Garrett manages to get near the stage, wildly bobbing his head, his white hair flying while playing his invisible guitar.

The singer screams, *"You say you don't care about me anymore, then just leave like you have before."*

Garrett's singing and rocking out around the stage and the singer laughs. "You," he says into the microphone, pointing to Garrett. "You know how to play 'Into the Dark'?"

Garrett drops his hands and flips his hair. "Yeah, man, totally."

"Come on up and show us, man."

Garrett climbs up onto the stage, grinning from ear to ear.

"Dude, what's your name?" The singer runs a black cloth over his sweaty forehead.

"Garrett Ritchie."

"You play guitar, Garrett Ritchie?"

"Yes, I do!" he shouts out to the crowd.

"All right, dude." The singer grabs a spare guitar from the stage and offers it to Garrett. "Let's see what you can do."

Garrett straps the guitar around his neck and instantly starts playing with incredible precision and confidence. The band joins in and it's like Garrett has always been one of the band members as he effortlessly plays their song like it's his own.

As he continues to play, he glides around the stage and his white hair glows like the moon underneath the bright lights. Garrett grabs an available mic from one of the stands and starts to sing, *don't come back this time, I can't take it anymore, cause you're right out of the jungle, girl, yeah.* The audience reacts by screaming out his name: *Ritchie, Ritchie.*

The lead singer starts jumping around on stage, screaming out the lyrics to his song into the microphone, maybe because he's worried Garrett's stealing his show.

What do you have to say now, Lara?

Thrashing his guitar, the lead singer shouts out to the audience, "Let's give this guy a hand!" But Garrett keeps playing and the thunder of clapping and shouting explodes around us—they want more *Ritchie.* Matt, Kylie, and I get in on it: "*Ritchie...Ritchie!*" We all shout until our lungs hurt.

The lead singer marches over to Garrett and says something in his ear. Garrett stops playing, slips off the guitar, and takes a bow as the crowd roars.

"I'm gonna be doing this one day, so don't forget my name: Garrett Ritchie!" Garrett shouts out to the crowd and the entire audience explodes.

"We'll be back in fifteen!" the lead singer says into the mic and heads off the stage, leaving the rest of the band members looking confused.

As Garrett jumps off the stage, he's bombarded with girls wanting his autograph. He signs his name on their arms and shirts, and amusingly, the band's CDs.

"Man, that was a rush!" Garrett says when he finally gets away from the crowd.

Matt throws an arm around Garrett's neck. "You're famous."

"I don't know about that, but this has got to be the raddest moment of my life." Garrett waves to a group of girls calling out how much they love him.

"Let's get a picture to remember the day you became famous." Kylie pulls out her phone.

As we squish in close, trying to fit into the frame, arms around each other, laughing and poking each other, it feels like we've been friends our entire lives.

Thirty-Eight

WE EAT HOT DOGS on the pier and dance to the music until the sun sets in a blaze of orangey-red that spreads out over the ocean. When it gets late, we head back to the hotel, with only the glow of the moon guiding our way. We walk along the shoreline near the sleepy waves that tumble in and gently wash over our feet.

Sebastian and I walk hand in hand as we make our way down the beach in comfortable silence as the others walk ahead of us. I gaze up at the glowing white moon that appears to be following us. I think back to the times my mother would drive through the streets searching for a place to park for the night and I'd watch the moon follow us from the window. And when I curled up in the back seat, I believed that the glowing white ball in the sky was there for me, like a giant night light for when everything went dark.

I check my phone again. I've probably checked it a hundred times. I have a sinking feeling this isn't going to work out.

"Do you want to go back to the house and see if he's there?" Sebastian asks me.

I shake my head. "It's late and he must have come back by now, and found the note. Maybe he doesn't want to see me. Maybe—"

"Don't think like that. There's gotta be a reason why he hasn't called. We'll go back in the morning." His voice is reassuring. "If he's not there, we'll wait until he comes back."

I nod. But I'm scared I'll be waiting forever.

We pass fire pits with dancing yellow flames and people sitting around them talking, laughing, and even roasting marshmallows. As we get closer to the hotel, there's no one on the beach.

"This place is dead," Kylie says.

Matt checks his phone. "It's one in the morning."

"Let's hang out here, guys." Garrett heads over to a lone pit with an active fire and rubs his hands over the flames.

Matt goes over and stands beside Garrett and holds his hands out too.

"Who wants to go back to the room?" Amber says.

"I'd like to stay a little longer." I'm the first to answer. I'm not tired. I doubt I can sleep. He still hasn't called. What if I don't get to see him?

"Okay, but we gotta get some sleep." Amber wraps her arms around herself. "I'm cold."

"I'll go gather wood to make heat for woman." Garrett beats his chest with his fists.

Amber giggles.

"I'll help," Matt offers and catches up with Garrett.

Sebastian and I sweep the sand around the pit with our feet.

"Wish I had a beer," Garrett says when he returns, dropping a pile of sticks by the fire pit.

Matt comes back holding a piece of driftwood.

"Really? I didn't take you for a drinker." Kylie squints at him.

"I'll have a beer sometimes when I'm at a party." Garrett plops down on the sand.

"You're not going to be one of those screwed-up rock and roll stars, are you?" Amber sits next to him.

"Nah, I just like a beer once in a while."

"That's how it starts." Amber shakes her head. "My friend Aaron drank so much he ended up in the hospital."

"Is he okay?" I ask.

"Yeah, he's been in a twelve-step program for teens. I personally stay away from anything that could harm my body." Amber looks at each one of us thoughtfully. "You know what we need? *A truth circle.*"

"What's that?" Garrett tosses a pile of sticks into the fire.

"It's a way to get to know each other better, and well, bond." She smiles over at him.

"Eww, so, like spilling our guts," Kylie says.

Amber rolls her eyes. "More like we share things we haven't told anyone."

"You mean like telling secrets." Garrett cocks his head.

"Here, give me that stick." Amber reaches for Matt's driftwood.

"It isn't *just* a stick." Matt waves it around. "It's a magic wand… Although it doesn't seem to be working."

"Whatever." Amber yanks it from his hand. "This will be the truth stick we pass around and when you have it, you tell something about yourself, something you haven't told anyone else."

"Why the hell would we want to do that?" Kylie frowns.

"Like I said, it'll help us, you know, to bond," Amber says. "Okay, I'll give you an example. *Soooo...* When I was in Girl Scouts, I was bullied by the other girls."

Kylie leans in. "And why on earth was Miss Amber bullied?"

"Really, Kylie." She shakes her head. "I don't know, maybe because I'm pretty." She shrugs. "But anyway, after we did the circle, they were much nicer to me after that."

Kylie shakes her head. "Okay, like why would they be nicer to you?"

Amber lets out a heavy sigh. "Well, it seems my mama cheated, so I'd win the prize for the most sold cookies and when they found out it was her, not me, it helped."

"How'd she cheat?" Garrett asks.

Amber looks down and rubs the stick between her palms. "My mama bought every box I was selling, saved all year for it too. And in case you don't know it, those cookies are expensive."

"Thin Mints are my faves." Garrett licks his lips.

"Your mom's a little nuts, Amber," Kylie says.

"I don't think you should be judgmental when I'm baring my soul." Amber pushes the stick into the sand.

"This is lame and I'm not doing some trick circle." Matt shakes his head.

"Truth circle," Amber says.

"Whatever the circle's called, I'm out." Matt stretches his arms out in front of him and yawns.

"Yeah, I don't see how telling bad stuff about ourselves brings us closer. Seems the opposite could happen," Garrett says.

"No, Garrett, doing this will give us a deeper understanding of one another *and* ourselves, and that makes us all feel more humanly connected."

"Are you some spiritual nut or something?" Kylie asks.

"No, not at all, but I do believe that sharing brings on caring."

"Seriously, Amber." Kylie rolls her eyes.

"Give it a chance, *please*." Amber hits the stick against the firepit. "Look, I'll go first, to show you what I mean."

"I think you already went," Kylie reminds her.

Amber shakes her head. "I was just giving you an example of how it works." She holds the stick up in front of her. "Kylie, I've been upset since you said some things about me."

"Here we go," Kylie says.

"I want to take this opportunity to clear up a few things and this way, you can all learn more about me. First off, you're right, Kylie. For the most part, I mean. I am doing all this for my mama and, yes, I do want something that I'm afraid to admit to her… You know, because she'll probably get pretty upset after putting so much into me and this business. I just want her to be happy, but—I want to be happy too."

"I knew your mother was a pain in the—"

"Kylie, this is supposed to be a safe circle, so no judgment." Amber looks around at each one of us with dead seriousness. "We need to respect each other's feelings."

After a brief pause, she waves the driftwood. "I have a dream to be, well, a mechanic."

"You want to fix cars?" Kylie's eyebrows raise.

"Yes, Kylie Hanson, I want to fix cars. And I'm really hoping to one day open my own shop. I've already got a name and a slogan: *Amber's, a place your car can trust.*"

"That doesn't make sense, a place your car can trust," Matt says. "A car can't actually trust; it's just a hunk of metal, after all."

"It's clever and I happen to think it's perfect."

"I'm having a hard time picturing you all greasy." Garrett grins.

Amber frowns. "Don't you fix cars, Garrett?"

"Never." He shakes his head. "I don't do anything that might damage these." He holds up his smooth hands and wiggles his long, narrow fingers.

"I get it, about your hands. But if I get my chance, I'll show them how I can make an engine purr again. I'll be helping people get back on the road. Cars are important to our lives. Look at us— without Sebastian's old faithful, we wouldn't be here."

I smile over at Sebastian; he was the one who made this happen.

Matt shrugs. "I wouldn't know, we don't own a car."

"Yeah, but you do use the subways and taxis. And that's transportation, Matt. Hence: engines."

"Good point, Amber, I stand corrected." Matt nods. "How did you learn how to work on cars, anyway?"

"My daddy, of course. He taught me everything about motors. He's a mechanical engineer, and works for a big automotive manufacturing company. He's shown me how to diagnose problems with engines and how to fix them. He taught me what tool to use for any situation. He even bought me my very own impact wrench to make my job easier since I don't have the muscle strength. Not yet, anyway." She smiles. "He thinks it's just a hobby, but it isn't. It's what I want to do with my life."

"Are you going to be the first girl mechanic or something?" Garrett tosses a handful of sticks in the fire.

"Garrett Ritchie, you're obviously not up on your facts about women. There are plenty of women that can and do fix cars and all kinds of machinery and can do it as good as any man—and if you haven't seen one yet, you are looking at one right now."

"Okay, okay, Amber, chill."

"What's keeping you from following your dream?" Matt asks.

Amber shakes her head. "I don't know, I guess because my mom really hates it when I'm out there. Besides, she's got these big dreams for me, ones that have to do with me making it big in entertainment. Although I do like it, and obviously I'm very good at it, I'd rather put on those coveralls and get under the hood of a car." Amber falls silent and dips the stick into the fire. "Be gone." She passes the stick to Garrett.

Garrett takes it and twirls it like a baton. "Seems she'd just want you to be happy."

"She's got her own ideas of what my life should look like, I guess." Amber shrugs. "But enough about me. What would you like to share with us, Garrett?"

He throws his head back. "It's nothing, really. Guess I've been kinda afraid to tell my dad something."

"This is a safe circle. You can share your feelings." Amber rubs his arm.

Garrett gazes at the fire and lets out a chuckle. "It's dumb... I mean...I love my dad, which isn't dumb, and I'm grateful for all he's done for me, but—I kinda wanna know where I came from, *who* I came from. Thing is, my dad's always saying, *It's you and me against the world, buddy.* But I wanna know the part of the world I came from." He holds up the stick.

Amber takes his hand and squeezes it. "And you should if that's what's in your heart."

He looks down at her hand on his. "I didn't know I had such an effect on people." He tosses the stick into the fire.

"Garrett Ritchie!" Amber pulls her hand away. "Look what you did!" She attempts to get the stick out of the pit, but it's already burning up.

"Sorry." He grabs another stick from the pile and hands it to her.

"Thanks." She takes it with a huff. "Okay, your turn, Bash."

"Nah, I'll pass." Sebastian shakes his head.

"This *can* change our lives," Amber appeals to us with an encouraging nod.

Matt shakes his head and says, "Saying something out loud doesn't change anything."

"Oh, yes it does, Matt." Amber squints over at him. "Have you not just witnessed what has occurred tonight?" After a long dramatic pause and no response from Matt, she turns her attention back to Sebastian. "There's so much we don't know about you."

"I did something like this once." Sebastian looks out over the fire. "When I was in group therapy after my mom died."

"What did she die of?" Garrett asks.

Sebastian bows his head.

"Send it out into the universe, Bash." Amber hands him the stick.

Sebastian takes it and fidgets next to me. I look over at Amber and think about telling her to leave him alone with all this nonsense; all this prying is making me angry. I'm not sure why we're doing this, anyway; what good will it do?

I rest my hand on his leg and he glances over at me. "You don't have to," I whisper.

"It's okay." Sebastian breathes out a heavy sigh and says, "When I was little…my mom was killed." He gazes at the fire. "And I've been living with my grandma ever since, but she got sick and I just took her to a place that can take better care of her. Now it's just me and I'm trying to figure out the rest of my life."

"Do you know who killed your mom?" Garrett asks.

Sebastian nods. "Yeah, it was my dad. He's still in jail."

Everyone is silent.

I'm shaking when I reach for his hand. Sebastian looks over at me, his eyes brimming with tears. "Sorry, I didn't tell you everything." His voice is so tender my heart breaks. "I guess I was scared. But I don't want to be scared anymore. I just want to make my mom proud."

I squeeze his hand. "She's already proud of you, and so am I."

"That's so horrible," Amber says, sniffling. "You're so strong, Bash."

"This is getting way too intense." Matt swipes at his eyes. "We should stop."

Sebastian gazes over at me and hands me the stick. "You do what's right for you," he says.

What's right for me? How do I even know what that is? I take the stick from him.

I can do this, I tell myself, gazing at the fluttering orange flames inside the pit, and I realize that so much has already changed in my life and I don't want to ever go back to how it was. I look up from the fire and they're all watching me. "I'm not sure why, but my mother's always denied my father even existed. I used to live with my mother and my Uncle Richard until he died a few years ago and, well, life's been anything but easy. But now, after everything that's happened, my father has been found—and hopefully—I'll see him for the first time tomorrow."

"Maybe your mom's protecting you from something," Amber says. "You know, like he's a bad man."

"I've thought about that, I've thought of all kinds of reasons for why she's kept him from me, but I have to find him. I believe—I believe he's a good man." I rest my eyes on Amber. "So here I am."

I pass the stick to Kylie and after she takes it and squeezes my hand, she gazes out over the group. "Sorry to disappoint, but I've got nothing astonishing to confess."

"Kylie, we know there's something eating at you," Amber says.

Kylie grits her teeth. "You don't know anything about me."

"Then tell me."

"First off." Kylie looks at each one of us, shaking her head. "It's kinda weird how you're all willingly baring your souls?"

Amber raises a hand. "Talking about it helps us understand ourselves better and the people around us."

Kylie's laughing now. "Understand ourselves better? You mean like you wanting to stick your head under the hood of a car with your trusty hammer is something we all have to try and understand?"

"For your information, Kylie, it's an impact wrench," Amber corrects her. "And yeah, because even though that's what I want to do with my life, it's complicated."

Kylie shrugs and hands Matt the stick.

Matt holds the stick up in the air and gazes out at the dark sky. "Oh mighty stick, free me from the secrets within me." He pauses, then looks back at us and frowns. "I don't actually have any secrets."

"We all have secrets," Amber says.

"Well, I don't."

Amber shrugs. "Okay, fine, then tell us what you wish for. You're a really good actor, we all saw that on the show. Is acting really what you want to do, or is there something else?"

"No, ma'am." He salutes Amber. "Theater is my sole desire. Just give me the stage."

"Have you done a lot of stage acting?"

"Yes, I have."

"Like what shows?"

His face softens. "There's too many to list, but the best was *Les Miserables* on Broadway."

"Really? That's an amazing play." Kylie smiles. "Although, I'd have to say my favorite was *Phantom of the Opera*."

The closest I came to seeing a musical was *The Sound of Music* on TV. It was one of the rare times my mother, Uncle Richard, and I did something together. While my mother hummed along to the songs, Uncle Richard cried through most of it. But, being a stupid little kid, I marched around the living room singing along with the Von Trapp kids.

"Now tell us what's on your heart," Amber says to Matt.

"Can't think of a thing." He shrugs.

"Come on, Matty, whatcha hiding?" Kylie says.

"What do you care, Kylie? Seems you have your own problems in your plastic Barbie doll get up."

Kylie sucks in air. "My life isn't as perfect as it looks. But it's okay because I know what I want to do with my life."

"Become the next top model," Amber says.

Kylie frowns. "No, Amber, I don't want to spend my life modeling. Do you even know what it's like? I have to be perfect all the time: don't slouch, don't gain weight. What the hell, is that a pimple? Like I can't do anything that changes me because I have to be *perfect...perfect...perfect*!"

"I'm sorry you're going through that." I rub her shoulder.

"It's okay." Kylie clears her throat and smooths her hair back over her shoulders. "And for your information." She focuses directly on Amber. "I do have a wish or a dream or whatever the crap you call it. Hair. I love hair and I've been working my ass off trying to start a product line with this hair remedy I developed. I've come up with a miracle conditioner, and it can change the health of someone's hair at any stage. So, like yeah, that's what I want to do."

"I'd buy it. My hair's important to my image." Garrett runs his fingers through his silky white hair.

"You're lucky, Garrett, you have incredible hair." Kylie smiles now. "Most people struggle with hair issues—too thin, too dry, too oily, split ends, frizz. I want to help them get hair-healthy. So like yeah, I'm counting the days until I'm eighteen so I can stop modeling and start my brand, *Radiance*."

Matt leans forward. "Why don't you just stop modeling and do that now?"

"Modeling happens to be my family's way of life. My grandma was big in the industry and my mother still is. But she's getting older and plans on passing the torch to me—and I'm expected to follow in their footsteps."

Amber tilts her head to one side. "Is that why you don't eat… To be what they want?"

"Seriously!" Kylie leaps up off the sand. "You don't know what the hell you're talking about, Amber." She shakes her head and storms off.

"I'll go check on her," I tell them and make my way down to where she's standing just feet from the water, staring out into the wide expanse of the ocean. "You okay?"

She turns to me, her eyes glistening with tears. "I'm a mess." She kicks the sand and sits down. I sit next to her on the cold, moist sand.

"Amber's right, Skye. I'm just so damn hungry. I hate seeing everyone eat what they want all the time."

"I know what it's like to be hungry, but for different reasons," I tell her. "My mother and I have been in and out of homelessness for years now."

"What the—"

I shrug.

"And here I am throwing up all that good food." Kylie frowns. "Thing is, I want to stop, but I don't know how."

I drape an arm around her back. "But you want to, Kylie, and that's a start." I pull her close. "You're going to be okay."

She drops her head on my shoulder. "Yeah, we both will, huh?"

"Hey, got room for me?" Matt scoots in between us.

Kylie tousles his hair. "What's bothering you, Matty?"

Matt breathes out a heavy sigh.

"You know what you need?" Kylie says.

He pulls his legs close to him and looks over at her. "What?"

"This." She leans over and plants a kiss on his lips.

He pulls away. "What was that about?"

"You're a good kisser, Matty, even if." She licks her lips.

"Even if what?"

"Even if you won't admit that you're gay."

"What the hell, Kylie?" Matt scrambles to his feet.

"Why're you hiding it, anyway?"

Matt throws his head back and lets out an exaggerated laugh. "You don't get it, Kylie. If my dad finds out, he'll hate me."

"I'm sure he'll still love you. You're his son, silly."

Matt winces, shaking his head. "You don't know him. My dad already disapproves of me. He hates that I don't do sports, that I dress the way I do, that I talk the way I do, and what he really hates is that I take ballet, says real men don't twirl around. I'm pretty sure he'll disown me if he finds out."

Kylie jumps up and slips her arm around his waist, pulling him close. "I think he probably already knows."

Matt yanks himself out of her grip.

"Ah, come on, you know I love ya." She jumps around the sand. "Come on, Matty, show me some of those fancy dance moves."

"You're ridiculous, Kylie." He chokes out a laugh.

"Come on, you know you want to." She dances around him, waving her arms above her head.

Matt takes off running and leaps into the air, twirling maybe two feet off the ground before skillfully landing on the sand.

"That was on point." Kylie runs over to him and they dance together.

I look away from them long enough to check my phone. No messages. No matter what happens, I'm not leaving here until I see him. I only hope he'll be happy when he sees me. And maybe, when he finds out how I've been living, he'll want me to come live with him in his pretty yellow house.

Wrapping my hand around the bracelet, I close my eyes and promise myself I'll never give up on my father.

"Skye, come dance with us," Kylie calls out to me.

As I make my way over to them, I can hear Amber, Sebastian, and Garrett calling out as they head toward us.

And soon we are all together, dancing and singing and laughing on the beach as if we don't have a care in the world. And as for our dreams, at least for now, they are put on hold.

"Group hug," Amber says.

As we gather around each other—I look at each one of the faces I've come to know and care about and for a brief moment as we cling to one another, it's as if we're holding up the world.

Thirty-Nine

MELODIC WAVES RISE AND crash like a symphony, filling my eager heart with a longing I must fulfill. Cradling the cool grains of sand in my hand, I let the smooth pebbles sift through my fingers. I think about what Sebastian told us and my heart aches for him and all he's been through. Opening my eyes to the morning light, I'm surprised to see a large gray and white seagull just inches from me.

I watch him watching me and the memory of Mama Bird rests heavily on my heart. Nervously, I pull out my phone from my backpack—no messages. My heart sinks. As I rise, I'm careful not to wake Sebastian sleeping next to me or the others, peacefully asleep around us.

When I take a step forward, the bird spreads his wings and takes off. I run along the sand after him, but when I reach the water's edge, I can only gaze up at the bird as he soars across the sea.

I startle when my phone rings inside my hand. I look down at the screen, only to drop to my knees as I fumble to answer it. "Hello?" My heart pounds inside my ears.

"Is this Skye?"

"Yes, yes, it's me, Skye."

"Hi. I'm Jason and I got your note. I was surprised, first hearing from the show and now finding the note at my door…from you."

I turn away from the loud crashing of the waves and walk up the sand so I can hear him. "I didn't mean to go to your house unannounced, but I tried calling a few times and when I couldn't get through, that's when I left the note."

"It's funny because I actually just got my phone fixed, literally picked it up this morning."

That explains him not responding to my calls and texts. "Do you really think you're my father?" I blurt out and freeze the second I say it.

"Oh, man. Wow, that sounds—I mean, your mom. She called me years ago and said she had a baby girl, said that she was mine."

And I'm that girl! I'm your girl! I shout inside my head.

"Are you still there?"

"Yes, yes, I'm here," I say, tears spilling from my eyes.

"May I ask how old you are, Skye?"

"Sixteen." I sniffle hard.

"Wow, this is just so… Huh, I mean, the last time I spoke to your mom was in what…? 2002. So yeah, about sixteen years ago. What has your mother told you about me?"

"Um, well, she hasn't."

"Really?"

"She's… a very private person," I blurt out. "So what happened? I mean, why were you never around?"

"Truth is, I really didn't know her very well, and I couldn't contact her because I didn't know her last name."

"It's Perry. Our last name is Perry." My heart's beating out of my chest.

"Perry." He sighs. "Could you put your mom on the phone?"

"I would but—" I panic, I have no clue what to say. "She's not here right now—she's out running an errand."

My first lie to my father.

There's a long pause before he says, "What do we do now?"

"I, um, I was hoping we could meet."

Another long pause. "How long will you be in the area?"

"Just today. Does that work for you?"

"Today, yeah, sure." He clears his throat. "How about lunch… around 12:30?"

I can't believe I'm going to see my father. "Perfect! Where should we meet?"

"There's a place called Corner Cafe on Bexley, right next to the bank. Do you need the address?"

"Corner Cafe on Bexley. I can find it."

"By the way, how is your mom?"

"She's—good."

"That's good to hear. When I was contacted by the show, I wanted to find out more about you and your mom, and I asked for a private meeting, but then they called me back and said it wasn't going to happen, wouldn't tell me why, or give me any information, but now it looks like we're going to finally meet…" After a short pause he says, "I had better get back to work. I'll see you this afternoon?"

"Yes, at 12:30."

"I look forward to it. Bye."

I press the phone against my chest and close my eyes, waiting for the world to stop spinning. Today is the day my whole life is about to change.

The sound of my friends' voices caresses my ears... Voices that have become familiar to me, ones that I have found comfort in. When I open my eyes, they are there, waving for me to come back.

I take one last glance at the ocean and I head back.

"Guess we didn't need the room after all," Garrett says when we're back in our room.

"We still have time to use it." Matt collapses on one of the beds. "Wake me when it's time to go."

"Can't believe you talked to your dad, Skye." Amber hugs herself. "This is so exciting. Our trip has brought two people together."

"Let's make sure it's happily ever after," Kylie adds. "I'm showering and then—" Kylie points to me. "I'm going to get you ready."

"I can get ready on my own," I tell her, pulling out my dress and shoes from the closet.

Kylie shakes her head as she makes her way to the bathroom. "You gotta trust me on this," she says and shuts the bathroom door.

Sebastian flips through the menu on the table. "Think I'll get food for everyone." He looks over at me. "What would you like, Skye?"

"I'm not hungry." I try to swallow the wave of nausea that's moving up my throat.

"I'm starving," Garrett says. "I'll go with you, Bash."

Sebastian nods and comes over to me and takes my hand. "This is your big day. It's going to be okay." He hugs me.

"I hope so," I whisper, feeling a little unsure now that Jason Mackey is expecting to see my mother too.

"I'll be right back." Sebastian smiles at me. I nod and watch him make his way over to Garrett, who's waiting for him by the door.

"Large coffee with two sugars and four creams for me, Bash," Matt says sleepily from the bed.

"I wanna go too," Amber says and follows Garrett and Sebastian out the door.

I take the dress off the hanger, hold it up to my chest, and gaze at myself in the full-length mirror outside the bathroom. I look tired and frizzy-haired, but the dress is pretty.

Kylie comes out of the bathroom wrapped in a fluffy white towel. "This is your big day, and you are going to look fabulous." She hands me a pink bottle. "After shampooing, put my conditioner in your hair and leave it on for three minutes. Rinse, and it'll like take care of this." She grabs a clump of my hair and shows me what is obviously a mess. She frowns, shaking her head. "It's like your hair is starving for nutrients. You could use a trim to get rid of those god-awful split ends. But for now, we'll do this."

I open the bottle and sniff, detecting a hint of coconut and maybe honey. *"Mmm*, it smells delicious. What's in it?"

"I've mixed in a few things like coconut oil, which not only helps your hair feel smooth and soft, it helps each strand grow stronger and it nourishes your scalp. People don't realize we need to take care of our scalp, that it's skin too, and our hair grows from there. And then there are follicles and glands that can get clogged. I have a remedy for that too. I also added honey, lemon juice, rose water, and a secret ingredient that I can't reveal to anyone; it's a miracle plant and literally heals hair to a lustrous shine and texture."

"Impressive. Where can I find it?" Matt calls sleepily from the bed.

"Thanks, Matty, but my product isn't out yet, but it will be as soon as I turn eighteen and can get the money that's sitting in my trust. After my product takes off, I plan on developing something for the skin as well." Kylie beams and turns her attention back to me. "Now let's get you ready."

When Kylie's done with me, I have silky hair and flawless skin. Besides her miracle conditioner, she used the makeup she keeps in her purse, saying she never leaves home without it. "Now, there's one more thing we gotta do." She tries to take my bracelet off my wrist.

"What are you doing?" I yank my arm away.

"Like, you gotta take that off. It's ruining your look."

I shake my head. "I'm not taking it off."

"Skye, it's ugly."

"No, it isn't and it's *never* coming off."

"Okay, okay. It's just some stupid rubber bracelet you can get anywhere for free, but okay, have it your way."

I turn away from Kylie. I don't tell her that those three words on the bracelet have kept me going, that I only have two things that mean anything to me: Lil' Monkey and this bracelet.

When I finally step out of the bathroom, Kylie announces, "Here she is." The expressions on each of their faces make me feel how Cinderella must have felt when she was transformed by the fairy godmother for the ball.

"Skye, you're so beautiful." Sebastian comes over and kisses me.

"You're a knockout," Garrett says, munching on a breakfast sandwich.

Matt gives me a thumbs-up.

"Oh, Skye, you are a true princess," Amber cries.

I can't stop smiling; I feel like I'm about to burst with happiness. Today is going to be the most important day of my entire life.

All because I never gave up.

Forty

WHILE SEBASTIAN DRIVES THROUGH the sprawling metro area of San Jose, I can't stop shaking.

"It's going to be okay." Sebastian glances over at me.

"Yeah. I'm just a little nervous." I force a smile and stare out the window, worrying I misled Jason Mackey into thinking he's seeing my mother too. When he realizes I lied, will he hate me?

I have to believe when he sees me that all of that won't matter. I have so many questions to ask him. But what if I'm too nervous to remember them? I pull out a notepad from my backpack and write:

How did you meet my mother?

Did you hope I'd find you?

Do you want me in your life?

The last question scares me. I never considered the possibility that when I found him, he might not even want me.

Sebastian parks and everyone scrambles out of the car and wishes me luck. "You coming, Bash?" Matt calls as the others head down the street toward the farmers' market.

"I'll catch up." He waves over to Matt.

Anxiety has set in, the kind that makes my chest tight, and makes me think I'm having a heart attack. I pull at the straps of my dress that feel like a boa constrictor around my neck.

"Are you okay, Skye?" Sebastian asks.

"What if he doesn't like me?"

"Impossible." Sebastian shakes his head and looks at me with an assurance I can almost hold on to. "When I first saw you smelling those flowers on the tree, and you looked over at me, you stole my heart right then and there. And that's what's going to happen to your dad."

The place is crowded. The hostess has me follow her to a table a good distance from the entrance. I choose the chair facing the door.

Will I recognize him right away?

Will he recognize me?

I'm ten minutes early. I'm feeling queasy. My hand shakes as I organize the sugar packets according to color and straighten the menus on the table. I check the door. It's getting hard to breathe and my heart is pounding. As I take deep breaths in and exhale slowly, the server comes over, asking if I'm okay, and places a glass of water and a straw on the table. I tell her I'm fine and she asks for my order. I tell her I'm waiting for someone. When she's gone, I check the door.

I twirl the straw in the water and take a sip. I check the time on my phone. He's three minutes late. I'm afraid he isn't going to show. But when I check the door again there's a tall man dressed in black jeans and a pale blue button-down shirt with the cuffs folded at his elbows. He scans the room and when he sees me, he waves.

How does he know it's me in a crowd of people? Tears prick my eyes, but I will not let them fall. I don't want him to think I'm a baby.

I wave back and as he walks toward me, I stumble up from the chair.

"Skye," he says when he's standing right in front of me.

I look up into the eyes of my father and my heart flutters. "Hi."

"Wow, you're as pretty as your mom," he says.

I startle at his words; I look nothing like her. But it doesn't matter because my father called me pretty.

"Where's your mom?" He scans the room.

"Um, she couldn't make it."

His lips pinch together. "Why is that?" His bluish-gray eyes are staring at me now.

My mother has blue eyes too. What are the chances of two sets of blue making brown?

I have to sit down; my legs are wobbly. He takes my cue and sits across from me.

He's watching me, waiting for an answer.

But I don't know what to say.

"What can I get you?" The server is standing over us now, tapping a pencil on her pad of paper as if she's in a rush.

Jason Mackey turns his attention to her and orders coffee and a cheeseburger. I steal a glance at his face; he doesn't look like I imagined he would. He has a long oval face and a long sharp nose. I search for similarities between us, but nothing jumps out at me.

The girl scribbles it down on a pad of paper and then turns her attention to me. "What'll you have?"

"A burger and Coke."

"You want cheese on that?"

I nod.

The second she walks away, he leans in toward me. "Why didn't your mom come today?"

Shifting in my chair, I can tell by the look on his face that he's disappointed. This isn't how I imagined it would be. "She didn't come on the trip with me."

His face collapses like a stack of blocks. "I don't understand."

What should I tell him? I think she hates you for some reason? Why else would she tell me you never even existed?

"Is your mom married? Is that why she's not here?"

"No. Are you?" My leg shakes under the table.

He nods. "Maybe I can talk to your mom on the phone."

This is getting complicated. I don't want to tell him another lie. "She doesn't actually know I'm here with you."

"What do you mean?" He runs his fingers through his ultra-short brown hair.

"I wanted to meet you. Does it really matter if she knows or not?"

His right eye twitches. "Well... I have...you know, questions."

"Of course. I mean, you knew her. You and her... Well, I just wanted to meet you…first. I'm sure she wants to see you. It's just that—I wanted to meet you—first."

"Really? Okay, that's good. And yeah, I'm curious about what happened."

You and me both.

Our server comes back and sets down our drinks and two plates with burgers and fries.

I clear my throat. "What happened to you and my mother?" My right eyelid twitches. Something we have in common.

"I'm not totally sure. What has she told you?" He sips his coffee while looking directly at me.

"Honestly, she hasn't told me anything." *Twitch.*

His eyebrows raise and he looks—well, bummed. "Really."

"She's a very private person. I was hoping you could tell me everything, you know, like how you two met."

"I can see her being a private person, although I didn't know her that well." He looks past me, his eyes shifting back and forth like he's looking for someone or something. "I'm not sure if it's my place to talk about what happened."

"Please, I'd like to know and really, I don't think she would mind."

He peers down at his plate. "Not sure what's going on here, Skye."

"Just a girl wanting to know about her father." As soon as it comes out of my mouth, I regret saying it.

He rubs his head like it hurts.

This isn't how it's supposed to be. "I'm sure she'll call you after

I tell her how it went."

He pushes his plate away and leans forward. "Okay, I'd like that." His mouth curls up into a smile. He has a nice smile, but I still don't see a clear resemblance. "If I'm being perfectly honest, your mom is someone I've never been able to forget. She really never told you *anything*?"

I shake my head. "Maybe you could tell me how you met."

"I remember it as if it were yesterday." His head bobs as he speaks. "I met her when I was working construction; I was twenty-four at the time." He places his smooth and very clean hands flat on the table. Definitely not the hands of a construction worker.

"Your mom was singing and playing the guitar on the corner where I was working. All the guys pooled some money, and I offered to give it to her; think she made a bundle that day." He chuckles.

"She doesn't know how to play guitar," I tell him. I had wanted to buy a guitar at a thrift store once, but she said it was a waste of money.

"Oh, she could play, *and* her voice… Beautiful." A huge grin spreads out across his face. "I was so glad she agreed to have coffee with me and we ended up spending the entire evening together."

For now, I'll ignore all the stuff about my mother singing and playing guitar. "What did you talk about?"

"Hmm." He rubs his rather large forehead, unlike my small one. "She mostly talked about how she was trying to make it as a singer, how she moved from Oregon to L.A. to try to make it in the music business, said she was planning to move to Nashville."

"My mother has never been out of Los Angeles."

Jason Mackey lifts his burger and takes a big bite. He chews and swallows. There's a little bit of grease on the corner of his mouth.

"Then what happened?"

"We—we were together that whole night." He blushes. "But then she was gone when I woke up."

"You saw her again, though, right?"

"Uh-uh. She never gave me her number and, as I said on the phone, I didn't know her last name."

"Then how did you know she had me?" I glance down at my untouched burger.

"I gave her my number on the restaurant's receipt. It was maybe a year later when she called me, and told me she had a baby girl, my baby—and that she was having a hard time and she needed help. But the phone went dead, and it came up as an unknown caller. I never heard from her again."

Are those tears in his eyes?

"Now here we are after all these years. And I'd like to know what happened myself." He rubs his eyes.

Tics. I break out into a bunch of them. First, my leg shakes under the table, and then my other eye twitches. And then there's the worst one: my leg jerks up and my knee slams into the table, rattling everything on it.

"Sorry," I say, deflated, and slump back into the chair.

"You look so much like your mom," he says.

Why does he keep saying that? "I don't look anything like her." I stare back unapologetically at Jason Mackey.

"Yes, you do, right down to your eyes."

"Guess you don't remember what she looks like."

"I've never forgotten her." He shakes his head. "Especially her pretty brown eyes."

Brown? Anger builds inside me as I level my gaze on Jason Mackey. "You mean blue—she has *blue* eyes." My voice is raised and people at nearby tables are staring at us. "For your information, my mother doesn't sing, she doesn't play guitar, and she definitely doesn't have brown eyes."

Startled, he straightens his spine. "I'm not sure what's going on. Let's talk to Kary."

Kary? "You mean *Mary,* her name is Mary." Something catches in my throat and I start to choke.

"Are you okay?" He reaches for me. I throw my hand out to stop him.

Jason Mackey combs his chin like he's got a beard he's trying to tame. "Are we talking about the same person?"

I clear my throat. "We obviously are not. But for the record, I have a picture." I drop my backpack on the table, rip open the zipper, dig inside, and pull out my box. Throwing open the lid, I sift through the papers until I find the picture of my mother and me that was taken at the mansion the day we arrived. It's a nice picture too; we're both smiling.

I hand him the photo. He examines it carefully, shaking his head the whole time. "That's *not* her, that's not Kary."

I fall back into the chair.

"Look, I don't know what's going on, but the girl I knew, the one who had you, isn't this woman in this photo."

A lump forms in my throat.

Snatching the photo from his hand, I leap up from the table and my chair tumbles over and hits the floor. "You're *not* my father, can't you see that?" I shove my box into my backpack and run through the restaurant and out the door.

Someone calls to me as I run down the sidewalk. I wipe tears from my cheeks and turn around. Jason Mackey is running toward me. "Skye, stop! Please stop!" he calls out but I turn back and keep running but he manages to catch up to me; he's obviously a good runner.

Whirling around, I scream at the top of my lungs, "Leave me alone!"

People on the street stare at us. *Now* the whole stupid universe cares. A woman nearby gives Jason Mackey an accusing look and asks if I need help. Suddenly embarrassed at the scene I'm causing, I tell her I'm fine. She nods and turns back as she crosses the street to check on me.

He's bent over now, his hands on his knees, trying to catch his breath. "Look, I'm sorry." He peers up at me. "It's just that I know for a fact that isn't the woman I knew. The woman you look like."

Why does he keep saying that?

He straightens back up and scratches his head. "There has to be a reasonable explanation for all this. We need to ask your mom if she knows Kary."

The only explanation is you're probably not my father. "I'll talk to her when I get back."

"Yeah, okay." He nods.

"I'd better go," I murmur.

He asks me if I need a ride. I shake my head. I don't take rides from strangers. "Did you want to walk back with me?" he asks.

I shake my head.

"You've got my number. Please call me after you talk to your mom. Okay?" He touches my shoulder.

"Yeah, okay." I nod.

"Okay. Let's talk soon." He pauses, holding my gaze for a few seconds before he turns to go.

I stand there on the sidewalk, frozen in place as I watch him walk away from me. When he turns the corner, I stand there as cars whiz by and people walk past while a sense of dread builds inside of me, one where I fear I will never find my real father.

A man bumps into me and turns to say he's sorry. I move away from the middle of the sidewalk and a few unwanted tears escape my eyes. There's something really wrong, and it has to do with my mother. There's something she's keeping from me, I'm sure of it now.

And that something scares me.

Forty-One

SEBASTIAN DRIVES DOWN A long stretch of road into a world that no longer makes any sense. I rub my fingertips along the cold glass and gaze out at the cloudy sky as it grows darker. The last question on my list that I planned on asking Jason Mackey means nothing now.

I glance behind me. Both Matt and Kylie are propped up against each other sleeping. Amber found her way into the back with Garrett and every once in a while, I hear them giggle.

Sebastian glances over at me and asks me again if I'm okay.

I nod and drop my head on the headrest and close my eyes, grateful no one is asking me any more questions like they did when I got back to the car.

"Tell us everything." Amber held her breath.

"What was he like?" Kylie asked.

But I couldn't tell them we came all this way for nothing.

So, I told them it went well, but that it'll probably take some time for us to get to know each other. That seemed to work. That and the mention of going to Starbucks before heading home.

Sebastian isn't fooled, though. He keeps checking to see if I'm okay.

"Looks like we're heading into a summer storm." Sebastian peers out the window. The sky has changed dramatically since we left, from gray scattered clouds to inky, dark rain clouds looming above us. "Hopefully, I can make it out of here before it breaks." He turns on the headlights. But not more than a mile down the road, lightning shoots down from the sky. One, two, boom!

It's close.

Rain pelts down on the car like we are being shot at with a BB gun. Sebastian struggles to see out the window as the windshield wipers struggle. Finally, he pulls off the road and parks in a dirt lot.

"I'm going to wait until it subsides." He switches on the hazard lights.

Across the way is an open field of tall yellow grass spreading out as far as the eye can see. I'm mesmerized by the way the long, thick blades sway and bow under the weight of the rain like some sacred dance.

Lightning strikes the sky, followed by a thundering boom. Amber screams. Kylie talks over Garrett who's singing—*thunderbolts and lightning*—while Sebastian's reading from his phone for another possible route. There's too much noise in the car, too many voices, and without thinking, I fling open the door and stumble out of the car. I take off running toward the field. I make my way through the sheets of rain, barely able to make out the muffled voices in the distance calling to me. S*top! Come back! Where are you going,*

Skye?

But I don't stop, I keep running, and when I reach the golden field, I submerge myself in the icy cold grass that clings to my skin like wet ice. Lightning shoots down from the murky haze. Closer. I've heard stories of people getting struck by lightning and living to tell about it. Most had some sort of scar; they said it was a reminder of the moment that changed them forever. Some said they had been zapped of the things that plagued them like a slate wiped clean.

I desperately want what plagues me to be wiped clean and as my sandals struggle through the soaking wet mud, I wave my arms toward the phantom sky. "It's me! Skye! Come get me! We're kindred spirits!" I cry out. But my voice gets lost inside the cascading rain.

I was probably born on a day like this one, where wind gusts push the coiled clouds, and then... In a split second, it happens... Lightning strikes—the crackling light flashes so bright that for an instant I am blinded and the air is knocked out of me. Collapsing upon the bed of quivering grass, my body burns like it's on fire.

"Skye!" His familiar voice penetrates through the sheets of rain.

I pry open my eyes and see Sebastian as he falls to his knees beside me. "What the hell are you doing?"

"It worked!" I cry. "It worked!"

"What are you talking about?" He shoves strands of his drenched hair from his eyes. The look of fear on his face takes my breath away.

"I think I was struck." I search for a mark, a cut, a burn, something that proves it, but it's impossible to see through the pounding rain.

"You could have been killed!" he cries.

"You don't understand." My teeth chatter as I try to speak.

"Nothing makes sense anymore. I'm just so scared."

"I'm sorry things don't make sense right now!" he shouts over the thunder. "But this isn't the answer."

"I don't know what else to do," I sob.

"We'll figure it out, okay?" He takes my hand. "Now let's get the hell out of here before we both fry."

As we make our way out through the sopping wet field, tears stream down my face.

But I can't taste them.

They're mixed with the rain.

Forty-Two

ONE BY ONE, GARRETT, Matt, Amber, and Kylie get out of the station wagon, groggy and tired. I don't get out with them. I don't have the strength.

"You scared me," Kylie says through the open window. "I couldn't bear it if anything happened to you. Call me if you want to talk."

I nod. "I'm okay, really."

"Good." She pats my arm. "Okay, guys, let's get ready to face the firing squad," she says and they all wave goodbye to Sebastian and me before heading over to their hotel.

"Where should I take you?" Sebastian asks.

"I don't want to go back tonight. Can I stay with you?"

"My place then." He puts the car into drive.

I reach for my bracelet, but it isn't there. I look down at my wrist and gasp.

"What's wrong?" Sebastian looks over at me.

"My bracelet, it's gone," I say and frantically search around the seat and floor and shuffle through my backpack.

"When did you last see it?"

I close my eyes and try to remember the last time I saw it and I think… I'm sure it was on my wrist when I went into the field. It must have slipped off then. I want to go back and find it.

But I know I can't.

Back at his apartment, I peel off my muddy, stained dress and shower I let the hot water run down on me and sob, clinging to my wrist where my bracelet used to be.

When I'm dried off, I brush my hair and put on the T-shirt and gym shorts Sebastian left out for me. As I tie the drawstring tight around my waist, I can hear him talking on the phone in the other room; he sounds happy.

I find him in the kitchen chopping garlic. He peers up from what he's doing and smiles at me. "Your thoughts on spaghetti?"

"Sounds good. What can I do to help?" I ask and he hands me the jar of Ragu. "Is this another family recipe?" I make myself grin.

We both laugh.

While the pasta boils, Sebastian puts on some music from an old vintage radio on the counter. He asks if I like classical music. I tell him I'm not sure, and while we work together in the kitchen, the beautiful music begins to soothe the ache in my heart. We prepare bread with butter and fresh garlic and after Sebastian puts the tray in the oven, he reaches over and kisses me so sweetly.

"Skye," he says when our lips drift apart. "I don't mean to pry, but don't you want to talk about what happened with your dad?"

I take a deep breath in and say, "It's just that…When I was with him, he said things that didn't make sense. It was like he was talking about a completely different person, not my mother at all. If what he says is true, there's no way he can be my father."

"I'm sure there's got to be a logical explanation." He caresses my cheek. "Maybe you need to talk to your mom."

"Yeah." I nod, although I'm afraid that any explanation that comes from my mother will be anything but logical. But I've got to find out why Jason Mackey said those things about her.

Maybe she had a whole other life before I was born and she didn't want to tell me. But why? I have a sinking feeling that whatever I learn about her past, it'll mean he isn't my father.

"I heard you on the phone earlier. It sounded like good news?"

"I think so. When I stopped in at the university, I asked what I needed to do to reapply for next year. I explained why I didn't accept admittance when I had the chance and that I knew I had probably lost my scholarship." He takes the pot of cooked pasta off the stove, heads over to the sink, and dumps it into the colander. "I figured it was a long shot, you know, figuring out a way to be close to my grandma while I go to school." He piles spaghetti on our plates and looks over at me. "The call was from Susan with college admissions. She said she wants to meet me the day after tomorrow, and said she might be able to get me in this fall *with* a scholarship."

"Sebastian! That would be amazing." I smile over at him as I take the crispy garlic bread out of the oven. "You'd be close to your grandma while you go to school."

"Wouldn't that be something?" He grins. "Things may just work out after all." He pours sauce on the spaghetti and sets our plates down on the table.

I have to look away for a second. I don't want him to see the tears welling up in my eyes. It would mean he'd move away, that I'd lose him too. Swiping my eyes, I take the piping hot bread over to the table and sit down.

"I'm starving." Sebastian grabs a piece of garlic bread and takes a bite.

I gaze down at my food.

I'm not hungry anymore.

Sebastian pulls into *The Aires* parking lot and drives around while I look for her car. Part of me hopes it isn't here, but then I see the back end of her beat-up old Toyota parked between two cars.

"You want me to come in with you?"

I shake my head.

He nods and gazes out the window. "I don't want to leave you, but I'll be back tomorrow night." He shuts off the engine and removes his key ring and yanks a key off. "This is the key to my apartment, just in case you need a place to stay."

"Thank you." I wrap my fingers around the key. "I'll see you when you get back." I unlatch the seat belt and pause.

"You gonna be okay, Skye?"

"Yes." I give a convincing smile so he doesn't worry. "Good luck on your trip. It's going to work out. I just know it."

"Thanks." He leans over and kisses me. "Let me know how it goes with your mom."

"I will." I nuzzle my head into his neck and close my eyes. Everything disappears.

I don't know how long I stand outside the door squeezing the card key between my fingers, but when I finally swipe it through the slot, the door unlocks. The room is pitch black and I'm hit with a mix of raunchy tobacco and a pungent smell that tells me she hasn't bathed since I left.

When I push the curtain open, she moans and pulls the bedspread over her head.

I go straight for the nightstand and sift through the clutter of empty bottles of booze, a TV remote, two empty cans of diet Coke, a bag of butterscotch candies, a Musketeer wrapper, and a glass filled with cigarette butts.

I find her bag on the floor and I drop to my knees, yank open the flap, and spill its contents on the carpet. I sift through her toothbrush inside a crinkled baggy, a brush, a bottle of aspirin, keys, the envelope with what's left of the money, a pile of matches and assorted lighters, a pack of cigarettes, a wad of toilet paper, cherry-flavored Chapstick, a stale sugar cookie wrapped in a tissue, a knitted brown beanie, and her beat up, old wallet. I rummage through the wallet and pull out an ID—Mary Perry—and a driver's license—Mary Kenny. What?

I recognize the name Kenny; it was Uncle Richard's last name. He said my mother and he had different fathers. I remember now when she signed me up for homeschooling, the woman behind the desk said her name didn't match the one on the birth certificate and my mother had laughed, explaining that her name was actually Mary, that someone had made a mistake at the hospital and put a K instead of an M and she hadn't gotten it legally fixed.

I search her bag. I've got to find my birth certificate, even though she claims she lost it a couple of years back when I asked to look at it, hoping to find out my father's name. But Rayna saw it. So, it must be somewhere. There's a zipper inside the bag and when I unzip it, there's a folded white envelope inside.

Glancing over at her, I check to see if she's still asleep before I pull out the envelope and open it. There's a paper inside and a small blue card— my social security card. I unfold the paper and there it is, my birth certificate.

I take in a breath and scan my finger down the document. *Child: Skye Lark Perry. Date of birth: 01/11/2002 at Los Angeles County Medical Center.* The father section is blank. *Mother: Kary Ann Perry.* Kary Ann? *State of birth: Oregon.* But my mother never lived in Oregon. *Birthdate: 8/18/1982.*

I check her license again. Mary Kenny, born March 13, 1980. The birth certificate's name and birthdate are different from what is listed on her license. What's going on?

I remember Rayna said his name was written on the document.

I examine the front, nothing. I turn it over and there, on the back written in the lower left-hand corner in tiny letters is the name Jason Mackey.

It's true then. Jason Mackey is my father.

Then who is my mother?

"Skye! Where have you been?" The sharp edge in her voice jolts me. I raise my head and make myself look at her.

"I was with my father."

"Your father?" She sits up. Her glassy eyes stare at me. "What are you talking about?"

"I showed him a picture of you, and he said you *are not* my mother."

Her eyes get big and she pulls herself up and out of bed, wobbling back and forth as she tries to steady herself. She's still wearing the same stretchy pants and yellow shirt she was wearing the day I left.

"Who are you to me?" I demand.

Her hand trembles as she rubs her cheek. "Why the hell is my stuff all over the floor?"

"I'm trying to find out who you really are."

"Who *I* am?"

"What's your real name?" I hold up her IDs.

She squints over at the IDs in my hand. "Mary Kenny. I'm Mary Kenny."

"So you and Uncle Richard are not half siblings." Why would they lie about that? What is going on?

She shakes her head.

"Did you adopt me?"

She shakes her head.

"Are we even related?"

She murmurs, "It doesn't matter now."

"What doesn't matter?" I stiffen, suddenly afraid of what I might hear. Maybe I don't want to really know. Maybe I shouldn't know.

She gets up and staggers to the bathroom and slams the door.

I call to her but she doesn't answer. I go over and try opening the door, but it's locked. I collapse on the chair and wait. It seems like an eternity before she comes out. Her face is crumpled and her eyes are red.

"Tell me what happened."

"Richard told me never to tell you." She drags her feet across the room and drops down on the bed.

"Never tell me what?"

"That was a long time ago." She sucks in air and sputters out a cough. "What do you want from me?"

I look down at my wrist where my bracelet used to be. "I need you to tell me the truth."

"I told Richard…" She picks up the pack of cigarettes. Her hand shakes as she pulls one out, lights it with the gold lighter, and tosses it on the nightstand. "I told him not to do it, but he wouldn't listen." She takes a drag from the cigarette.

"You told him to not do what?" I'm shaking so hard my teeth are chattering. "Please, just tell me what happened. It'll be okay."

She looks over at me. "That's what my brother said. He was always saying it would be okay."

"What did he say would be okay?"

Her head jerks as she inhales smoke deep into her lungs. "That it was okay that he kept you." Smoke seeps out of her mouth as she speaks. "He said you had no one, said he made it so you could stay with us and there was nothing to worry about."

"I don't understand what you're saying."

She stares off into the distance. "He told me that you were everything he ever hoped for."

"What do you mean?"

"All because that girl across the hall knocked on our door." Her hand shakes. "Back then my brother could get around, he wasn't sick, and when he answered the door, there she was, telling him she had lost her phone and wasn't feeling good, and then… She just collapsed right there in the hallway with you in her arms. She was crying, begging him to take you, and to get your bottle from the apartment because you were screaming at the top of your lungs."

"Why did she have me?"

"Damnit, Skye, you were her baby," she says in a way that is so matter-of-fact it frightens me. But it can't be true. There's no sense to it. Why is she telling me these lies?

I'm doubled over, clutching my stomach. "Then where is she? Why am I not with her?"

She rubs her nose and sniffles hard. "She died on the way to the hospital. Richard didn't know what to do, said the baby didn't have anyone—he went over to her place and packed all the baby things and we moved to a new place within days."

Why is she lying? "Stop it!" I cry. "Now tell me the truth."

She drops her head in her hands. "That's the truth."

My throat constricts. I can't get enough air into my lungs. "You're trying to make me believe that…Uncle Richard stole me."

"No one stole you, Skye." Her voice quivers. "You needed us, and Richard made it so you could stay."

I'm worried my heart is about to push through my chest. "So you got some legal papers, like a guardianship or something?" I try to breathe, try to calm down, telling myself there has to be some logical explanation.

"Richard got me an ID that made it all work out and told me there was nothing to worry about."

"How the hell did you decide Uncle, Mother? Why not Father, Aunt!" I'm yelling so hard my throat feels like it's burning up.

She collapses on the bed. "I don't know. My brother thought you needed to have a mother figure more than anything else."

I choke out a laugh. "Why the hell did you agree? Because you've been a lousy mother!"

I blink, and she's already off the bed and coming toward me with her arms wide open. No. It's too late. I stumble up and throw my hand out to stop her. "Stay away from me—I mean it!" I shout. She stops in her tracks and looks at me like a deer in the headlights.

"You both kidnapped me!" I blurt out.

She takes a step back. *"No,* that's bullshit, Skye. *Nobody* kidnapped you. Richard said you were given to us for safekeeping. He found your birth certificate and social security card in the diaper bag." She's shaking hard now. "I remember he said, *Mary, she needs us and we're gonna keep her and we're gonna make it legit.* That's what he said."

"Stop it, stop it!" I shout. I don't want to hear any more and push past her, barely making it to the bathroom before I vomit.

When I come back out, I find her sitting on the edge of the bed, smoking. "How—how could you do something like this?" I stumble over to the edge of the bed and sit down.

She doesn't look at me when she says, "Richard said you made us a family, that you'd be in an institution without us, and he took damn good care of you, said we saved you. He did everything for us until he died on me…leaving me with nothing."

"Is that what I am to you? Nothing?"

She shakes her head. "He promised he'd take care of everything."

"Why did you keep me after he died?"

She looks right at me. "I couldn't bear to be alone. I've never been alone." She drops the cigarette into an empty cup. "After my mother disappeared, I went to live with my brother and when he died—you were the only one left."

I stare at her and it's like I'm looking through her, a hollow shell. "Mary Kenny, you oughta be in jail." I look around the room. The walls are closing in and it's getting harder and harder to breathe. I have to get out of here.

"I can't go to jail!" She throws up her hands. "I didn't do anything wrong," she cries. "It was Richard… It was all Richard—" She collapses on the bed. "It was him," she moans, covering her face with her hands.

I get up and grab the envelope filled with money. *My* money, and I start counting it.

"What're you doing with that?" She peeks out from behind her hands.

"I'm taking my money—I'll leave you half—but after it runs out, you're going to have to figure out a way to get your life together because I'm done taking care of you." I pick up the envelope with the birth certificate and social security card.

"Where are you going?"

"Don't worry about me." I shove the money and envelope into my backpack.

"You *can't* leave me. I'm your mother."

I stare down at her, and I'm hit with the weight of her desperation as she gives me one of her *you gotta save me* looks. Not this time. This time, the only one I'm saving is me. "My mother is dead." I gulp down my tears, toss my backpack over my shoulder and head toward the door.

She lets out an ear-piercing scream, one that shakes me to my core, but I keep walking…right out the door and down to the landing even though I can hear her begging me to come back. Her desperate cries cut through me like a knife, but I don't stop.

Descending the stairs, I hold on to the railing to steady myself and count aloud each step that takes me further away from her and her harrowing cries—*One…two…three… I'm free… Four…five… six…pick up sticks.* When I get to ten and my feet touch the ground, I head straight for the parking lot.

I lift open the trunk and gaze down at the TV. I shouldn't have gone back to her after the birds died. But I did because I believed she was my mother. She never even asked what happened with the birds or where I had been. She was too drunk. And when she sobered up, all she worried about was the damn TV.

"This is the end of the road for you." I grab hold of the TV and lift it out of the trunk. Like the Incredible Hulk, I raise it high above my head with a strength I've never known before. Grunting, my arms tremble under its weight. I count *three…two…one* before I throw it as hard as I can, but it doesn't go far before it crashes to the ground.

Gazing up at the night sky, I'm surprised to see the moon smiling down at me.

Forty-Three

I STEP INSIDE SEBASTIAN'S apartment, kick off my shoes, and climb into his bed.

If only he were here with me.

The room is stifling hot, but I can't stop shivering. Pulling the covers up to my shoulders, I squeeze my eyes shut. Everything she told me races through my mind like the lines from a script, yet they are all jumbled and don't make any sense. The only thing I'm sure of now is how everything about my life up until now has been a complete lie.

Especially Uncle Richard. He was the worst lie of all. I believed he was a good and decent man, and the one person I could trust. Thing is, I never belonged to him at all. He tricked me and lied to my face every day we were together. How could he have done such a horrible thing?

How can I ever know what's real? Who I can trust? But somewhere in all of these lies, I realize there is one thing that is real—my father. Although I'm not so sure he even wants to know me. Jason Mackey hoped to find someone too...but that someone wasn't me.

It was my mother.

But my mother is dead.

Reaching for Lil' Monkey, I press him against my face and weep. As I drift off, a soft voice brushes across my ear and whispers... *Surrender.* Opening my eyes, I look around the room, but there's no one there. My mind must be playing tricks on me. What more can I surrender to, anyway? I'll never get a chance to know my mother.

By morning, I'm left hollow and numb. A persistent snapshot plagues my mind, one of my mother's eyes, and the desperation that has always lived in them.

But then...she was never my mother.

But she's all I've ever known.

There's a voice message from her on my phone. I tell myself not to listen...but I do anyway. Her voice quivers. *Skye, I don't know what to do. Stop doing this to me. I'm going to the shelter. Come meet me. What happened isn't my fault... Richard told me it was okay. Just forget everything and come to the shelter.*

Sobbing, I throw the phone down on the floor. I will *never* go back to her. Never! But what's going to happen to me now? My phone pings. I drop to the floor and crawl over to the phone and pick it up. There's a text from Sebastian. He says he's at the college, and says they accepted him for the fall with a full scholarship. He says he hopes I'm doing okay and that everything worked out with my mother and that he'll call just as soon as he starts his drive home.

I'm going to lose Sebastian, too.

I know now that Jason Mackey is my father. Don't I need to tell him the truth? He asked me to, and I said I would. Maybe…maybe if I tell him, he'll come and get me.

But I'm afraid…afraid that he won't.

I start to text him, but I end up deleting whatever I write. If I tell him Kary died, I might never see him again. *It's Skye. I'm sorry to tell you that the woman who I've been living with isn't my mother. She told me Kary died when I was a baby. That means you're my father.*

I delete *that means you are my father* and I type *I hope to hear from you. Skye.* Send.

I watch the screen, waiting for him to text me back. I bring the phone to the bathroom and shower. Still no text. I dress in one of Sebastian's T-shirts and brush my hair. My phone pings and I drop the brush. It's from Jason Mackey!

I take in a breath and read slowly: *I'm really sorry about this devastating news. My heart is broken.*

My hand shakes as I read it over and over, hoping to find some hidden meaning, one that lets me know he wants to see me. I don't want to lose him. But then, I've never had him to lose.

I text back: *My heart is broken too. You should know I'm no longer living with the woman you saw in the picture. I'd really like to talk again sometime and get to know you better. Skye.* Send.

I wait. But he doesn't text back.

When Sebastian walks through the door, I fall into his arms. He searches my eyes and says, "Skye, tell me what's wrong. What happened with your mom?"

And like a dam that can no longer hold the weight of the water against its side, I break—and it all comes flooding out. And while I speak of things that frighten me and things I still don't understand, I'm afraid I might drown.

But Sebastian is right here to keep me afloat.

"I can't help wondering what she looks like. Jason Mackey said he sees her in me."

"If you want, we could try finding her picture on my computer."

"Yes, yes, please."

Sebastian takes his computer out of his bag and sets it on the kitchen table. I sit beside him and watch him type her name into Google search and scroll through the images of people named Kary Perry. I study each photo hoping to find some recognition. But how can I be sure? Just as my heart begins to sink, realizing that there's no way I can ever be sure it's her, I see a picture... A picture of a young girl, not much older than me, and her eyes are the exact color and shape as mine. She's even got an acoustic guitar propped up on her lap.

I know in my heart that I'm looking at my mom's face for the first time. I point at her picture. "That's her. That's my mom."

"Oh, wow, Skye, you look so much like her."

"I do, don't I?" I gently touch the screen with my fingertip and trace the outline of her face. "Mom," I whisper, overwhelmed with an agonizing sadness, for I will never get the chance to know her. "She's so pretty."

"She's pretty like you, Skye," Sebastian says.

I fall into his arms and weep.

Forty-Four

THE AIR IS HOT and sticky and my arms are beginning to ache from carrying the heavy pot of water. I consider pouring some of the water over my head, but I'm careful not to spill even a single drop.

"This is for you, Lillian." I pour the water all around the trunk. The thirsty earth sucks it up in a matter of seconds. I wonder who will water the tree now that Sebastian won't be here anymore.

I startle when my phone rings in my pocket. I'm still getting used to having it. I quickly pull it out and accept the call.

"Hey girl, your texts are worrying me," Kylie says on the other end of the phone. "All you keep saying is you're fine but I know something's going on with you."

"I am fine. Really," I say as convincingly as I can.

"*Hmm*, okay," she says into the phone, not totally believing me. "Hey, BTW, Garrett won the whole thing. Can you believe it? The dark horse found the light." She laughs.

I'm not surprised, thinking back to the pier when all the girls were clawing at him. "That's so great. He deserves it."

"Yeah, he is kinda cool," she says. "So like, what's going on with your dad? You were so upset when you ran out into the field that day. Was he mean to you?"

"No. It's just that…things are kind of complicated right now."

"Yeah, I get it, parents can be a pain. Like, my mom's being a pill, she's lining up all these modeling jobs for me, and like I don't have time for it, not to mention I don't want to do it."

"Maybe you should tell her how you feel, about what you want, I mean."

"I don't know. I'd be letting her and my grandma down." She sighs. "Crap, I'd better get going. My mom's trying to call me."

"Okay, talk soon then." I shove my phone back in my pocket and pick a handful of flowers from the tree before heading over to our old place.

There's no one in the hallway as I stand at the door and set the pot down on the floor. I knock hard on the door and wait. If someone answers, I plan to tell them about the birds and that I'd like to leave flowers on the windowsill.

I gaze down at the wilting flowers in my hand. I don't have a plan if no one answers. A door slams in the distance. I glance up; the landlord is heading toward me. "May I help you?"

He's the reason the birds are dead. "I'd like to go inside."

"Ah, I remember you. Have you come for the television? Because I think someone stole it."

I shake my head. "I'd like to go inside for a second."

He pulls off a key ring from his belt, sifts through a bunch of keys, and opens the door. I follow him inside.

The walls are bright white and the room smells like fresh paint.

"I'm going to leave these flowers on the windowsill for the dead birds, so hopefully you won't be an asshole and throw them away too." I attempt to force the window open, but it must be stuck shut from the paint.

At first, he looks confused with his eyes all wide and his mouth hanging open. But then he breaks out into a grin and starts banging on the frame with his fist until it loosens. After he pushes up the window and steps aside, I look out, hoping it was all a big mistake and I'll see Mama Bird peering up at me, wondering why the hell it took me so long to come back.

But she's not there.

"Mama Bird, I'm so sorry," I whisper.

"Ahh." He nods. "The birds flew away. It was very nice."

I pull my head back inside. "What do you mean they flew away?"

"Yes, they flew into the sky."

"But the nest is gone."

"I took it down."

"Are you *sure* they flew away?"

He nods and closes the window.

I can't believe it! The birds made it out into the world! I throw my arms around the unsuspecting man. "Thank you! Thank you so much!"

"No problem." He chuckles.

I finally let him go and hand him the wilted flowers.

He looks down at them. "Thank you." He takes the sticky stems from my hand. "I am very sorry about the television."

"It's okay," I tell him. "She won't be needing it anymore."

Forty-Five

WE SPEND THE NEXT few days packing up everything in the apartment. Most of the things are packed for The Thrift Angels' pickup.

Sebastian plans to take photo albums (his eyes well with tears when he shows me his family photos), her books, records, and her antique Victrola record player over to his grandma's new place. He tells me they will make her feel more at home. During our breaks, we dance around the room to his grandma's Frank Sinatra records.

Nancy, Veronica, and the baby arrive in the afternoon to go through some of Marion's things that Nancy might want. The baby laughs when he's handed a cookie. His name is Sam, and he smiles at me every time I look at him. He's all gums and crumbs.

Nancy is a lot younger than I expected. Her dark hair is pulled back in two pigtails. She wears shorts so short I can see her silk underwear. She tells us at least four times that she's only thirty-eight and too young to be a grandma. She's right, she looks like she could be Veronica's sister.

Veronica sits on the couch with the baby and stares at her phone. "Don't mind my daughter," Nancy tells me when she sees me staring. Veronica yells at her mom to take the baby because he's getting fussy.

"I'll take him," Nancy agrees. "But you gotta help."

Veronica narrows her eyes. "No way, I'm not doing that. It's not my stuff."

"Then take care of *your* baby!" Nancy snaps.

Nancy likes to talk. I learn that she had Veronica at eighteen. She goes on to say she didn't want her daughter to follow in her footsteps, but here she is with a baby and no man. She said it loud enough for Veronica to hear, but when I glance over, Veronica doesn't seem to be listening.

Nancy has a few pieces of furniture and two large boxes by the door that she plans to take. Before Nancy leaves, she rushes over to Sebastian and, after throwing her arms around him, she starts bawling about how much she's going to miss him.

"I'm going to miss you guys too," Sebastian says, wiggling out of her lengthy hug.

"Honey, we're going to miss you more." Tears stream down her face. "You are a wonderful grandson. Marion's lucky to have you."

"She's more than I could have ever hoped for." He's sniffling now.

Nancy gazes up at him and holds his chin in her hand like she wants to make sure he pays attention. "You stay focused as you attend to your life. That's what Marion would want." Sebastian nods. "Keep in touch, okay?" Nancy pats his cheek affectionately.

"I will." He swipes at his eyes.

Sam starts to wail.

The next morning, Sebastian tells me he wants to take me to see fireworks. I didn't even know it was July fourth. I haven't been keeping track of the days.

I was fourteen when I asked my mother to take me to see a fireworks show somewhere in the city. I had never seen a live show while Uncle Richard was alive. He rarely left the apartment. I was so excited when she agreed, telling me that she knew of a park on the other side of the city where she had gone as a child with her mother and brother. But by the time evening came, she had had too much to drink and couldn't drive.

Maybe I should have snuck out, found a place where I could see them, but back then I was afraid…afraid of all the things she told me about how I could disappear without her by my side. I never questioned why someone would want to take me in the first place. Now I realize she and Uncle Richard had already made me disappear.

We stop at 7-Eleven to get hot dogs and Slurpees. It's still hot and muggy at eight-thirty at night and we have the windows rolled down as he drives us to a place he promises has a spectacular view of the fireworks show. The warm air blows through my hair and the radio plays a song I've never heard before. The singer's voice is pure and the words have to do with having found what they were searching for.

I found what I was searching for, but he didn't want me.

Sebastian drives through winding roads up to the Hollywood Hills and parks on the side of a mountain. We can see the entire city of Los Angeles and all the lights down below glittering like fallen stars. We sit on the hood of the car and eat our hot dogs in silence.

"I'm starting to feel good about things." Sebastian gazes over at me with eyes that hold all his hopes and dreams. "I mean, when I visited my grandma, she remembered that I draw, she asked me how college was going. It felt like a confirmation, you know, that this is the direction I'm supposed to go in."

I'm in awe of the clarity he has for his life. But I can't help but wonder what will happen to me when he's gone. I've never felt so lost in all my life. "You're on your way to making your dreams come true and you deserve it." I caress his face and smile.

Sebastian reaches for my hand and threads his fingers with mine. "That means everything coming from you, Skye Girl."

I try to hold my smile steady as tears burn against the back of my eyes. Sebastian leans in and kisses my lips so tenderly that my heart aches even more.

"I've been thinking about the birds," he tells me after our lips drift apart. "They ended up okay, you know, and I think it's like a sign—that we're going to be okay too. I believe that. Don't you?"

I nod. I want to believe that there are signs that help us know we're on the right path. But how can I believe in anything when everything's gone so wrong? I don't see how anything in my life will ever be okay again. And to make it worse, Sebastian was the one thing right with my life, and now I'm losing him too.

Arizona might as well be a million miles away.

Fireworks suddenly ignite the sky. Sebastian scoots closer to me and we watch as stunning bright lights burst into the velvety darkness and blaze colors and patterns that take the shapes of flowers, stars, and more. We *ooh* and *ahh* and shriek in delight while laughing and kissing between each explosion. As the sky shimmers with teardrops falling down from the sky, Sebastian says my name.

"Hmm?" I look away from the sky and over at him, and I'm moved by the expression on his face. "What is it?"

He gazes into my eyes. "That day you stood at my door and told me about the birds. That was the day you had my heart." He gently caresses my cheek. "All I'm really sure of is that I love you, Skye."

An explosion bursts above us, red, all red, flowery red. I tremble, not because of the explosions, but because of the words he has just spoken, words I can only recall ever hearing from Uncle Richard. And then, it's as if I'm being filled up, and the empty space in my heart is no longer empty. I smile into his glistening eyes, my own eyes brimming with tears. I want to tell him, tell him how I feel, even if I'm afraid. "I love you too, Sebastian."

He breaks out into a huge smile. "We can do this, Skye," he says breathlessly.

I'm not sure what he means, but he looks so happy and I'm about to burst myself. "Do what?" I ask, wiping my eyes.

"We can be together. I'll have a place off campus, and I want you to come with me. Will you come with me, Skye?"

I'm not sure if I heard him right. "You want me to come with you to Arizona?"

"Yes, yes, I do."

My mind gets fuzzy. "Are you sure?"

"I've never been more sure of anything in my life." He slides off the hood of the car and lifts me up, pulling me to him. "I don't want to be without you, Skye. Come with me." He bites his bottom lip, searching my eyes, waiting for me to answer.

But he doesn't have to wait long before I smile up at him. "Yes, Sebastian, I'll go with you."

He breaks out into the biggest grin. "I'm so happy," he says breathlessly and holds me close.

The sky is filled with a fury of lights, booming and crackling one after the other, and soon the entire sky is lit up in a magnificent array of colors. And when the lights disappear and the sky turns a smokey black, I'm still here.

Forty-Six

THERE'S SOMETHING I NEED to do before we leave for Arizona.

I give Sebastian directions to the shelter. He makes a right onto Marbella and parks down the street from the house. I stare out the window, thinking about everything and nothing all at once.

"I'll be right here," he tells me.

"I won't be long." I grab my backpack and get out of the car. I make my way up the block and stop in front of a house that looks like any other house on the street. The plain one-story white house with brown trim is a clever disguise for a shelter, one that hopes to keep the bad guys away, the kind who hurt women and children.

Pulling up the latch on the wooden gate, I make my way up the path, climb the steps, and stand on the porch in front of the black metal screen door. After pressing the buzzer, I check my backpack for the letter.

"Can I help you?" A voice comes out from the speaker on the wall.

"Yeah, I called earlier and I'm here to see my… I mean, Mary Perry."

"Your name?"

"I'm Skye Perry, her—daughter." My eyelid twitches.

It takes forever before Ms. Arthur opens the door. She squints at me through the slits in the screen. "Skye. I'm glad you're here." She unlatches the two locks and steps back. "Your mom will be glad to see you. And you're in luck, we just had a bed open up."

I stand in the entranceway, staring at the blue eyeshadow caked like half-moons above her pale blue eyes. I don't tell her that Mary isn't my mother and that this part of my life is over. I shake my head. "I just wanted to give her something before I go."

Her eyes narrow. "Where are you going?"

"I'm going to stay with a relative."

"I see." Her eyebrows raise. "She's doing better…your mom. Come with me."

I follow her long, swaying ponytail past the counter where people are required to check in and through another door and down a hall that smells like a mix of ammonia and lemon. She takes me into a room I've been in before. It's the screening room, where the women are questioned: Why have you come here? Do you fear for your life? Do you have any family to stay with? Do you have any money? A job? A car?

"Your mom said some troubling things when she first got here, something about a stolen baby. Do you know what she's talking about?" Ms. Arthur looks ready to call the cops if she can get enough information.

Flinching a little, I shrug.

The woman rubs her arms like she's cold. "How old are you, Skye?"

"You don't need to worry about me," I assure her.

"I see." She studies me like I'm under a microscope—first my face, then my body, even down to my shoes. "Your mom must have told you she's on kitchen duty."

I shake my head. "What does that mean?"

"It means Mary has been working in the kitchen, and if she keeps it up and goes to classes, that will allow her up to a hundred and twenty days to stay. If all goes well, we'll help her with transitioning after that."

"Why couldn't you have done this before?"

"Done what before?"

"Helped her."

Ms. Arthur seems surprised. "She didn't want to participate and we can't force someone to help themselves. Now, can we?" She scratches her head. "Where will you be staying?" A guarded smile moves across her face when I don't answer. "Perhaps when Mary finishes the program, she can come stay with you?"

"No." I shake my head. "I can't take care of her anymore."

The woman tilts her head to one side and clasps her hands in front of her. "What do you mean?"

I start to open my mouth, but then it occurs to me I don't have to answer to her.

"You know, we offer services for *you* as well." She rocks back and forth; her long gray ponytail swings like that of a temperamental horse.

"Do you think you can help her?"

"Well. As long as she wants help."

I pull out the envelope from my backpack. "Please give this to her."

"Don't you want to see your mom?"

I had thought about seeing her, and part of me wants to...but I can't, not now. I hand Ms. Arthur the envelope.

She takes it and we both gaze down at the words written on the front: *To Mary Kenny (Perry), CONFIDENTIAL.* She peers up at me.

"Thank you for trying to help her." I turn away and make my way down the hall.

"Skye," she calls. I turn back.

"When your mom came here, she was really distraught, she kept insisting she didn't do anything wrong. Do you know what she meant by that?"

I shake my head. "Did she say anything else?"

"She kept talking about a piece of paper with information on it that can be found with a birth certificate."

I don't know what to think. I doubt *she* even knows what she's talking about. I took the papers out of the envelope and there was only my birth certificate and my social security card. "She's not used to being alone. Don't kick her out this time, okay?"

Ms. Arthur stares down at the envelope.

"*Please*, help her."

"I'll do my best."

"Thank you." I nod. "And she has my number if you need to contact me... In case, you know, just in case." I turn around and walk down the long hallway.

"Should I tell her when you'll be coming back?" Ms. Arthur calls after me.

I press the buzzer that opens the door and I walk through it.

Not everything needs an answer.

Forty-Seven

PULLING OUT THE ENVELOPE, I remove the birth certificate and social security card and tear open the flap, and there inside like she said, is a small white piece of paper stuck in the corner. There's a name written in Uncle Richard's scratchy writing: Evelyn Cory. A phone number is scribbled below it.

Who is Evelyn Cory?

I call the number right away and a woman's voice answers.

"Hi." I clear my throat. "I'm looking for Evelyn Cory."

"This is she."

"Oh… I—I was wondering, do you happen to know…Kary Perry?"

Silence.

"Hello?"

"Yes, yes, I do… She is—*was* my daughter. Who, may I ask, wants to know?"

"I'm Skye and I just found my birth certificate, and I've learned I'm Kary's daughter."

"Oh, my!" she cries. "I've been hoping and praying you'd find me someday. Are you okay?"

"Yeah, I'm okay. So…you knew about me?"

"I knew Kary had a baby. She told me her name was Skye." Her voice quivers.

"I don't understand. If you knew about me, where have you been?"

"I didn't know where your father took you."

"My father?"

"Yes, I assumed he had you. But I didn't know who he was."

"I was never with my father."

"Then who took care of you?"

My heart stings and I don't know what to say as I suck back tears. "I was…I was raised by people who knew Kary."

"I wish I had known." She starts to cry.

"What made you think I was with my father?"

Evelyn Cory blows her nose. "Our last phone call, my daughter told me she was tired of being mad at me and that she was sorry she didn't tell me about the baby. She said she wanted to come home, but first she needed to see what the father of her baby wanted. I assumed they got back together, and that he took you after she died. It only made sense when I went to her apartment to pack her things. I found pictures of you, but there was nothing in the apartment that belonged to a child, which seemed rather strange. I asked the police, and they said they didn't see anything either and assumed she lived alone. It only made sense to me that he took you."

I suck in air, trying to process it all. "How did she die?"

"An aneurysm. It was sudden." She blows her nose again.

"Where is she buried?"

"My baby's buried here in Oregon."

"I don't understand any of this."

"Nor do I," she says.

Part of me feels bad for making her sad. But I need to find out about Kary. "Can I ask why she was mad at you?"

There's a long pause before she says, "When Kary was sixteen, her father and I separated. Kary was very close to her dad and she wanted to go live with him but his new girlfriend wouldn't have it, and Kary was so hurt she blamed me, insisting that I should have somehow fixed things with her dad. A couple months before her eighteenth birthday, he died in a car accident and Kary was so distraught she left for L.A., said she needed to leave this place, and was planning to pursue a singing career."

Not only do I have Kary's eyes, but maybe her voice.

"I remember thinking, okay, I'll give her time to find herself, and then she'll come home." Evelyn weeps into the phone now. "But she never came home."

"I didn't mean to upset you." I chew on my bottom lip.

"Oh, no, you're not sweetie. It's just that it still feels like yesterday when I got that call and I thought I had my daughter back—but then she died within a week after that call and I didn't know how to find you."

I'm not sure how I'm supposed to feel. My mind is a blur, and my heart's beating so fast I press my hand to my chest.

She clears her throat. "You said someone who knew Kary is

taking care of you?"

"She's gone now. I'm staying with a friend."

"Oh, sweetie, I'm so sorry. Where are you right now?"

"I'm in L.A., been here all my life. I'd really like to know more about Kary."

"Skye, I would love to tell you everything you want to know, and I have pictures, lots of pictures, and videos. Perhaps I can come out to see you sometime, or maybe…you could come here?"

"I would like that very much."

"Oh, that's so wonderful to hear. Would you like to come here?"

"You mean to Oregon?"

"Yes, of course." Her voice brightens. "I'd be happy to get you a plane ticket."

"I've never flown before."

"Whatever form of travel makes you feel comfortable. And Skye, when you come here, you are more than welcome to stay as long as you like. After all, you are my granddaughter," she says. "Oh, dear, I must sound so pushy."

My eyes prick with tears. "Oh no, it's okay. I'm glad, I mean, that you want me to come."

She sniffles. "I want that more than anything. I'll be here when you're ready."

"Thank you again. Well, I better go."

"Alright, sweet girl, and…I'm so happy you found me. Please don't hesitate to call me if you need anything or just want to talk."

"I will, thank you."

"Goodbye for now, dear."

"Goodbye."

When we hang up, I don't even try to stop the tears from rolling down my face.

Forty-Eight

I'VE IMAGINED WHAT IT would be like to live with Sebastian in Arizona. But I'm not sure how I'd fit into his world. I'm still a minor, which means I can't enroll in school without a legal guardian. And I'm not even sure I have a legal guardian.

I don't belong to anyone now.

Unzipping my backpack, I pull out my box and a little slip of paper falls out when I open it. I recognize it right away; it was from my fortune cookie, the fortune I never read when Kylie was throwing up. I glance down at it and read: *Follow the direction of your heart.*

Crumpling the paper, I'm not so sure I believe in things like that. But then I remember Iris, a woman that Ms. Arthur had invited to the shelter and introduced as a *Meditation Guru*. The woman was tall, around six feet. She decorated herself in a yellow tunic and a dusty rose kimono, and her dark hair was wrapped in what she called a meditation scarf.

She said she was there to help heal our wounds and show us how to discover our truth. She said we not only must listen to our hearts but open ourselves up to the sacred place inside of us that can change our lives… That is, if we will only listen. Iris compared the human body to the Earth's center of gravity. She said all the experiences from our past, good or bad, are stored within us and they serve as a way to help us find our way. She claimed it was the only true way to set ourselves free.

I'm willing to give it a try to see if Iris's theory works. I lie flat on the floor and shut my eyes and try to recall her steps… *Cleansing breaths, slow, deep… In through the nose, out through the mouth, in…out…in…out.* I begin naming each of my body parts one by one, telling them to relax, and telling myself I am where I need to be. *Breathe…* I envision my muscles going limp… *Breathe…* Trust the process… Repeat. I'm surprised when I start to feel a tingling sensation come over me like my entire body is going to sleep. I begin drifting into a kind of weightlessness, and soon my body doesn't feel like mine anymore. I continue to consciously breathe in and out. As I move into total calm, everything inside of me goes quiet.

And it's then that I find I am able to listen to the calling of my heart.

When Sebastian comes back from the bank, he takes one look at me and asks what's wrong. My eyes well with tears.

"You're scaring me, Skye." He tucks his hair back behind his ears and sucks in his lips.

I take his hand and squeeze it. "Don't be scared. I've just been thinking since I found out I have a grandmother... There's so much I want to know about Kary—there's so many things I need to understand." I stare up at him; he looks as if he's about to cry. "Evelyn said she wants me to come and stay with her, and she'll tell me about my mom."

Sebastian bows his head, and his hair falls in waves over his face. He breathes out a heavy sigh before looking up at me. "I get it. You're searching for a part of you that's missing. You're trying to find your home."

I nod. I wanted my home to be with him, but I've got to learn more about my mom and I can only do that with my grandmother.

He drops his head and rests his forehead against mine and I can feel his warm breath on my face. "Maybe things aren't aligned right now for us, but we'll find our way back, won't we, Skye Girl?"

"Yes, we'll find our way back," I say softly, needing to believe it too.

Forty-Nine

"I DON'T THINK I'M ready for this," Sebastian says, squeezing my hand.

I look over at him as he drives toward the train station. "I'm not either." I lean over and rest my head on his arm. It feels impossible to think about being without him even though I've only known him a short time. It's like he's always been there and now we are about to say goodbye.

"Just wish we had more time," he says.

"Me too. But we can text and call whenever we want, right?"

He nods and for the rest of the ride there, we both are quiet. There's so much I want to say to Sebastian but I'm afraid if I do, I'll break down and cry.

I don't want that image of me to be the last thing he remembers.

His phone pings while he's parking. Sebastian cuts the engine and reads the text. "It's Adam," he tells me. "He said his mom's making my favorite, homemade chili and cornbread, and they're going to wait on dinner until I get there."

"Sounds like fun," I say, grateful Sebastian will be surrounded by people who care about him.

"I can't wait for you to meet them and show you around campus." He smiles at me.

"I'd like that," I tell him and before he can see the tears welling up in my eyes, I grab my backpack and get out of the car.

We hold hands as we make our way over to Will Call. My grandmother has a ticket waiting there for me. The man behind the glass hands me an envelope with my name on it and as he smacks his gum, he tells me the train is running late.

"I'll stay until you board," Sebastian says.

I shake my head. "It's okay, you have a long drive ahead of you and people are expecting you."

"I don't want to leave you here alone."

I look up at him, my heart aching. I'm not sure how I can be without him now that he's moved into my heart in ways I have never felt before. But I know it isn't our time, that we're both trying to find our way in the world and we're on different paths. "Kylie will be here any minute," I reassure him.

He cups my chin in his hand. "I selfishly wish you were coming with me."

"I'd be a thorn in your side," I say, half laughing as my heart breaks.

"You'd never be a thorn anywhere in my body." His grin lasts only for an instant before it fades. "No matter what happens, I've got you right here." He thumps his fist over his heart. "I'm gonna miss you like crazy, Skye Girl."

"I'm going to miss you so much, Sebastian." I smooth back the hair from his face and his eyes look as sad as I feel.

"Wish you were coming with me."

A big part of me wants to stay with him. But I have to see Evelyn Cory, the only person who knew my mother. And maybe the only person who can help me now.

"I have something for you," I tell him and unzip my backpack and pull out my trusted friend. "This is Lil' Monkey." I hold up the one thing that holds all my memories in his little worn-out body. "He means the world to me, and I want you to have him."

Sebastian shakes his head. "I can't, Skye. I can't take something that important from you."

"*You* are important to me, Sebastian." I hold out Lil' Monkey.

Sebastian wipes his eyes and takes the stuffed monkey from me and holds him to his chest. "Until we find each other again—I promise I'll take good care of him."

And we hold each other for a long time, Lil' Monkey squished between us.

I sit on a bench in the middle of the busy courtyard that's buzzing with people. Everyone here has somewhere to go.

I have somewhere to go now too.

Absently touching my wrist, I gaze down at where the bracelet used to be. Like Jackson, I don't need it anymore.

"There you are," Kylie calls out to me.

I look up and see her gliding through the crowd toward me, looking stunning in a pink halter top and white skirt, showing off her extra-long tan legs.

Kylie throws her arms around me, squeezing me tight.

"Means a lot, you being here." I hug her back.

"You okay?" she says.

I hug her tighter. "Yeah, I'm good."

Kylie knows what happened. I called her when she texted me and said she had a dream about me falling from the sky and disappearing. She was crying, which surprised me. First, I reassured her that I wasn't going to disappear, because I've since realized if anything, I've been found. Then I told her what happened, and it did sound like some made-up story. But it isn't... It's my story. We both cried together over the phone. She said she wanted to see me before I left.

I'm so glad she's here.

"Your hair is so silky soft." She runs her fingers through it. "You've got to tell me what you're using." She grins playfully.

"If you must know, I'm using a new product. It's called *Radiance*." I play along. "Have you heard of it?"

We both laugh.

"You know, Skye, I want you as my poster girl for great hair because it just so happens I met with a major manufacturing and distribution company yesterday, with the help of my mom I might add." She smiles. "They want to work with me to get *Radiance* out. They're already talking about a shampoo and fragrance line."

"Kylie, that's amazing!"

"Thanks, I'm really excited." She grins. "You know how you've been open with me?" Kylie's smile has faded. I nod. "Well, I think you should know I ended up in the hospital after we were last together."

"What happened, Kylie?"

"Really, I just had low iron and something with my blood sugar, but I'm glad it happened because it made me think about what I'm doing to myself. So, I'm getting help, you know, to work on my relationship with food, and it feels good. I wanted you to know because…I think of you as my most real friend."

I throw my arms around her. "I feel the same way about you."

"Okay, like, this is getting way too sappy." She chokes out a laugh. "New subject: how's that guy of yours, anyway?"

"He's good. He's on his way to Arizona." I suddenly burst into tears. "I already miss him and it hurts so much. I don't know if I'll ever see him again."

Kylie slings her arm over my shoulders and pulls me close. "From what I could see going on between you two, you'll find your way back to each other."

"Yeah, we will." I wipe my eyes, wanting to believe that.

"Hey, I've got something that'll cheer you up." Kylie pulls out her phone from her purse and makes a call. "Yeah, she's here," she tells someone on the other end. "Everyone here? Okay, cool."

"What's going on, Kylie?"

She grins over at me. "We wanted to surprise you." She holds up her phone and I can see tiny squares showing Garrett, Amber, and Matt's faces. They all start talking at once.

"One at a time," Kylie insists.

We all laugh.

"I can't believe this, guys," I cry. "Hey, congratulations, Garrett."

"Thanks, Skye. I must admit I'm still kinda surprised, and I'm pretty jazzed seeing how they're already talking about incorporating my music into the show, something like Brax trying to be a musician and starting a band kind of thing."

"That's so stinking perfect." Kylie grins.

"Kinda rad." He laughs. "Now I don't have to start a band back home."

"You deserve all of it and more, Garrett," Amber says.

"Right back at ya." Garrett grins. "Hey, Skye, I hear you're going to meet your grandma for the first time."

"Yeah, I am."

"That's cool. You get to meet family. I was wondering if you have any advice for when I find my biological parents?"

"*Um.*" I'm not sure what to tell Garrett. Finding my father didn't turn out the way I thought it would. And because of that, my whole life has changed. "I guess be realistic about it. I had this picture of how it was going to turn out with my father, but it didn't even come close. But it'll be okay, I mean, even if it turns out different, because now I'm about to meet my grandmother."

"Yeah, I get that. I'm gonna keep it real, thanks, Skye."

"That's something I'm trying to do," Matt says.

"You doing okay, Matty?" Kylie peers into the phone. "Did you clear up that matter of yours?"

"I'm still working on it. I'm taking the necessary steps to

embrace the real me."

"What do you mean, embrace the real you, Matt?" Amber says.

"It's nothing, really."

"Oh, it's something," Kylie says. "I gotta tell you, Matty, I'm really proud of you."

"Thanks, Kylie. I appreciate that."

"Well, I've got news about embracing the real me," Amber declares. "I told my daddy I want to be a mechanic, and he wasn't surprised. He said he was proud of me and he wants to help me figure out what I need to do next."

"What about Mama Bear, did you tell her?" Kylie asks.

"Not exactly, but I did tell her I don't want to act anymore."

"How'd she take that?" I ask.

"Better than I thought she would. I think she's relieved after being on the show."

"Guess Garrett's the one that's going to be too big for us one of these days." Kylie grins.

"Hey, did you forget, we've all made it, remember," I say. "Our picture is up there on Mama's wall of fame."

Everyone laughs.

Kylie peers down at the screen. "Okay, guys, it's been fun, but we need to wrap this up or Skye is going to miss her train outta here."

"Well, no matter what happens, from here on out, we have to keep in touch," Amber says. "We should get together, maybe once a year or something, until we grow old."

"I'm in," Garrett says.

"Me too." I nod.

"Why not?" Kylie shrugs, smiling.

"Sounds good" Matt agrees.

An announcement booms out from the intercom: "Oregon-bound boarding in effect."

"I guess I'd better get going." I wave to my friends on the phone and after everyone calls out their goodbyes and good luck, Kylie ends the call. As we make our way over to the train, it hits me hard that what I'm about to do is very real and that my life has become more uncertain than ever. After my visit with Evelyn Cory, I'm not sure what's going to happen to me. What if I'm making a big mistake? I wish I was with Sebastian, driving to Arizona and having chili and cornbread.

I stop walking.

"What wrong, Skye?" Kylie says, standing in front of me now.

"I'm really scared. I mean, maybe I'm making a big mistake going there."

"Oh, Skye, of course you're scared. You're going into a whole new life, but it's going to be okay."

"I want to believe that." I swipe stubborn tears from my eyes.

"I've got something for you." Kylie reaches into her purse and pulls out a tiny gold box. "Here, open it."

I open the box and inside is a necklace that has my name spelled out in silver letters. I look up at Kylie, and her eyes are filled with tears.

"This is who you can believe in." She touches the letters of my name. "I don't want you to ever forget who you are—'cause you're amazing just the way you are." She sniffles. "I sound like that Bruno Mars song, huh?"

I let out a choked-up laugh and lift the necklace out of the box.

"Here, let me." She takes the necklace from me, drapes it around my neck, and latches it.

I turn to face her. "Perfect." She smiles.

"Thank you." I throw my arms around her and we both cry as we cling to one another.

"Come on, you don't want to miss your ride to your new life."

I shake my head and swipe tears from my cheeks.

"You're going to be okay, Skye, more than okay."

"Yeah." I nod. "We both will."

"Hey." She sniffles. "We gotta remember this moment." She holds up her phone.

I lean in and smile.

Fifty

AS I MAKE MY way down the aisle to find my seat, I'm about to leave everything I've ever known behind. As Kylie said, I'm heading to a new life. One that both excites and scares me.

There's no one in my row. In fact, the train isn't even half full as I move into my seat and pull my backpack onto my lap. When I spoke to Evelyn last night, she asked if I played the guitar. She said she has Kary's guitar, and that it was one of the things she took from her apartment after she died. And then she asked if I wanted it.

At first, I was speechless, that I would be given such an incredible gift, the very possession that my mom loved, the very instrument she played as she sang and touched other people's lives. Like my father's.

I said I would be honored to have my mom's guitar.

My phone buzzes; it's a text from Kylie. She sent the picture she took of us. I smile at the photo of the two girls that look as if they're ready to take on the world.

I save it into my photos with the picture of us at the pizza place that Sebastian sent me and a selfie of Sebastian and me that we took on the hood of the car the night we said we loved each other. I miss him already. But I know he's headed to where he belongs, and with Lil' Monkey at his side.

I wonder if Mary read my letter yet. I hope she feels reassured that no one is coming to take her to jail. I told her I hope she'll do what it takes to have a better life for herself. I told her I forgive her.

Taking my box out from my backpack, I lift up the lid and take out the only photo of me as a baby. I now know it was Kary holding me all along. Next, I take out the image of her beautiful face that Sebastian printed off the computer and I place it behind the ripped photo. Tears prick my eyes as I gaze at my mom's face as she cradles me in her arms.

When my phone rings, I'm jolted from my thoughts and, thinking it's Kylie again, I answer with, "You miss me already?"

But it's not Kylie's voice that I hear on the other end, but a man's nervous chuckle. "Skye, it's me, Jason."

"I'm sorry, I thought you were someone else," I say breathlessly.

"That's okay. I hope I'm not calling at a bad time."

"No, not at all." I can't imagine a time when I wouldn't want to get a call from my father.

"That's good. I'm calling you because—you've been on my mind and I've been thinking about your text." He clears his throat. "I wanted to ask you what you meant when you said you're no longer with the woman who raised you?"

He really doesn't know. But how could he? "It's complicated. But what matters now is that I'm not with her anymore."

"May I ask who is looking after you?"

"I'm looking after myself. But, I just found my grandmother, and I'm going to Oregon today. I'm actually on the train right now, to visit her."

"That's incredible. Are you planning on staying?"

"I'm not sure. I'm still trying to figure things out."

"I get that. I've been trying to do that as well. Oregon's what, only around a few hundred miles from San Jose?"

"Yeah, it's not too far," I say.

"I want to be honest with you, Skye. After I got a call from that show, I was worried about telling my wife—her name is Angie, by the way. But I decided to tell her everything. I mean, meeting your mom happened before I ever met her. So, I was thinking maybe we can see each other again sometime, and we could get to know each other under better circumstances. What do you think?"

Cradling the phone to my ear, I cling to every word. "Yes, I would like that very much." I cover the speaker with my hand so he can't hear me cry.

"That's great," he says. "I think we're off to a good start, don't you think?"

I clear my throat and take my hand off the speaker. "Yes, definitely."

"All right, well, you have a safe trip, and let's keep in touch."

"I will and thank you… Thank you for calling."

"I'm glad I did. And if you don't mind, maybe you could let me know you made it there safely."

"All right, I will."

When the call ends, I hold my phone to my heart and watch the train pull out of the station. As familiar streets disappear from view, I wish I could see Mama Bird one last time, so I could tell her goodbye. I imagine the birds as their wings take them out into the world and to a life that belongs only to them.

I'm not exactly sure where I'll end up, but it feels like I'm headed in the right direction.

I close my eyes and wrap my fingers around the pendant, and as I caress the letters of my name, it occurs to me that I, Skye Lark Perry, have wings.

And like Mama Bird's babies, I too am ready to fly.

About the Author

Dorothy Deene has lived most of her life in the L.A. area and is no stranger to the entertainment world. She spent years writing and directing plays and working as a column writer for the Gazette. It wasn't until her daughter landed a spot on a reality show at CBS Studios that centered around a group of talented teens and their parents, did Deene begin writing her debut novel, *The Gravity of Lies*. To learn more about the author, you can find her at and follow her on Twitter @dorothydeene.

www.dorothydeene.com
www.facebook.com/dorothydeene
www.instagram.com/dorothy.deene
www.twitter.com/dorothydeene

Acknowledgements

I owe a debt of gratitude to Sword and Silk's Laynie Bynum and MaryBeth Dalto for believing in *The Gravity of Lies* and that Skye's story should be told. Thank you to Jennia Herold D'lima for your keen eye in the editing of my story, ensuring that Skye and the cast of characters were at their best. To Celin Chen for the incredible cover art that perfectly depicts Skye's journey. And to everyone behind the scenes at Sword and Silk who helped get *The Gravity of Lies* ready and out into the world.

A heartfelt thanks to my husband Kevin and kids Julianna and Justin for your inspiration, patience, and constant love and support as I chased my dream. To my sister, Carole, my sounding board to all things, especially my stories. To my dad for cheering me on. To my friends Janice and Diana, who were always eager to hear about Skye's story even before it was written. To my mom, the first person who ever believed I could make my dream come true. Mom... wherever you are, I did it!

And finally, this story is dedicated to anyone who is searching.

I hope you never give up.

CPSIA information can be obtained
at www.ICGtesting.com
Printed in the USA
LVHW051621190723
752839LV00001B/69